"Will you be relieved to see us gone?"

When Lydia met his gaze, Gideon looked as if she'd handed him a time bomb set to explode.

Laughing, she said, "I suppose there's no diplomatic way of answering that."

His eyes creased in amusement. "I grew up with sisters. I've learned to recognize a loaded question."

"Then let me rephrase. I know your duties will be simplified. But I wonder if you'll miss us in some small way."

He studied her for a moment, then nodded. "I dare say this valley will miss all of you. You've brought a measure of joy to what would have been a dreary winter."

Lydia supposed she shouldn't put too much import into his words, but she couldn't ignore the warmth that settled in her heart.

"I'm glad we weren't a complete chore."

He shook his head. "Not a *complete* chore."

When she would have glared at him, he laughed. "You mustn't take yourself too seriously. After all, our time together is limited."

Yes. But did it have to be?

Lisa Bingham is the bestselling author of more than thirty historical and contemporary romantic fiction novels. She's been a teacher for more than thirty years, and has served as a costume designer for theatrical and historical reenactment enthusiasts. Currently she lives in rural northern Utah near her husband's fourth-generation family farm with her sweetheart and three beautiful children. She loves to hear from her fans at lisabinghamauthor.com or Facebook.com/lisabinghamauthor.

Books by Lisa Bingham

Love Inspired Historical

The Bachelors of Aspen Valley

Accidental Courtship
Accidental Family
Accidental Sweetheart

LISA BINGHAM

Accidental Sweetheart

⟨H⟩ **HARLEQUIN**® LOVE INSPIRED® HISTORICAL

Recycling programs
for this product may
not exist in your area.

LOVE INSPIRED BOOKS

ISBN-13: 978-1-335-36968-0

Accidental Sweetheart

www.Harlequin.com

Printed in U.S.A.

The blessings of thy father have prevailed
above the blessings of my progenitors
unto the utmost bound of the everlasting hills.
—*Genesis* 49:26

Dedicated to Joyce, my mother.

Thank you for always believing in me.

Chapter One

February 21, 1874
Utah Territory

Gideon Gault sensed trouble. Something strange was happening in Aspen Valley, something…unsettling. A thread of agitation ran through the community surrounding the Batchwell Bottoms Silver Mine. It bubbled beneath the surface, filling him with anxiety—even though, for the life of him, he couldn't figure out why.

Pausing at the entrance to the mine, he planted his hands on his hips and squinted against the sun. For the hundredth time that day, he allowed his gaze to sweep over the street beyond.

"Problems?"

Glancing over his shoulder, Gideon acknowledged Charles Wanlass, the mine's blasting foreman, and recent newlywed.

"I don't know. Do things feel…odd…to you?"

Charles smiled. "Odd? In what way?"

"I don't know. I just…"

Charles's grin grew even broader, and Gideon grimaced. The man grinned a whole lot these days. Ever since

Charles had married and adopted twin babes, Gideon's friend existed in a perpetual bubble of happiness that was beginning to grate on Gideon's nerves. Especially since Gideon seemed to be surrounded by miners who were afflicted with the same brand of besottedness.

"There's something going on," Gideon groused, trying again to explain the fact that, each day, he grew a little more skittish, a little more suspicious. He woke up with the sensation that something was off-kilter with Aspen Valley and went to bed sure that he'd missed something important.

But what?

"Maybe it's the good weather that has you out of sorts," Charles offered. His tone was a little too tongue-in-cheek for Gideon's liking.

No, it wasn't the weather. After months of snow, bitter cold and whipping winds, the valley had begun to enjoy a temporary thaw. For weeks, they'd basked in unseasonably bright sunshine. Seemingly overnight, the man-high drifts of ice that had once been pushed up against the buildings had melted to dirty mounds, while the thoroughfares grew thick with mud. Deep puddles made it hazardous to stand too close to the street since the passing wagons threw dirt and grime in every direction. And crossing the road…well, if a man didn't want to lose his boots, he needed to use the wooden boards that had been laid down to provide a temporary bridge from the Miners' Hall to the cook shack.

But all that was normal for Aspen Valley in the spring. *So, what had him feeling so antsy?*

Gideon knew why the other men were restless. They lived in dread of the moment when the pass cleared and the fifty mail-order brides who'd been stranded at Bachelor Bottoms for the winter were forced to leave the valley.

Gideon couldn't wait for that day. He'd finally have the women out of his hair, his unit of Pinkertons guarding the silver rather than the ladies' dormitory, and his life back to normal.

"Maybe you're just grumpy," Charles said.

The man had the all-out gall to laugh and Gideon scowled. "Very funny."

"You could drop by the house for something to eat. Willow was planning to bake today. She'd love to fatten you up."

Tempting as that thought might be, Gideon shook his head. The last thing he needed was to follow Charles home right after the man's shift. Although Charles and Willow tended to be reserved in public, Gideon knew they'd be goo-goo-eyed in their own row house. In his present mood, that was more than Gideon could handle.

"Maybe later. Right now, I need to get to the bottom of this."

Jamming his hat on his head, he rested his hand loosely on his sidearm and strode to the boardwalk. Once there, he sauntered in the direction of the cook shack. Maybe Charles was right. Maybe he was hungry. He hadn't eaten that morning, and he was feeling peckish. This late in the day, he probably wouldn't find any hot food, but he could grab some biscuits and cold ham and make himself a sandwich. That and a glass of milk ought to chase the restlessness out of his system and help him think clearly.

Ahead of him, he could see a pair of miners heading toward the Pinkerton offices and he grimaced. Hopefully, they'd keep walking.

Please let them keep walking.

If the men stepped into the Pinkerton building, Gideon would have to forgo the cook shack and head into the office to see what they wanted. His guards were already stretched too thin with their current duties. And if the miners sought the Pinkertons out, it was usually to ask for help in settling a minor dispute.

This day was going from bad to worse.

"Good morning, Mr. Gault."

Gideon turned at the soft call, his hand leaving his revolver and lifting to his hat when he saw Stefania Nicos and Marie Rousseau, two of the mail-order brides who often volunteered to help prepare the morning meal.

"Miss Nicos. Miss Rousseau."

The women shared a secret, inscrutable glance.

Where were their guards?

He turned back to call to the miners and ask them to alert his office that he needed one of his men, only to discover that they were nowhere in sight. That meant Gideon would have to escort the ladies safely home.

"Miss Nicos, I—"

The women had disappeared as well.

What on earth?

He glanced down the nearby alley. *Nothing.* Checked inside the door to the company laundry.

Nothing.

Where had they gone?

He hooked his thumbs into his belt and surveyed the street from one end of Aspen Valley to the other. Not even a stray dog roamed the boardwalk. It was as if the inhabitants of Bachelor Bottoms were being plucked out of thin air, and the mining community was gradually becoming a ghost town. There were no stray workers, no women, no wagons, no horses. If not for the dripping of the melting icicles, Gideon could have believed he'd been dropped into a painted backdrop for a melodrama.

Which only added to his uneasiness.

Gideon resumed his walk, his gaze restlessly scanning back and forth. Maybe it was time to get a team of men together and sweep the area. He wasn't sure what he was going to tell his men to look for, but he'd think of something.

Sighing heavily, he gave up on the thought of a sandwich for now, passed the cook shack and headed to the three-story frame building that housed the Pinkerton office and their barracks. Opening the door, he called out, "Dobbs! We've got a pair of runners! Miss Nicos and Miss Rousseau are on the loose."

Except for the echo of his own voice, there was no response.

Gideon had a unit of thirty men who'd been hired by the mine to guard the silver ore and provide security for the shipments being sent to Denver. But, since December, Ezra Batchwell had insisted that the Pinkertons spend their time hovering over the mail-order brides "for their own protection."

Gideon snorted. In his opinion, the fifty-odd women who'd been marooned here when their train had been pushed down the mountain by an avalanche didn't need any protection whatsoever. It would have been easier to guard the miners. In the past few weeks, the women had been testing their boundaries even more than usual—a result, no doubt, of the fact that Ezra Batchwell had broken his leg and had been confined to his home. Without his bullish insistence that the ladies be kept at bay, the brides seemed determined to challenge the willingness of Gideon's men to corral them.

To be honest, the Pinkertons hadn't tried that hard to rein them in. With the warmer weather, everyone in the valley knew it was only a matter of weeks before the women would be forced to leave. When that moment came, Aspen Valley would return to an all-male population. Even worse, they would lose the joy that the brides had brought with their fine cooking, bright smiles and effervescent personalities.

But that was the way things worked at the Batchwell Bottoms Silver Mine.

"Dobbs! Winslow!"

Nothing.

The chance for a sandwich seemed to be getting further and further out of reach.

Gideon stepped outside. Once again, the hairs at the back of his neck prickled. The roads, the boardwalks, were empty.

He knew that production had stepped up in the mine since a new tunnel had been blasted. Crews were larger, shifts longer. As soon as the canyon had cleared enough for repair crews, the railway lines would be restored and then the ore they'd amassed the past few months would be shipped out of the camp.

But that didn't explain why there was no one around today.

A trio of miners exited the Hall, relieving Gideon's misgivings slightly. Maybe things weren't quite as strange as he—

"Mr. Gault."

He stiffened. Without turning, he recognized the voice of Miss Lydia Tomlinson, one of the marooned women. As a self-professed suffragist, she'd become the unofficial leader of the ladies in the past few months. In Gideon's opinion, the woman meant trouble with a capital *T*. She had a way of putting…*ideas* in the other brides' heads. And since she didn't have much regard for authority, she could be a handful.

Gideon mentally prepared himself, knowing that any conversation with Miss Tomlinson would prove to be an intellectual skirmish. She could talk a mule into surrendering his left hind leg if she had a mind to do so—and the mule would give it up willingly.

He leaned in to the Pinkerton office one more time—as if by some miracle, one of his men would appear and relieve him of the need to match wits with Lydia. But there would be no such deliverance. Instead, he was forced to step outside.

Automatically, his gaze swept the boardwalk, looking for the miners who'd come out of the hall—but there was no sign of them.

He was losing his ever-loving mind.

In the meantime, Miss Tomlinson scrutinized him from the tip of his hat to his dusty boots, then regarded Gideon as if he were slightly daft.

Sighing, he touched a finger to the brim of his hat. "And how are you this lovely morning, Miss Tomlinson?"

One of her brows lifted. Clearly, she'd caught the thread of resignation in his tone.

"Quite well, Mr. Gault. Nevertheless, I wondered if you and I could have a word."

Gideon seriously doubted such a thing was possible. Lydia Tomlinson didn't exchange a *word.* She talked and talked and talked. To be fair, she was an intelligent creature with a good head on her shoulders. But she could be so *bossy.*

"About?" he asked cautiously.

Her eyes narrowed. "You needn't look like I'm proposing to escort you to a firing squad."

Apparently, she could read minds as well.

Gideon purposely relaxed the line of his shoulders and tried his best to make his hands hang loose at his sides.

"There was no such stuff in my thoughts."

"Mmm-hmm." Her lips thinned. "I wish to discuss a matter of business with you."

Gideon couldn't imagine what kind of "business" the two of them might share. But he supposed that since Ezra Batchwell was unavailable, and Jonah Ramsey had been quarantined at home with measles, Gideon was probably the next company man on her list with whom she intended to argue.

"What can I do for you?"

She shifted, her gaze roaming the streets around them. For a moment, sunlight slipped over her cheeks and highlighted the delicate curve of her jaw. She really was a pretty woman—tall, slim, with honey-colored hair. If she weren't so...*snippy*...

"I would rather divulge the subject inside. Away from prying eyes."

One last time, Gideon allowed his gaze to roam Main Street, from the mine opening to the slopes of the Uinta mountains in the distance. Near as Gideon could tell, there wasn't a soul in town who could "pry." But there was no use arguing the point.

He held the door wide. "After you, Miss Tomlinson."

"You may call me Lydia, Mr. Gault."

Gideon was pretty sure that if he used Lydia's Christian name, his own mother would roll over in her grave. Clotilde Gault had been a stickler for proper social customs and morés, and an unmarried gentleman did not take such liberties with an unmarried woman—even if she did spout on about the emancipation of women and the equality of the sexes.

"How can I help you, Miss Tomlinson?"

Her lips pursed, ever so slightly, but thankfully, she didn't press him into dispensing with the formalities.

"The ladies have been discussing the rapid melting of the snow."

She paused, clearly waiting for a reaction, so he offered a noncommittal, "Oh?"

"By our reckoning, it seems as if most of the drifts have wasted into nothing. If this continues, we're worried that the standing puddles around the Dovecote will soon flood into the house."

So, she did have a logical reason for her visit.

"Jonah Ramsey and I have been keeping our eye on the water levels—or we were until he took sick. If necessary, he's given orders to dig a series of drainage ditches to the river. But at this point, such efforts would probably be premature. Here in the high Uinta mountain range, spring can be unpredictable. These high temperatures could give way to a Utah blizzard at a moment's notice. I've seen the weather change from freezing cold to blazing heat, to snow, hail and rain, all within a single afternoon."

Lydia looked skeptical, but she didn't push the point. Instead, she said, "The women would be more than happy to help dig should the need arise. I know with the new tunnel that manpower has been spread thin."

Gideon's mouth opened, but for the life of him, he couldn't think of anything to say. Somehow, he couldn't bring to mind the image of Lydia or the other girls slogging through the mud with pickaxes and shovels, fashioning a trench that would stretch the hundred feet from the Dovecote to the Aspen River.

"I don't think that will be necessary, Miss Tomlinson. I'm sure that the mining company could gather a crew should we need it."

She nodded, then lapsed into silence. Her gaze roamed the room, taking in the utilitarian office.

Unlike many of the other buildings in town, this one had not fallen under the women's purview. While the cook shack, the Meeting House, and even the Miners' Hall had been scrubbed and polished until they gleamed, this space was clearly run by men. Mud streaked the floors and the desks were littered with papers, logbooks and coffee mugs. The only nod to neatness was the rifles lined up on a rack against the far wall.

For some reason, the untidiness caused a warmth to steal up Gideon's neck. Judging by the way Miss Tomlinson invariably dressed to perfection in frilly dresses with nipped-in waists, he'd bet she was a stickler for orderliness. Today, she looked especially fine in a red gingham dress with black braid trim.

"Was there something else, Miss Tomlinson?"

Rather than speaking, she moved restlessly around the room. Despite the warmth of the day, she wore delicate kid gloves the exact shade of crimson as the capelet that graced her shoulders.

Where did a woman find red leather gloves?

As she moved, Gideon felt compelled to shift to face her—until he had the sensation of becoming a sunflower tracking the orbit of the sun.

"I suppose that leads me to my main question," she said, regarding him from beneath her lashes.

The look she offered him didn't seem very…businesslike.

Gideon couldn't help folding his arms across his chest. He instantly regretted the movement, wondering if she would interpret it as a defensive gesture.

Once again, he felt a prickling sensation. His instincts told him that Miss Tomlinson was up to something.

But what?

Gideon's men had already relaxed their guard substantially since Batchwell's accident. Short of allowing the ladies to wander all over town at will, what more could she want of him?

"Have you sent anyone to check the pass?"

Of all the questions he might have suspected she'd ask, that was the last one that would have popped into his mind. Even so, Gideon hesitated.

"Not yet. I'd planned on riding up that way later this afternoon."

"Excellent. When should I meet you at the livery?"

It took a full second for her query to sink into his brain. *She wanted to go with him.*

Not knowing how best to respond, Gideon stalled.

"Meet me?"

"Since the condition of the pass will determine the fate of the women, I think it's only logical that I accompany you."

He held out a hand. "Oh, no. No, no, no. This isn't a jaunty buggy ride in the countryside, Miss Tomlinson. Despite the fact that the roads have become clear in the valley, up by the canyon, the slopes will be treacherous at best. The debris field left from the avalanche will be unstable and full of the rocks and broken tree limbs that were brought down from the higher elevations. If we can get into the canyon at all, we'll be headed into terrain kept in shade most of the day. That could mean encountering ice and even the threat of another avalanche."

Lydia's eyes seemed to snap, even though she maintained her neutral expression.

"Do you take me for a fool, Mr. Gault?"

How was he supposed to answer that question without getting himself into trouble?

"No, ma'am."

He mentally grimaced when his tone emerged with a hint of a question.

Again, her eyes narrowed, but she didn't remark on his inflection. Instead, she said, "I wasn't proposing a buggy ride at all, Mr. Gault. I am fully aware of the hazards and consequences of the weather—which is why I intended to meet you at the livery. I'm certain that Mr. Smalls could be persuaded to loan me a mount. Rest assured, I'm a qualified rider."

"We don't have sidesaddles here at Bachelor Bottoms," Gideon said with what he hoped was a negligent shrug. Inwardly, he congratulated himself on his quick thinking. There was no way that Miss Fancy Pants could get on a horse with all those ruffles and gathers and lace unless she used one.

Unfortunately, the moment she scowled, he realized that he'd managed to irritate her even further.

"I didn't think that you would, Mr. Gault."

"And you can't be going anywhere in…*that.*" He made a vague gesture to the frilliness of her attire. "You'd freeze to death the minute we hit the shady patches."

"What time, Mr. Gault?"

Her tone reminded him of Sister Grundy, his childhood Sunday School teacher. Miss Grundy's voice had held the same thread of steel when Gideon had tried to bring a frog to church under the guise of "educating one of God's creatures."

He sighed and glanced at the clock over his desk. In the silence, the tick-tock of the timepiece seemed overly loud—and Miss Tomlinson's toe tapping impatiently against the floor merely served as an accompaniment.

"How about one o'clock?"

The appointed time was less than an hour away—and by his standards, he doubted that any woman could get herself changed into suitable clothes and return to town. His sisters had never managed such a feat.

"Very well. One o'clock."

With that, she strode past him in a wave of something

that smelled like lemons and gardenias. In doing so, she managed to hook the door and pull it closed behind her with a resounding *slam!* that rattled the windows.

Gideon couldn't help chuckling. Lydia Tomlinson might be a pain in the neck most days…

But she was like a firecracker with a faulty fuse. A body never knew what might set her off.

And oh, what fun it was to see what it took to get her to lose control.

Lydia marched down the boardwalk, a secret smile twitching at the corners of her lips. She really hadn't meant to slam the door quite so hard…

But she'd needed to signal to her friends that Gideon Gault was no longer being distracted.

Within seconds, Stefania and Marie joined her, and the three of them walked down the boardwalk, heading out of town toward the Dovecote.

"Any progress?" Lydia asked.

"We were able to get five more men."

Lydia shot a glance at the other girls, catching their barely submerged glee. "Five? How?"

"We threw a blanket over each of them and hauled them into the cook shack. From there, we explained the nature of our protest and how they could help."

"And they all agreed to join our cause?"

"Klute Ingraham is still thinking about it. But Iona started plying him with pie, so I think his stomach will declare its allegiance soon enough. If that doesn't work, Iona is prepared to mourn the fact that the stuffed ferrets he provided for decoration in the Dovecote need a new set of clothes for spring."

Since Klute had a passion for taxidermy and dressing his creations in fanciful clothes, Lydia supposed that would keep him from comprehending the true nature of his situation. In essence, he was a prisoner to the mail-order brides. He and the other men they'd taken hostage would remain in their control until their demand was met: an end to the "no women" clause in the mine's rule book.

"Well done! Where are you keeping this batch?"

"At the infirmary for now. Since Sumner has been forced to remain home with Jonah during his quarantine, we figured that no one would bother to look there."

"And who do you have guarding them?"

"Greta and Hannah."

Lydia laughed. Greta was a plump Bavarian woman who knew very little English. What words she knew, she offered in a big booming voice. Even if she bellowed her orders in German, she more than captured a man's attention. Hannah was a sturdy farm girl from Ohio. The pair of them should be more than capable of guarding their captives.

"That brings our total to…"

"Thirty-seven!" Stefania offered proudly.

Lydia chuckled. "See what you can do this afternoon to bring that number even higher. I have an appointment to meet Mr. Gault to examine the pass. We should be gone at least an hour, but I'll do my best to keep him out of the town proper for two."

Marie and Stefania both offered her mock salutes. Then, they turned to retrace their steps so that they could relay their "orders" to the women who would lie in wait for the next batch of men who foolishly sought a meal, a haircut or a game of checkers in the company store.

Lydia knew that the ladies' efforts wouldn't remain undetected for much longer—she hadn't thought that they would last this long. Indeed, she was surprised that the dip in the mine's workforce hadn't already become a problem. But with more and more snow disappearing every day, the brides had been desperate to find a way to get Ezra Batchwell and Phineas Bottoms to revise the company's strict rules for employment.

In order to work at the prestigious and profitable Batchwell Bottoms Silver Mine, the men had to sign an oath that they would abstain from drinking, smoking, gambling and cussing. And most egregious of all, in her opinion, women were forbidden on company property. That meant that married men were forced to live apart from their wives and families. And if a man happened to fall in love once he came to the territories, he was in big trouble.

Unfortunately, the owners of the mine hadn't counted on a trainload of mail-order brides being stranded in their community. Despite the Pinkertons, who had been ordered to guard them night and day, many of the men had begun to form attachments with the ladies. Two of their own— Sumner Ramsey and Willow Wanlass—had even managed to marry a couple of the men. But those relationships— as well as so many others that had begun in secret—were already in jeopardy. If something wasn't done—*soon*— these men would be faced with the loss of employment or separation from their families.

Such a situation was untenable, even to someone like Lydia, who had sworn off matrimony or any other forms of romantic entanglements. Therefore, she'd been assigned the task of keeping Gideon Gault in the dark about their efforts for as long as possible. She was to distract him, waylay him, monopolize his time, no matter what it took to do so.

Casting her eyes skyward, she offered up a quick prayer.

Dear Lord, please bless us in our efforts to keep these families together.

And please, please, don't let me lose my temper with that insufferable man.

Chapter Two

Well before the appointed time, Lydia stood next to a docile gray mare, the reins held loosely in her hands. She was glad that she'd made the effort to arrive early. As she'd suspected, a quarter hour before they were meant to meet, Gideon Gault burst out of the Pinkerton offices and ran in the direction of the livery.

She wasn't sure if he was considered off-duty or if he'd merely hoped to arrive at the livery incognito, but he'd changed his clothes, donning a pair of worn boots, brown wool pants, a brown leather vest and a brown shearling coat.

Perhaps the choice of so much brown was an attempt at camouflage, given the mud in Bachelor Bottoms. If that was the case, it didn't work. In all that well-worn gear, there was no disguising the man's musculature. Gideon Gault had long legs and broad shoulders—making Lydia wonder what sorts of activities were entailed with becoming a Pinkerton. A man didn't get that kind of physique by trailing a bunch of women around Aspen Valley in order to keep the miners at bay.

"Good afternoon, Mr. Gault."

He'd been so mindful about missing the puddles in his

dash across the street that her greeting brought him up short and he skidded to a halt, nearly plowing into her headfirst.

Automatically, he reached to lift his hat, but the action merely emphasized the montage of emotions that raced across his features: surprise, dismay, then utter resignation.

"Miss Tomlinson."

"I see you were hoping that I would forget our errand."

"No, ma'am, I—"

Even he must have realized the halfhearted objection because his lips twitched at the corners. "I had expected you to take a little longer."

At least he had the grace to admit that much.

"And why would you think that?"

"Experience."

"Oh. So, you're one of the men at Bachelor Bottoms who's been forced to live apart from a loved one?"

He shook his head. "No, ma'am. I grew up with sisters. Five of them."

Her brows rose. "It's a wonder you survived, Mr. Gault."

He didn't miss her sarcasm. If anything, it made his smile even wider. "I've got battle scars, Miss Tomlinson. But, yes, I survived."

The livery door opened and Willoughby Smalls walked out, leading a strawberry roan gelding.

"Thanks, Willoughby."

Smalls grinned, his gaze bouncing from Gideon to Lydia. An accident at the mine had crushed the gentle giant's throat years ago, robbing him of his ability to speak. But he still managed to communicate his thoughts by waving a finger between the two of them.

"Yes, we'll be riding out together."

"Despite the fact that Mr. Gault worked so hard to leave me behind," Lydia muttered under her breath.

Smalls made a chortling noise, then moved to Lydia's side. Bending, he offered his laced hands to help boost her into the saddle.

"Thank you, Mr. Smalls. You are too, too kind."

She shot a glance in Gideon's direction in time to see his ears redden ever so slightly.

As soon as her boot rested on Smalls's palms, he hoisted her up as if she weighed no more than a feather. She barely had time to throw her leg over the mare before landing unceremoniously in the saddle.

This time, it was her turn to feel a tinge of heat seeping into her cheeks as Gideon's keen brown eyes raked over her form.

After she agreed to host a series of speaking engagements on women's suffrage up and down the California coast, Lydia's aunts had insisted that she be outfitted from head to toe in a proper wardrobe for the occasion. Because of that, Lydia had been burdened with more clothing—and trunks—than decency permitted. But for once, Lydia was grateful that her guardians had seen fit to provide her with a split riding skirt and tailored jacket—as well as a wool greatcoat to wear over the top. Granted, the matching hat was a trifle fussy. But she couldn't miss the fact that Gideon was looking at her less like an annoyance and more like…

Well, like a woman.

"As you can see, Mr. Gault. I am more than prepared for the rigors of our outing."

His mouth—which had dropped open ever so slightly when she'd sat astride the horse—snapped shut.

"We'll see about that," he said. Then he offered a soft clicking noise to his horse and headed the animal out of town.

"Thank you again, Mr. Smalls," Lydia offered.

The man beamed up at her and waved.

Although Lydia had always been an avid rider, it took several moments to accustom herself to the mare and the unfamiliar tack. But once she'd loosened her grip on the reins and settled more firmly into the large saddle, she was able to relax and move with the animal.

"Is this something you do every year?" she asked, catching up to Gideon.

He looked at her questioningly. "What?"

"Ride out to examine the pass?"

He nodded. "Usually Jonah and I make the trip once or twice a week until we can see a possible path to the adjoining valley."

"So, it's not unusual to be completely cut off? Even with the railroad coming through?"

"The railway company tries to keep the tracks clear as long as they can. But eventually, even they have to call it quits. For the last couple of years, we've only been isolated for a few weeks. This year has been…unusual."

Unusual.

That was one way of describing the situation. Nearly three months had elapsed since the avalanche. And this winter, the miners had been forced to contend with more than fifty stranded passengers who were living in their valley, eating their stores, using their supplies. In many ways, it was a blessing that spring had come early, even though there were those who weren't looking forward to the consequences.

"Will you be relieved to see the back of us, Mr. Gault?"

When she met his gaze, Gideon looked as if she'd handed him a time bomb set to explode.

Laughing, she said, "I suppose that there's no diplomatic way of answering that, is there?"

His eyes creased in amusement. "Like I said. I grew up with sisters. I've learned to recognize a loaded question."

"Then let me rephrase. I know that your duties will be simplified. But I wonder if you will miss us in some small way."

He studied her for a moment, then nodded. "Yes, Miss Tomlinson. I dare say that this valley will miss all of you when you've gone. You've brought a measure of joy to what would have been a dreary winter."

Lydia supposed she shouldn't put too much import into his words, but she couldn't ignore the warmth that settled into her heart.

"I'm glad we weren't a complete chore."

He shook his head. "Not a *complete* chore."

When she would have glared at him, he laughed. "Come now, Miss Tomlinson. You mustn't take yourself too seriously. After all, our time together is limited."

Yes. But did it have to be?

"I don't suppose that your views have changed?"

He arched a brow. "What do you mean?"

"When we first arrived, you and Jonah, Mr. Batchwell and Mr. Bottoms…well, you were all so certain that having females in the valley would be the ruin of the mine. Do you still think that way?"

She liked the way that Gideon didn't answer immediately. He seemed to consider the question for some time before saying, "I would say that we've managed to make things work."

"Are production numbers down?"

"No. From what I've seen, they've increased."

"And the safety issues. Has there been a marked increase in injuries?"

She knew by the way he stiffened in the saddle that he had figured out the gist of her argument.

"No. We've had some problems—the tunnel collapse in December and the incident with Jenny Reichmann—"

"Which had nothing to do with the rest of us at the Dovecote."

He inclined his head in agreement.

"Overall, I'd say that the men have been mindful of the risks of their job and have done their best to avoid any dangers they've encountered."

"So, there is no hard evidence that the women have proven to be a distraction."

"I can assure you that the men are plenty distracted, Miss Tomlinson. But there's been no sign of it in their work. *Yet.*"

"On the other hand, there have been definite advantages to having us here, I believe. Take the food, for example…"

Gideon drew his mount to a halt, forcing her to do the same.

"I take it that you're building up to a grand finale in this debate, Miss Tomlinson. Why don't you cut to the chase?"

She reached to pat the neck of the mare.

"I meant nothing of the kind. I merely wanted to know—in your expert opinion—if you felt that men and women could coexist here at Bachelor Bottoms."

He sighed and squinted against the bright sunshine that radiated from the upper slopes of the mountains.

"It doesn't really matter what I think, Miss Tomlinson. I'm a hired man, like the rest of the miners. If you want to make headway with your argument, you'll need to take it up with the owners."

"But I would like your views on the matter, Mr. Gault. If the Misters Batchwell and Bottoms were to come to you and ask the same question, what would you say?"

He met her gaze so completely, so directly, that she nearly looked away.

Nearly.

"Honestly, Miss Tomlinson, I think that Aspen Valley would be better off with the women gone."

The words clutched at her heart like an unseen fist. She should have expected such sentiments coming from one of the Pinkertons tasked with guarding the mail-order brides, but she'd thought—no, she'd *hoped*—that Gideon Gault might look past those challenges to the ways the girls had helped the community. Even he must see that a measure of happiness had come to Bachelor Bottoms, and the women were responsible for helping to make that happen.

"Now, how about we go check out that pass so you have an estimate for the rest of your stay?" Gideon said, urging his mount forward.

And for a moment, the chill that seeped into her body had nothing to do with the wind gusting down from the snowy peaks.

Gideon knew without being told that he'd disappointed Lydia with his answer. Although she tried to keep a blank face, he saw the light fade from her crystal-blue eyes only to be replaced with something that looked very much like…hurt.

As he led his mount up the slope, Gideon pushed that thought away. He was nothing to Lydia Tomlinson—so why would she care one way or the other? For the past few months, he'd been a thorn in her side, just as she'd been one in his.

Nevertheless, he couldn't seem to shake away the feeling that—in his haste to get things back to normal again—he'd inadvertently denigrated the good the women had done.

His eyes automatically scanned the debris field left by the avalanche even as his mind worried over his conversation with Lydia. Despite what he'd said, he would be the first to admit that the ladies had improved Bachelor Bottoms— and he wasn't merely referring to the change in their diet. The food they served at the cook shack—two hot meals and cold meats and cheeses for lunch—were above and beyond anything that Stumpy, the old mine chef, had ever prepared. During the past few cold winter months, the men had learned to treasure time spent over savory stews, rich breads and hearty soups. Gideon probably had a better idea than most the way that the women had carefully planned each repast to make the most out of the community's dwindling supplies. They'd stretched the foodstuffs as far as possible, all without lessening the taste.

There were other ways the ladies had contributed even more. They'd nursed many of the men through illness and injury, brought order and warmth to their surroundings. Even the daily devotionals had grown sweeter from the sounds of their voices and Lydia's touch on the pump organ. Gideon had no doubts that Aspen Valley would become quite dismal again when they left.

But they would have to leave.

Those were the rules of the mine. No drinking, smoking, cussing or women.

Perhaps Phineas Bottoms could be persuaded to take a second look at the requirements for employment, but Ezra Batchwell would never agree. Not in this lifetime or the next. The man was an ardent, confirmed bachelor—had been for as long as Gideon had known him. Gideon knew all about the rumors that the other miners whispered about the bearlike man who had helped to open up one of the most successful silver mines in the territories. That, as a young man, he'd been the victim of unrequited love—and after being refused, he'd vowed to live a life alone.

Gideon was sure that the story was so much hogwash.

Ezra Batchwell was a businessman, through and through. He'd set his course on lifting himself out of the coal mines of Aberdeen and making his fortunes. And he'd done that. But that feat would be the very reason why he wouldn't change his methods. Why would he tinker with success?

"Are things so very bad?"

Gideon jerked from his thoughts to find that Lydia remained by his side. Even more unsettling, she'd been watching him carefully—probably in an effort to read his thoughts again.

He forced himself to take in the slopes around him, the path of rocks and broken limbs. Up ahead, he could see the hulking shapes of the ruined railway cars poking through the drifts, looking like beached whales marooned from a sea of white. It wouldn't be long before the carriages would be completely exposed. Once they were, a crew would salvage whatever the railroad might find useful. Then the twisted rails would be dragged out of the way so that the rail beds could be repaired, regraded, and lined with ties. Thankfully, the damage didn't look nearly as bad as he and Jonah had supposed. Locomotives could probably start heading into the valley by summer.

But the women…

The women would be long gone by then.

He urged his mount the last few bounding strides to the top of the hill so that Gideon could look down, down, into the canyon below. For the first time in months, he could see the glint of the river and the muddy beginnings of a trail. There were still a few spots where negotiating the hairpin turns would be treacherous. But if the weather continued to warm up the way it had…

The brides could be carried out of the valley in a series of wagons by the end of the month.

"Gideon?"

He realized too late that she'd asked a question and still waited for an answer.

"Are things bad?"

He shook his head. "It's melting a whole lot faster than any of us had anticipated."

Her cheeks seemed to pale.

"How much longer do we have?"

He took a pair of field glasses from his saddlebags and peered through the lenses.

"If it doesn't rain again? I'd say a week. Ten days at the most."

He thought he heard her gasp. But when he lowered the glasses, her face was expressionless.

"That soon?"

Again, he couldn't tell from her tone if he'd offered Lydia good news or bad.

Stuffing the field glasses back into place, he nodded. "You'd better tell the girls to start packing. As soon as we can get a rider through the pass to alert the railroad, and the trail looks steady enough for a team and wagon, we'll start the evacuation."

The word *evacuation* seemed wrong, somehow. As if the ladies were being taken somewhere better. Safer. But even though he knew they had to go—for the miners' sakes as well as their own—Gideon couldn't help thinking that, given the chance, the men of Bachelor Bottoms would have done everything in their power to make them feel at home.

The sky was growing dark before Lydia had a chance to relay the information she'd gathered from her trip up the mountain. By the time she'd helped Mr. Smalls take care of her mare, checked in with the women preparing and serving the evening meal, then played the pump organ for the evening Devotional, her brain was a-swirl with the myriad tasks that still needed to be accomplished. Only then could she and the other mail-order brides announce their demands and begin a proper protest.

Did they have enough time?

As she hurried toward the Dovecote, she could see the glow in the windows caused by the myriad lamps. She'd probably missed dinner with the other girls, but she had no doubts that one of the women would have placed a plate of food in the oven for her. Hot tea, coffee or cocoa would be waiting on the stove.

She stumbled, coming to a stop. Now that the sun had dipped below the mountains, the air was brisk, and her breath hung in front of her like a gossamer cloud. Overhead, the skies had become cloudy again and a light misting rain was swiftly turning to sleet.

For a moment, Lydia peered at the Dovecote, seeing the building for what it was—an old equipment shed that had been converted into a haphazard dormitory. The outer boards were rough and peeling. The yard was a series of puddles and matted brown grass. Planks had been stretched over the worst of the mud to give the brides a walkway to a front door that looked like it belonged to a feed store more than a residence.

But the Dovecote had become a home. Even from yards away, Lydia could hear female voices, snatches of singing, laughter.

For a girl who'd never known the company of sisters—or young women at all, for that matter—the dormitory had proven to be an adventure. Lydia had learned so much about herself—how to have patience and understanding, to share the burdens and accomplishments of others. It was for that reason that she'd been persuaded to organize their current plan.

Had they started too late? Would they be able to do

enough to disrupt the routines of Bachelor Bottoms and its owners? Would Batchwell and Bottoms realize the extent of the sacrifices they demanded of their men? Could Lydia get them to see that denying their employees of their wives and sweethearts didn't just lessen the man, it lessened the entire community?

The door opened and Iona Skye, a regal widow in her sixties, poked her head out. "Is something the matter, Lydia?"

"No! No, I'm coming."

Lydia hurried the last few yards, dodging into the warmth of the Dovecote.

As she'd anticipated, she was immediately inundated with the rich scents of perfume, baking bread and a hint of cinnamon.

Iona reached to help Lydia with her coat. "Let's get you out of those wet things. You'll catch your death."

"It started drizzling as I turned down the lane."

"Come here by the fire."

Before Lydia quite knew what had happened, she found herself ensconced in a comfortable chair, a quilt draped over her lap, and a steaming cup of tea cradled between her palms.

"I'll have your dinner ready in no time!" Marie called from the small kitchen area.

"No rush. Really."

Lydia knew that her friends were trying to give her enough time to unwind from her busy day. Although they pretended to be involved with their own tasks, there was no disguising the way they hovered nearby. She saw no reason for prolonging their misery.

"I have news, so gather round."

Immediately, the brides grabbed their chairs, upended crates, and even a few barrels—using the seating arrangements they'd managed to cobble together in the past few months.

"As you probably all know by now, I rode with Gideon Gault up the mountainside to check the pass."

"And?" Stefania asked breathlessly.

"It's worse than we thought. The snow has been beaten down by the heat and the rain. According to Mr. Gault, we have only a week—maybe ten days—until he and his men will organize a wagon train to force us out of the valley."

"He said those very words? That we'd be forced out?"

Lydia held up a hand. "No. He didn't say that *exactly*." She sighed. "But I did manage to ascertain his true feelings. He thinks that we should all leave as soon as possible."

"So, we can't count on his becoming one of our allies," Myra Claussen said mournfully. Her identical twin, Miriam, gripped her hand.

"I don't see how we can change his mind. He seemed very adamant."

"Which means we're going to have to proceed very carefully. If Mr. Gault stumbles across our plans before we can get everything into place…" Iona murmured.

"He will do his best to stop us," Lydia confirmed.

"What should we do?" Emmarissa Elliot asked from the opposite end of the room.

Lydia thought for a moment, her finger unconsciously rubbing at the ache between her brows.

"We're going to have to step things up. In my opinion, we need at least a hundred men to join sides with us. Anything less won't cause a pinch in the staffing of the mine." Lydia pointed to Anna Kendrick. "Were you able to talk to Sumner?"

"Yes, but only briefly. She said that Jonah's getting restless and it's only a matter of time before he ignores her insistence that he remain quarantined from the rest of the men."

Lydia turned to Millie Kauffman. "What about Charles Wanlass?"

"Willow said that he's behind us a hundred percent. He's even willing to talk to his own crew once we're ready."

"Good. What about Phineas Bottoms?" She turned to Iona and was surprised when the older woman blushed.

"I have tried to develop a…rapport with the man at the cook shack."

"And…" Lydia prompted encouragingly.

"Do I have to?" Iona whispered.

"You know how important this is to us all."

Iona shifted uncomfortably in her seat, but nodded. "I'll ask him to join me for lunch tomorrow."

"And…"

"And I'll arrange to dine with him…*alone*…in the private room in the cook shack."

"Do you think you can keep him occupied?"

Lydia didn't miss the way Iona's hands trembled before she gripped them in her lap.

"I'll do my best."

"Excellent. That means the rest of us will need to strike the storehouse tonight."

She glanced up at the mantel clock, noting the hour. "Those of you who are willing and able, dress warmly, and we'll meet down here at midnight. Agreed?"

The women grinned and spoke together.

"Agreed!"

Chapter Three

Darkness hung thick and black as Lydia and the women crept toward the storage house.

So far, they hadn't encountered any men—but the fact that they'd brought their number of "hostages" up to thirty-nine by the end of the night might have been partially responsible.

Marie Rousseau stumbled over a crack in the boardwalk and Lydia grasped her elbow to keep her from falling. The Claussen twins, Myra and Miriam, giggled, then corrected the path of the pumpkin wagon they pulled behind them.

"Shhh," Iona whispered. "We can't let anyone know we're in town, let alone that we're raiding the storehouse."

"I feel positively wicked," Millie Kauffman whispered with apparent glee.

"We've become outlaws," Hannah added.

"We can't be outlaws. We haven't done anything illegal," Miriam insisted.

"We've kidnapped nearly forty men," Myra pointed out.

"I don't think it can be considered a crime if they've agreed to the situation."

"We're about to burglarize the storehouse."

"Honestly, Myra. You sound like you *want* to be breaking the law." Miriam's exasperation was so apparent that Lydia could nearly hear the woman rolling her eyes. "Besides, we aren't taking anything, we're simply *rearranging* something."

"Shhh." Lydia lifted her hand, her eyes roaming the shadows. There'd been a noise coming from the alley. A soft panting.

A dog darted from the shadows, and she wilted in relief.

"Let's get this done as soon as possible and get back to the Dovecote."

Lydia took a key from her pocket and unlocked the heavy padlock that secured the door. Then, she allowed the women to slip inside while she watched the street.

Once they had all safely entered, she closed the door again and reached for the lantern kept on a hook nearby. After lighting it with a friction match found in the iron holder, she adjusted the wick, then whispered, "Find the ammunition as soon as you can and load up your baskets and the wagon. We can't stay here a moment longer than necessary."

They hurried down the aisles, using the hand-drawn map provided by Dr. Sumner Ramsey until they found the spot where crates of bullets had been stacked on shelves.

Lydia held up the lamp, revealing boxes and boxes labeled by type and caliber.

"*Ach.* So, so many," Greta murmured in her heavy German accent.

"Oh, dear," Iona sighed. "I had no idea that the camp armed itself this heavily."

"There's no way that we're going to be able to haul all of these back to the Dovecote, not even with the wagon."

"We'll take what we can, then come back tomorrow for more."

Greta was the first to grasp one of the crates, pry it

open with a cleaver from the cook shack, and begin removing the ammunition from inside. She quickly loaded an empty feed sack and placed it in the wagon. Beside her, the rest of the ladies sprang into action, filling baskets and pillowcases—and whatever else they'd managed to find to transport their booty.

Lydia hoped that such measures would prove unnecessary. She doubted that even Ezra Batchwell would resort to an armed confrontation in order to get the women to toe the line. But she didn't want to take any chances. She'd anticipated that the disappearance of the weapons would capture someone's attention, but she'd hoped that it would take them longer to realize that the bullets were gone. By that time, they would have hidden the ammunition so the men couldn't change their minds.

A rattling came from the front of the storehouse and the women gasped.

"What's that?" Stefania whispered.

"Shh!"

They froze.

Lydia barely dared to breathe as the rattling resolved itself into the unmistakable creak of the door.

"Give me the lantern!"

Marie scooped their only source of light from a nearby crate and handed it to Lydia.

"Stay here. I'll do my best to get rid of whoever it is."

She quickly strode down one of the side aisles, then cut back to the section of the storehouse that was reserved for food. Without even looking, she grabbed a bag from one of the shelves, then moved more slowly toward the front entrance.

Even though she'd been expecting to encounter someone on her trip back to the door, she jumped when a shape loomed out of the darkness. A gasp pushed from her lips when the lamplight slid over the man's face.

Gideon Gault.

"Mr. Gault, you nearly scared the life out of me!"

He seemed just as surprised to see her.

"Miss Tomlinson. It's after midnight. What on earth are you doing in the storehouse so late at night?"

"We had an…emergency at the Dovecote. One of the brides fell ill and we were out of…" Too late, she realized she didn't know what she'd grabbed from the shelf. Glancing down, she grimaced. "Beans. We were out of beans."

Gideon blinked at her with such a puzzled expression that she nearly laughed out loud.

"Beans?"

"Yes. It's well known that a poultice made of beans and…and vinegar…is an excellent cure for…"

For what? What?

"Female complaints."

In Lydia's wide experience, nothing quelled a man's curiosity faster than mentioning "female complaints." But she'd forgotten that Gideon had been raised with five sisters, so apparently, he was made of sterner stuff.

"Beans and vinegar."

"And mustard." Lydia fought to keep herself from wincing. "And a dash of bacon grease."

Lydia could feel panic beginning to flutter in her chest like a flock of moths, but she fought to keep her expression serene.

"And it couldn't wait until morning?"

"No. Not really?"

The man eyed her with those coffee-brown eyes, and she was sure that he could see the deceit hanging over her like a black cloud, but he finally sighed.

"Where are your guards?"

Locked up in the Miners' Hall.

"Guards?"

"The Pinkertons who are supposed to be watching the Dovecote."

"I… I've no idea. We haven't seen them all day."

Honestly, that should have been the last thing to admit.

Gideon lifted his hand to the crease between his brows and rubbed the spot as if he had a headache. For the first time, she noted the exhaustion that lined his features.

"Shouldn't you be in bed, Mr. Gault?"

"I could ask the same question of you, Miss Tomlinson."

She gestured to the door. "I was heading there now."

"Then I'll escort you home."

She balked at the idea, sure that he'd somehow divined that the dormitory was missing half of its occupants, but for the life of her, she couldn't think of a plausible reason for refusing his offer.

"That would be much appreciated."

She reluctantly blew out the lantern, knowing that she would be leaving her friends in complete darkness. Unfortunately, that fact couldn't be helped.

Gideon held the door for her, allowing her to step into the cool night air.

"Do you have your key?"

"Yes, of course."

To her consternation, he snapped the lock shut, effectively imprisoning the women who were still inside. Then he made a sweeping motion with his hand.

"After you."

They walked in silence for several minutes, but with each step, Lydia grew increasingly uncomfortable. There was something…companionable about having Gideon escort her home. Something sweet. And that was not something she wanted to feel about the tall Pinkerton.

"You mentioned you had five sisters."

There was a beat of silence and she realized she hadn't asked a question, but had offered a statement of fact. Thankfully, Gideon seemed willing to follow her lead.

"Anna, April, Addie, Adele, and Adelaide. All five of them are older by several years."

Lydia couldn't help laughing. "So why weren't you named Alfred or Abraham?"

"I think my mother was expecting another girl. She'd chosen the name Augusta. When I was born, she named me after my father instead."

"He must have been proud."

Gideon shrugged. "Unfortunately, my father had already passed of diphtheria."

So, Gideon truly had been raised in a house with nothing but women. No wonder he'd found the arrival of the mail-order brides such a trial.

"Then Bachelor Bottoms must have seemed like a masculine haven when you arrived."

Gideon shot her a look, and to her surprise, he didn't offer a pithy answer. "Actually, for a little while, I missed a bit of feminine fussing from my family. I'd spent years in the Army, so I'd had enough of an all-male environment."

His expression became strangely tight, his eyes shuttered.

"Then why did you come to the territories? Why not stay at home for a little longer?"

He shot her a glance, seeming to weigh whether or not he should confide in her. "By that time, my mother had died as well and my sisters had all married and scattered. I managed to visit them, but… I couldn't bring myself to be a burden."

"Family is never a burden, Mr. Gault."

He eyed her curiously. "That's not a response that I

would expect from a woman fighting for…how do you put it? Female equality and emancipation?"

She sniffed. "Neither of those issues rule out the possibility of a family, Mr. Gault. I believe that women should be given the same rights and opportunities as men. But I also understand that most ladies feel a keen need to be wives and mothers."

"*Most* ladies? Does that mean that you have no designs on ensuring such a fate, Miss Tomlinson?"

She opened her mouth, then closed it again. Somehow, they had strayed into perilous territory.

"That is neither here nor there."

"Mmm. So, you're afraid to commit one way or the other?"

They'd reached the end of the boardwalk at the edge of town and when Gideon stepped into the lane, she stayed where she was, needing the added height so that she could meet his gaze. Eye to eye. Man to woman. Equals.

"I have committed myself wholeheartedly to the Cause, Mr. Gault. In doing so, I spend most of my time traveling and lecturing. Neither activity lends itself to a happy marriage or family life. Therefore, I have chosen to remain… unfettered."

He seemed to consider her statement. "An interesting choice of words. *Unfettered.* Is that how you see marriage and motherhood? As a punishment or an impediment?"

"You're purposely twisting my words."

"No, I'm merely trying to understand them."

She folded her arms tightly in front of her. "There are many women who—"

"We're not talking about other women. We're talking about you."

"I…" She huffed. "I don't see marriage or motherhood in a negative light. I merely don't see it as part of my future."

"Because…"

"Because I doubt there's a man alive who would have the courage to put up with the likes of me!"

The words blurted from her mouth without any thought. But before she could retrieve them, Gideon Gault laughed.

"You may be right," he offered.

There was no sting to his voice, no negative inflection. If anything, she sensed that he found the male population lacking in courage rather than the other way around. In any event, he resumed walking, forcing her to trail along behind him.

"So, you'll be heading to California after this?"

She quick-stepped to catch up to him, nodding. "I begin my tour in San Francisco. Granted, many of my engagements have already passed and will have to be rescheduled, but I'm eager to get underway." Peering up at him in the darkness, she asked, "Have you been to California, Mr. Gault?"

He shook his head. "No. I've always wanted to go there, but so far, I've never had the chance."

"I hear that it's warm all year round and you can pluck lemons and oranges right from the trees."

"Will your itinerary allow you such luxuries?"

He was teasing her now, so she responded in kind. "Oh, I'll make time. I also want to stand on the shore so that I can write to my aunts and tell them that I've dipped my toes in the Atlantic and the Pacific."

"Aunts?"

"Yes. My aunts have been my guardians for nearly a dozen years."

"That must mean that you've lost your parents as well. I'm so sorry."

Yes, her mother had died soon after she was born. But her father…

He might not be dead, but he *was* lost to her.

"There's no need to be sorry. My aunts have been wonderful to me. They saw to it that I had the finest education and a loving home." Even more importantly, they'd helped her leave her shameful past behind.

They were almost to the door of the Dovecote now and Lydia's steps unconsciously slowed. For some reason, she felt reluctant to end their walk. Being able to talk to Gideon this way, openly, honestly, had shown her a different side to the man. One that was…companionable.

"Here you are," Gideon announced needlessly.

"Yes. Thank you."

"In the future, perhaps you would be so kind as to wait for your guards to escort you around town?"

There was no sting behind the words, only weariness.

"You do realize that there's no need for you and your men to trail us as if we had designs upon the company's silver, don't you?"

"I don't think the silver is Mr. Batchwell's main concern."

"What else could we take? By your account, we only have a few weeks left in the valley at most."

"Ah, but you and your friends have already stolen the affections of most of the men in Aspen Valley, which is why no one wants you to leave. That fact probably worries Batchwell more than his silver. So as long as I'm told to keep my men watching over the females in the Dovecote, that's what I'll have to do." He motioned to the door. "I'll wait here until you're inside, and I've heard the bolt hit home."

Lydia moved in a daze, entering and locking the door. After all her pestering and prodding, Gideon had admitted, of his own free will, that the women had touched the lives of the men in Bachelor Bottoms. Judging by his tone, he didn't seem to mind.

She hurried to the window, pushing aside the curtain in time to see Gideon pausing to look over his shoulder. He must have seen her, because he lifted a hand to the brim of his hat.

She waved in return, waiting until he'd disappeared into the darkness. Then, she tossed the bag of beans onto the table and meandered upstairs to her room.

Once inside, she lit the lamp and adjusted the wick. As she did so, she caught her reflection in the mirror. For some reason, her cheeks were pink and her eyes sparkled with an inner energy.

How very odd.

Up to this point, she'd thought of the Pinkerton as something of a nuisance. But tonight, she'd had a peek into the gentleman behind the uniform, and she'd been surprised by what she'd found. He really was an interesting man. Although she'd learned a little about his family, there were so many things she still wanted to know.

Her hands lifted to her hair and she began removing the hairpins one by one. Sitting on the edge of her bed, she glanced at Iona's empty cot and wished she could talk to her friend and get her opinion on the change in…

Iona.

The other girls were still locked in the storehouse!

Lydia jumped to her feet and raced pell-mell down the staircase. Then, after peeking out the front window to make sure that there was no sign of Gideon Gault, she ran as fast as she could back to town.

Gideon didn't bother going back to the Pinkerton office and the barracks on the upper floor. He'd only gone a short distance into town before the old familiar restlessness began to bubble up inside of him.

He had to get away.

He had to keep moving.

He had to feel the wind in his hair and the roll of a horse beneath him.

By the time he'd reached the livery and saddled his gelding, he was breathing heavily and his lungs felt as if bands of iron tightened around them. The past seemed to suck him back into that dark place where flashes of battle crowded into his brain, pushing everything aside. Try as he might to stay rooted in the present, the coppery taste of fear tainted his tongue. His ears seemed to ring with cannon fire, and the stench of gunpowder and blood lingered in his nostrils. Then, just as quickly, the sensations shifted into something worse. Far worse.

Death.

Disease.

Untold suffering.

Swinging onto the back of his mount, he spurred it into a gallop as soon as the animal had cleared the threshold. Then he was riding, riding, up toward the mine where the intermittent lanterns illuminated the road.

Once he'd passed the opening, he was forced into slowing his horse, even though he wanted to keep flying through the darkness so that he could chase away the ghosts of his past and the sensation of being trapped. He doubled back in the other direction, taking a rarely used road that was little more than a set of wagon ruts etched into the grass.

It wasn't until he found himself at the top of the slopes and looking down into the canyon that he brought his mount to a stop. Dragging the cool, damp air into his lungs, he closed his eyes, trying to push away the memories that seemed determined to wash over him and transport him to another time. He felt another mount beneath him, quivering as Gideon led it toward the noise and violence of the battlefield. He remembered the way it had reared back, unseating him, beginning a cascade of ill-timed events that would see him captured, then transported south.

To Andersonville.

His body and spirit railed against the images that flashed behind his eyes like malicious lightning bugs.

So much death.

Such despair.

As if his very soul depended on it, Gideon took deep breaths in an attempt to re-anchor himself in the present.

He would not give in to the past.

Not tonight.

Gradually, the sensations of misery and filth began to fade beneath the heady scent of pine and wet grass.

And something more. A faint hint of…

Gardenias and lemons.

An image of Lydia sprang into his head, pushing away the remembered ugliness of war. In his mind's eye, he saw her in a montage of poses: militantly regarding him with her hands on her hips, challenging him with an imperious stare and smiling up at him in the darkness.

That thought lingered, becoming more real as he remembered the way that the moonlight had slipped over the curve of her cheek and sparkled in her eyes. Crystal-blue eyes the color of the Aspen River first thing in the morning.

The woman was full of surprises, he'd give her that. Until today, most of their encounters had proven to be a battle of wits. She'd seemed to delight in slipping away from the Pinkerton guards, and Gideon found secret pleasure in hauling her back into line.

But tonight…she'd been more open. More…

Real.

A man would have his hands full with a woman like that. If he didn't keep her in line…

No. That kind of thinking is exactly what Lydia would expect of him. He could already hear her railing at him that the fairer sex wasn't meant to be controlled. They were meant to be…

Loved.

But Lydia had made it clear that she didn't want to be loved. At least not by a man. She intended to live her life as a champion for women's suffrage.

Which was too bad. Because a woman like that could be a formidable force. Exasperating, yes, but she would also be fiercely loyal and devoted. No doubt, she would love a man with the same passion as she fought for women's equality.

Gideon shook his head to rid it of such thoughts. Why was he even thinking of such a thing? Lydia Tomlinson was law unto herself. In a matter of days, she would resume her journey to California, and Gideon's life and routine could return to normal.

It was better that way.

Much better.

As he shifted in the saddle, his horse nickered slightly. And somehow, the noise sounded like the animal was laughing at him.

Gideon's gaze scanned the darkness of the pass one last time, taking in the glint of moonlight on the river below. And something more. A spark of light?

He leaned forward in the saddle, ruing the fact that he didn't have his field glasses with him. For long moments, he scoured the area below him until he was sure that the glow had been a figment of his imagination.

He'd decided to return to town when he saw it again. A tiny flicker down by the riverbanks.

A fire?

For nearly a quarter hour, he watched, and in that time, the light neither grew larger or smaller—which meant it was being tended. Occasionally, Gideon would lose sight of it altogether—as if someone or something blocked it from view. Then it would reappear.

The sight wasn't completely unexpected. The miners weren't the only ones to make Aspen Valley their home. There were trappers and hunters who lived or crossed through the area. Farther north, beyond the next mountain range, there were farmers and ranchers trying to eke out a living in the fertile lowlands. If the pass had opened enough for Aspen Valley to contact the outside world, it only stood to reason that the outer world could come to them. For all Gideon knew, it could be the Pinkerton offices or the railway company trying to make contact.

But something about the idea of a stranger only a few miles away, with the Bachelor Bottoms warehouses full of silver ore and the Dovecote bursting with single women, caused the hairs at his nape to prickle. All thought of sleep skittered away. He would return to his quarters, retrieve his field glasses and leave word with his men that he'd be gone until morning. It shouldn't take much longer than that to investigate what he'd seen and make up his mind whether added security measures were needed.

Chapter Four

Gideon hurried into the Meeting House with only seconds
to spare—which meant that the only seats available were
toward the front. He could feel the heavy weight of dozens
of eyes settling upon him as he dragged his hat from his
head and did his best to finger-comb his hair into place.

He probably looked a sorry sight. He hadn't slept at
all the night before, and his clothes were spattered with
mud. His hand rasped against the stubble at his jaw and
his stomach gnawed with hunger. After a fruitless morning where he'd been able to discover little more than the
still-warm ashes of the fire he'd seen the night before, he'd
needed the steadying influence of the morning Devotional
to begin his day.

Leaning back in his pew, he allowed the prelude music
to soak into his tired muscles. Around him, sunlight
streamed through the windows of the Meeting House,
forming bands of warmth that highlighted the crowded
pews. Since the hours at the mine had been extended,
there were only two shifts, rather than the usual three,
which meant that more of the miners attended the early
services. The benches were filled to capacity with men
who'd finished their work. Their weary, dusty faces butted

up against those miners who were clean and eager to get to their posts.

Gideon had always thought that the Devotionals were a symbolic leveler. Here, there were no rich men, no poor men, no handsome dandies or ugly mutts. They were simply children of their Heavenly Father seeking the influence of the Spirit.

His eyes skipped from row to row, stopping at the front pews on the opposite side of the room.

No, not just men. The women came as well. Since Ezra Batchwell had been sequestered in his house with his injury, the women had stretched the boundaries of their freedom—and he supposed that it was to their credit that they'd sought out the spiritual venue. This morning, they sat in two rows, wearing their best Sunday bonnets. Some of them glanced over their shoulders to smile shyly at the men behind them. But for the most part, they seemed lost in their own thoughts, enjoying the music being played by their leader, Miss Lydia Tomlinson.

Gideon would have been the first to admit that Lydia was a fine organ player. She managed to coax sounds out of the old pump instrument that he never would have believed possible. This morning, she was playing something lyrical, classical. Gideon had heard the melody before, although he wasn't schooled enough to know its name. He only knew that the melody seemed to chase itself from high to low then back again, bringing to mind soaring birds. Or playful cherubs.

The moment the thought appeared, Gideon pushed it away. Honestly, the lack of sleep was making him quite fanciful—yet another sign that the time had come for the women to leave the valley.

But even as he told himself to keep his mind on his job, he couldn't help watching Lydia as she bent over the keys.

She seemed lost to the music, her fingers flying, her eyes slightly closed as she played from memory. She'd removed her bonnet before sitting down and the sun wove among the coils and curls, gilding her hair until it seemed to glow.

So beautiful.

Stop it!

He tore his gaze away, focusing resolutely on his hat, running the brim through his palms. But just when he'd begun to control his thoughts, the congregation rose for the first hymn, and without thought, his eyes strayed back to Lydia again.

He couldn't account for the way he felt a sense of… peace when he looked her way, as well as a heady anticipation. He had no doubts that within moments of meeting up with her again, the verbal sparring would begin—and the thought gave him a jolt of energy that seemed entirely inappropriate.

Once again, he yanked his thoughts—and his gaze— away from Miss Tomlinson. With all his might, he concentrated on the benediction, then on the sermon being offered by Charles Wanlass.

Unfortunately, his friend chose today, of all days, to speak about love, commitment and faithfulness.

Gideon fought the urge to roll his eyes. The man had it bad. It was there in the way he gazed down at his wife, Willow, who sat on the front pew with her friends. Charles was completely and irrevocably in love with his bride and thoroughly besotted with the twins they'd adopted as their own. It was enough to make a body wonder what he was missing.

Almost.

Gideon would have to be blind not to see the transformation which had occurred in his usually taciturn friend— and in Jonah Ramsey as well. But that didn't mean that such ideas of marital bliss would provide the same happy ending for Gideon. Much as he might want a sweetheart someday, he had to be realistic. He had nothing that he could offer a woman save an uncertain future. He could never settle down enough to make such a woman happy. Not when his nights were still often haunted by dreams of Andersonville and the savagery he'd witnessed. There were times when he woke screaming, his body trembling, his skin icy with sweat.

No woman should be asked to share such burdens.

Especially not one so refined as Lydia Tomlinson.

"Is somethin' wrong, buddy?"

Gideon started at the whisper. Beside him, Gus Creakle eyed him with rheumy eyes.

"No. I'm fine."

Creakle grinned, his eyes nearly disappearing beneath a lifetime's worth of wrinkles.

"She's a pretty little filly, ain't she?"

"Shh!" Gideon glanced around to make sure the man hadn't been overheard. But other than Smalls, who sat to Creakle's right, the other men seemed tuned to the sermon.

"She'd make a fine little wife."

"I'm not looking for a wife, Creakle."

The man chortled, the white tufts of hair surrounding his bald pate quivering as if from an unseen breeze. "I don't suppose a man is ever really lookin'. Most times, the notion falls in his lap." He laughed again. "Either that, or the notion smacks him upside the head."

"This is Aspen Valley, Creakle. A man can't stay employed if he entertains such thoughts."

Creakle huffed dismissively. "Some things is more important than a job, you mark my words."

"I happen to like my job."

"But it don't make you happy." Creakle gestured to

Charles who had paused in his sermon again to wink down at Willow. "Look at yer buddy there. He was a big ol' lump o' misery until that little gal came along."

Gideon didn't think he would go so far as to call Charles a "big old lump of misery," but he had to admit that Creakle had a point.

"And Mr. Jonah. Well, now. That man has had his life handed back to him—and I'm not talkin' about the way the doc operated on him. He's finally lookin' toward the future instead of the past."

"I'll admit that Charles and Jonah have found something special, Creakle. But I'm not shopping for what they're selling. And even if I were, Miss Tomlinson would be the last woman I'd pursue."

Finally, Creakle sat back, his eyes twinkling. His only response was, "We'll see."

But Gideon wasn't paying attention any longer. He'd happened to glance toward Lydia, only to find that she was looking at him.

And there was something about her too-innocent expression that made his heart pump a little bit faster.

Lydia waited until the last miner had left the Meeting House before allowing her feet to still at the organ. The final chord died with a sigh, leaving a moment of heavy silence. Then, the women began gathering their things.

Iona brought Lydia her coat and bonnet. A wrinkle of worry had settled between the older woman's brows.

"It's only a matter of time before someone starts noticing that there are men missing from their shifts."

Lydia had spent the night mulling over the problem and had finally come up with a temporary solution.

"I know, but I think I've come up with a way to prevent anyone from pinpointing our involvement for a little longer. I assigned Myra and Miriam to make some quarantine placards. With Jonah already diagnosed with measles, it's not a stretch that there could be other cases."

Iona's eyes crinkled at the corners in delight.

"Not a stretch at all."

"And we wouldn't want the new cases to infect the rest of the population."

"No. That would be horrible."

"Make up a list of the men we have so far. As soon as we have the quarantine signs in place, we'll take it to the mine. Who's running things now that Jonah is being kept at home?"

Iona's gaze sparkled with amusement. "Charles Wanlass."

Lydia grinned, knowing that they had an ally who would take their list at face value, no questions asked.

"Wonderful. And you've arranged to have lunch with Phineas Bottoms?"

Iona's cheeks grew pink. "Yes."

"I know you'll charm the socks off the man."

The older woman offered a sound that was very near a girlish titter. "I doubt that, but I'll do my best."

"So that leaves…"

Lydia walked to the windows, watching as Gideon Gault strode across the street to the Pinkerton offices.

"What are you going to do with that one?" Hannah asked, nodding in the man's direction. "The other men have been easy to sway to our cause, but he'll never willingly concede."

"He's going to catch on and raise the alarm," Sophie added with a note of doom.

"Then we'll have to take him by force."

The other women regarded her with wide eyes. So far, the men had been easy to catch—a blanket thrown over their shoulders or an invitation to the Dovecote. After a quick explanation from the women, they'd been willing to play along. But Gideon Gault would not prove to be so biddable. Even if they managed to kidnap the man, they would have to find a way to keep him hidden and under their control.

"We're going to need those iron manacles we saw in the Pinkerton office," Lydia said slowly. "And some of Sumner's sleeping powders."

Sophie gasped.

Hannah smiled.

"When will you make your move?" Iona whispered, despite the fact that none of the men were nearby to overhear them.

"As soon as we can gather our supplies and I can get the man alone. Get everything ready and bring it to the Dovecote. I'll arrange to have the Pinkerton join us for a meal."

Gideon's stomach rumbled as he pored over the latest ore reports from the mine. With the rails damaged, there would be no trains arriving at the warehouse near the station in town. Batchwell Bottoms Mine employees were going to have to haul the ore through the pass, then far enough overland to hook up with the railroad. They would have to use teams and wagons for at least ten miles, maybe more. On Gideon's end, that meant double the guards, double the headaches.

The entire situation wasn't completely new to Gideon. He'd come to Aspen Valley a few years before the railroad had been completed, so he knew the challenges and dangers involved in shipping the silver by wagon. But with everything so unsettled in the mining community, and his morning spent looking for whoever had spent the night in the pass, his gut warned him there would be trouble ahead. Trouble with a capital *T*. Trouble with—

"Problems?"

He started, then burst to his feet when he looked up to find Lydia watching him with arched brows.

"So sorry. I didn't mean to startle you."

She offered him an innocent smile, but he wasn't buying it. This woman managed to set off his inner alarms more than the thought of hauling a warehouse full of silver out of the valley.

"Miss Tomlinson," he murmured, wondering how she'd managed to sneak up on him without a hint of warning. "I thought you promised me that you'd stick to your guard today."

"He was busy helping Iona in the cook shack, and I knew I'd only be gone a few moments."

She set a plate on the blotter of his desk along with a mug of coffee.

"I didn't see you come into the cook shack after the morning Devotional, so I figured I'd bring the food to you."

She lifted the napkin from the plate to reveal potatoes, ham, biscuits and two fried eggs with their glistening yolks staring up at him like eyes. Although Gideon wanted to tell her that her concern was unnecessary, his stomach rumbled in response. Too late, he realized he hadn't eaten much the night before and nothing this morning.

"A man can't work properly on an empty stomach."

To Gideon's consternation, she sat in the chair opposite, and it was clear from her posture that she didn't intend to move anytime soon.

"Go ahead. I'll keep you company while you eat."

Gideon was pretty sure that her suggestion was a bad idea, but after she'd been kind enough to think of him, he supposed it would be churlish to send her out the door.

He reluctantly returned to his own seat.

"Would you care for a biscuit?" he asked, gesturing to the pair upon his plate.

"I've already had my breakfast, but thank you all the same. Go on."

He bowed his head for a quick, silent prayer, then took up his knife and fork, but still couldn't bring himself to wolf his food down in front of her. "You're sure you don't want anything?"

"Positive. But I'll be a little put out if you don't taste things while they're hot."

With that admonition in mind, he gingerly cut his meat. Within minutes, the savory goodness of the meal banished the rest of his reservations and he began to dine in earnest.

"Where are you from originally, Mr. Gault?"

He looked up, but sensed no guile behind her question, merely a casual interest in keeping him company as she'd originally stated.

"Ohio."

"Really? When I think of Ohio, I picture rolling pastures and fertile farmland. Were you raised on a farm?"

Gideon shook his head. "My grandfather owned an ironworks, so I spent my younger days working with the smelters."

Her brows rose. "How fascinating. Somehow, I never would have pictured you as a factory boy. You seem so… at home in the wilds of the territories."

Gideon didn't tell her that he'd once planned on taking over the ironworks for his grandfather, that he'd intended to double the size of the foundry and make Gault Industries a household name. During his time in the war, he'd fantasized about investing in modern machines and training their workforce with newer methods.

But he'd only been home a week before he'd realized that he couldn't go back to the man he'd once been. As soon as he'd stepped into his grandfather's offices, the walls had seemed to close around him, cutting off his ability to breathe. And the heat from the smelters had smothered him like a hot Georgia night. His grandfather had been forced to pull him out of the building to stop his screams.

Gideon wrenched his thoughts away from that moment. Looking up, he found Lydia watching him curiously. "I guess the wide-open spaces have grown on me."

She opened her mouth, clearly intent on pursuing the subject, but to his surprise, she motioned to his plate instead. "Enjoy the potatoes and the ham," she said. "We've used the last of them, I'm afraid. We've only got a few more sacks of dried carrots and onions, then we'll be out of vegetables of any kind."

Her words made the food all the more delicious.

"You've managed to stretch things to the last. You and your ladies should be congratulated. I think we ran out of root vegetables about mid-January last year."

The compliment made her beam.

"Thank you, Mr. Gault. I'll be sure to tell the ladies. They were worried that they hadn't rationed things enough."

"I daresay we can survive on meat and baked goods until the pass clears. Once we manage to get through the pass and can hook up with one of the telegraph lines, we can send for fresh supplies."

The joy slipped from her features, and too late, he realized that his words proved to be a reminder that the women would be sent away long before such foodstuffs would arrive. He braced himself for an argument about why the women should be allowed to stay, but to his surprise, Lydia didn't accept the bait. Instead, she rose to her feet saying, "I'll send one of the other girls to fetch your plate in a little while. In the meantime, I wondered if you would be willing to join us at the Dovecote for a late lunch tomorrow…say three o'clock?"

His brows rose, and once again, he felt a niggling suspicion. Miss Tomlinson was up to something. He was sure of it. She was far too solicitous. Too…nice.

"Why?"

"Why what?" She blinked at him, her eyes so clear, so blue. And innocent.

"Why do you want me to come to the Dovecote for lunch?"

Again, she seemed to bat those incredibly long lashes.

"To eat?" she drawled as if he were rather dense.

"We could eat at the cook shack."

She sighed and folded her arms across her chest. "The women have some questions about their upcoming journey. I thought it would be more efficient if they could ask you themselves—without being overheard by every Tom, Dick and Harry having a sandwich in the cook shack."

Her explanation seemed logical—making his own response seem truculent. And yet…

He couldn't escape the feeling that he was walking into a trap.

"What are you up to, Lydia?"

She stiffened. "I don't know what you mean."

"Let's say you're acting out of character."

"Out of charac—"

Gideon stood. "Yes, out of character. Let's face it, we've spent most of the last few months bickering with one another." He waved to his empty plate. "And now, suddenly you're worried about whether I'm eating enough or sleeping enough or—"

"I'm simply being polite!"

"Well, stop it!"

The words echoed in the small room, reverberating in

a way that made Gideon realize he'd stomped right over churlish and marched on to childish.

"Fine," Lydia huffed. "I'll leave you alone—right now and for however many days I have left in this valley."

He sighed, his head dropping. "Look, I'm sorry. I shouldn't have been so…"

"Suspicious?"

He conceded with a nod.

"It's just that… I've got a lot on my mind and…" He met her gaze head-on. This time, she didn't regard him with a neutral stare. Instead, her eyes glittered with a mixture of pique and irritation. "And I'd love to come to the Dovecote for lunch tomorrow afternoon. I'll be there at three."

After a quick nod in his direction, she strode from the room in a rustle of skirts, the door slamming behind her.

He winced, then slowly sank back into his seat.

Once again, Lydia had barely navigated a few yards before being joined by a pair of women from the Dovecote. This time, Iona and Marie accompanied her on either side.

"Well?" Marie asked somewhat timidly.

"He agreed to meet for lunch at three."

Iona smiled. "That's a good thing, isn't it?"

Lydia tried her best to tamp down the emotions whirling in her breast—excitement, trepidation and most astonishingly, guilt. "Yes. It's a good thing. Because the man is already more suspicious than we'd supposed." Her mind swung to the countless things that still needed to be done. "Do we have the placards in place?"

"Yes. The quarantine is now official." Iona's eyes sparkled in delight. "And just in time. The 'measles' seem to be spreading."

"Oh?"

"Yes, a dozen men heard about our protest and volunteered to participate."

"Really?" Lydia's heart thumped at the thought.

"I believe Charles is responsible. He and Willow have begun inviting a few of the married men to their home. After plying them with Willow's cookies, they've outlined how they hope to persuade Batchwell and Bottoms to change the rules. So far, their efforts seem to be working."

"Wonderful. Are you ready for your lunch with Mr. Bottoms, Iona?"

The woman's cheeks grew pink. "I've made a special meal complete with his favorite dried cherry pie for dessert."

"And you'll remember to subtly ask him for information on his views about the effect the women have had on the community?"

"Yes. I made up a little card with possible questions which I'll keep tucked in my pocket. If I need to, I can peek at it under the table."

Lydia reached to squeeze the woman's hand, knowing that Iona felt uncomfortable being thrown into the role of femme fatale. But of the two owners, Bottoms was the most approachable, and Lydia had noticed of late that he seemed to follow Iona with his eyes. In Lydia's opinion, that spark of interest should be encouraged.

"Very smart, even if I doubt you'll need the prompts. Somehow, I think that you and Mr. Bottoms will catch on like a house afire."

Again, the older woman's cheeks flushed and Lydia knew that Mr. Bottoms wasn't the only one anticipating the lunch alone.

"Have we had any progress infiltrating Mr. Batchwell's home?"

Marie nodded. "A few days ago. He's been kept abed with his leg, and up to this point, the only people he's allowed inside have been the man he's got working as his personal servant and a few mining officials—including Charles Wanlass."

"My, my, my. Charles has been a busy boy, hasn't he?"

"As the temporary Mine Superintendent as well as lay pastor, Charles has had plenty of excuses to go to the top of the hill," Marie said with a sly grin. "Anyhow, for the last few days, he's brought Willow with him."

Lydia's brows rose. When Willow and Charles had impulsively claimed a pair of abandoned twins as their own, Mr. Batchwell had proved to be their most formidable foe. Although Willow had never said as much, Lydia knew that the brusque, burly man had secretly terrified her. But after Charles had openly declared he would rather lose his job than Willow, she'd gained a wealth of confidence which, apparently, had extended to her relationship with Mr. Batchwell.

"Anyway, you know Willow. At first, she tut-tutted about his leg, then about the state of his house, then about how cold his meals were once they were brought up from the cook shack. She's been going up for an hour or so every day since then to cook and tidy things up. According to her, Mr. Batchwell is as grumpy as ever, but he does seem secretly appreciative of her help."

Lydia clapped her hands together, then rubbed them as she thought things over.

"It sounds like our efforts are coming along much better than I'd imagined—and just in time, too." They had over sixty men purposely staying off the job through a fictional quarantine. Mr. Bottoms was about to be courted, and a spy had been inserted into Batchwell's home.

The entire situation was better than she could have ever hoped. But there still remained one opponent who could bring their plan down before it could do any good.

Gideon Gault.

He'd already made his views clear on the situation. He would never come to the women's aid. Not willingly.

Which meant that something had to be done about the man.

And much as she hated to admit it, Lydia needed to be the one to do it.

Chapter Five

Quincy Winslow stepped into the Pinkerton Office. He swept his hat from his head and thrust his fingers through his hair.

"We've got another warm afternoon on our hands, Boss."

Gideon leaned back in his chair. After several hours of doing paperwork and payroll vouchers, he found himself grateful for the interruption. He knew that once the sun came out, he'd feel the same itching as his men to get out of doors and get something done.

"Any sign of Willems and Arbach?"

"Yeah. They were down in the tunnels. They took over Hansen's and Clemente's shifts."

Gideon rubbed the aching spot between his brows. "Then where are Hansen and Clemente?"

"They've got the measles."

"What?"

Gideon knew that Jonah Ramsey, the Mine Superintendent, had been diagnosed with measles by his wife, the only doctor in the area. But as far as he knew, keeping Jonah at home had managed to control the contagious illness.

"Yeah, they're being quarantined in the Miners' Hall with a few dozen men. From what I hear, there's more at the infirmary."

"How did that happen?"

Winslow shrugged. "The whole thing seems to have come on rather sudden. Some of the women have volunteered to nurse the men and keep the others away. They hung up signs to warn everybody off."

Measles. How the illness had managed to take root this late in the season—after months spent isolated from the outside world—Gideon didn't know. But he'd lost two good men.

"Have Tabbington and York come see me."

"They're quarantined, too."

Gideon blinked at him. "You're kidding."

"And Billingsly."

That was five men gone—five men that he couldn't afford to lose.

"Is that it?"

"As far as I've been able to tell."

Knowing that it would be useless to finish up his paperwork, Gideon pushed himself to his feet and snagged his hat on the way out of the door.

"Where you going, boss?"

"I think it's time I got to the bottom of this."

The sun was warm against his face as he strode onto the boardwalk—making the air feel more like mid-May than the end of February. At this rate, they wouldn't be worrying about how long the pass would take to open up, they'd be worrying about flooding.

Gideon made a mental note to take another ride through the mouth of the canyon. This time, he wouldn't only be checking the road. He'd be examining the nearby stream as well. He knew full well that the Aspen River was already close to capacity. If the snowpack melted any faster, it would soon overflow its banks and Bachelor Bottoms would have a whole new problem on its hands.

Every time Gideon thought he finally had rudimentary preparations put in place, some new trouble popped up.

Like measles.

He had nearly made his way to the front steps of the Miners' Hall when a pair of women popped up from the rocking chairs they'd pulled onto the boardwalk. Greta Heigle pointed to a white placard nailed to the porch supports and pointed an uplifted hand in his direction.

"*Achtung!* Stop!"

Gideon couldn't account for the way he came to a halt so quickly his hat shifted forward on his brow. Settling it more firmly into place, he took a deep breath to ease the tension twining around his gut like vines.

"Ladies."

Hannah Peterman joined Greta. The two women were shorter than average, but sturdy, forming an effective blockade.

"Please don't come any further, Mr. Gault," Hannah said.

"Quarantine!" Greta barked. The woman had very little English to her vocabulary, but she enunciated the word in a way that made it clear she took her job as guard very seriously.

Gideon braced his hands on his hips. This was uncharted territory for him. As the company's hired law enforcement, he was usually the one in charge of security—for whatever reasons necessary. On one hand, he supposed that this…*quarantine* would fall under his purview. On the other hand…

He and his men were already shorthanded.

"What's this business about a measles outbreak, Hannah?"

He didn't bother to offer his comments to Greta. At the moment, her fierce expression warned him that she would remove him by force if she felt the measure necessary—and even though she was a good head smaller than he was, Gideon had an inkling that she could do it.

"I'm afraid we've had a rash of men coming down with the illness," Hannah said.

"How on earth…" Gideon bit off his words when his tone filled with frustration—something he didn't want the women to become privy to. If they knew how shorthanded the Pinkertons were becoming, no doubt they would use that information as part of their argument for allowing the women to remain in the valley for another month. Maybe two.

"I thought Jonah Ramsey was the only one affected—and he's been off company property for nearly a fortnight."

In truth, Gideon hadn't thought that Jonah had contracted the measles at all. He'd suspected that it was Jonah's way of lingering around the homestead for a few weeks as a makeshift honeymoon. But clearly, the man must have been ill—and now he'd somehow started a contagion.

"Are you sure these men actually have the measles?"

Hannah nodded. "Quite sure."

"*Ja!*"

"How can you be sure if the doctor hasn't been to town to see them?"

Hannah folded her arms. "She told us what to look for and how to treat anyone showing the symptoms."

"Then you wouldn't mind my examining the men?"

Both Hannah and Greta took a step forward—and their expressions grew even fiercer.

"If you go in, you don't come out," Hannah warned, a hint of steel coating her words.

"Quarantine!" Greta barked at him again.

"If I could speak to my men—"

"You don't go in. They don't come out."

Gideon opened his mouth to argue, but closed it again. If his own men had been this fierce in guarding the women all these months, Gideon probably wouldn't be in the mess he was in today.

"I need a list of all the men affected. And I want to be kept updated at least twice a day."

Hannah nodded, but Greta continued to glare at him in disapproval. Seeing no way around them, Gideon finally took a step backward and touched the brim of his hat.

"Good day to you, ladies."

He continued down the boardwalk to the infirmary, wondering if he'd have more success there. But he was yards away when another pair of women stood—and judging by the way one of them brandished her knitting needles, he'd get no closer than a few paces. Funny, none of the women seemed to be contracting measles.

Realizing that it would be useless to tangle with the women now, he decided to come back later. After the female guards had changed.

Sighing, he stood indecisively with his hands on his hips, staring out at the quiet street, the growing puddles, and the dirty piles of snow that seemed to wither away with each moment that passed.

He had so much to do.

But for the life of him, he couldn't seem to pull his thoughts into line. They kept zigzagging from his quarantined men, to upcoming shipments of silver ore, to the itchy sense that he was somehow being maneuvered around a chessboard by some unseen force.

And he didn't like any of it.

The tightness began in his chest even as his hands unconsciously curved into tight fists.

He needed to get away.

Now.

He altered his course, heading to the livery. With each step, he moved a little more purposefully, until he was nearly jogging by the time he reached the sprawling building.

Smalls had left the double doors wide open to catch the fresh breeze, and the animals inside must have found the scents of spring intoxicating. Over the edges of the stalls, Gideon could see the animals moving restlessly, their ears twitching, nostrils flaring. Apparently, the humans in the valley weren't the only ones who suffered from spring fever.

Smalls appeared from the end of the long corridor that led to another similar set of doors opposite. His silhouette hung there for a moment, distinctive and broad and somehow reassuring.

"Any chance I can take a rig for an hour or two?"

Smalls's eyebrows rose at the unusual request, but he immediately changed his course, holding up a hand with one finger lifted to indicate that it would only take a moment to hitch up a horse and a piano box buggy.

As he waited, Gideon moved to the stall where his own gelding was boarded. As soon as Gideon stepped into view, the animal dropped his head over the gate so that Gideon could scratch his ears.

"Hey, boy."

Gideon could feel the animal's eagerness to be saddled and taken out into the sunshine.

"Sorry, but you don't take too well to being in the traces. You know that."

The horse nickered softly, seeming to object.

"Next time. I promise."

Gideon couldn't account for why he'd ordered a buggy instead. When the pressure started to build inside him, he needed the power of a full-fledged gallop to chase the ghosts away. But today…

Today, he didn't know what he wanted. He only knew that he needed something…different.

He heard Smalls moving behind him and turned to help the man bring a gentle mare from a neighboring stall. After leading the animal to where the small buggy awaited behind the livery, Gideon helped to harness the horse. Then he settled inside and gathered the reins.

Once again, Smalls's brows rose questioningly. Gideon didn't need words to know that the gentle giant was asking where Gideon planned to go.

"I'm not sure yet," Gideon murmured as if the question had been asked aloud. "I need to check the state of the river, take another look at the pass, maybe see how the Dovecote is faring after all this flooding."

Smalls took a stub of a pencil and a stack of small cards from his pocket. After licking the tip of the pencil, he quickly wrote.

You feeling all right?

There were few people in the camp that knew the way Gideon sometimes struggled with the after-effects of the war. Willoughby had seen Gideon coming into the livery enough to know that sometimes, battle seemed only a heartbeat away and Gideon found himself needing to escape. "Soldier's Heart" was the name some people used. Gideon would have thought "tormented" was a better term.

In either event, over the years, Smalls had seemed to instinctively know when Gideon needed to ride alone and when he'd needed a companion. On more than one occasion, Gideon had caught the man watching him from a distance, making sure that he didn't become so immersed in his memories that he became a danger to himself.

"I'm fine, Willoughby. The weather's getting to me, I think—same as it is everyone else. We've got the women we need to get out of the valley, then the ore."

Smalls nodded, then bent to write again.

You take care of yourself.

Gideon nodded. "I intend to do that. We can't afford for anyone else to catch this measles epidemic that's sweeping through town."

A grating chuckle caused Smalls's shoulders to shake, even though Gideon didn't quite catch the humor in anything he'd said.

The man stood back, offering a small salute.

Offering one last nod to his friend, Gideon slapped the reins on the horse's rump and headed out into the mud and sunshine.

Lydia had barely reached the outskirts of town before she realized that she'd loaded her basket with far too many items. She still had quite a distance left to the Dovecote and her arms were already trembling. It wasn't so much the foodstuffs that were making her muscles ache. It was the sugar sack that she'd packed with bullets. She should have known better than to bring them along.

Hearing the clop of hooves behind her, she moved to the grassy verge of the road. When the rider didn't pass, she glanced over her shoulder, only to find a buggy pulling up alongside her. And who should be driving, but Gideon Gault.

"Can I give you a lift to the Dovecote?"

She debated the question for only a moment—and only because the bullets seemed to be burning a hole in her conscience. But the thought of carrying them all the way to the Dovecote when she'd been offered a ride…

"Thank you. I'd be beholden to you."

"Hand me your basket."

Again, she hesitated, but seeing no way to refuse without arousing suspicion, she used the last of her strength to hold it toward him.

The basket dipped slightly as it exchanged hands, and Gideon frowned.

"What on earth do you have in here?" he asked as he set it on the floor of the buggy.

"F-foodstuffs," she answered vaguely, hoping he hadn't heard the faint rattling sound coming from the sack.

He still appeared curious, but she gathered her skirts and pretended not to notice. Then, she offered her hand and he pulled her up onto the seat beside him. As soon as she was settled, she changed the subject.

"I don't think I've ever seen you take anything but your horse, Gideon."

He clucked softly to the mare, urging the animal into a walk. "You'd be right about that. I can't think of the last time I borrowed a buggy."

One of her brows lifted. "I do believe you made an issue of taking a buggy over the muddy roads not so long ago."

He had the grace to laugh. "So, I did. But it's fortunate for you that I made the unusual request."

"Oh?"

"If I'd been riding my horse, I couldn't have offered both you and your basket a ride." His eyes sparkled. "I might have chosen to take the basket."

She huffed slightly, but it emerged in a sound that was more laugh than ire.

"What has you riding around town in a buggy, then?"

"I thought I'd check the riverbanks and see the extent

of the flooding. It's been warm today. A little too warm for my liking."

The thought caused her to glance up at the mountain peaks. Although the foothills were nearly bare, plenty of snow still waited above.

"What would happen if this weather continues?"

Gideon squinted up at the peaks as well.

"We could be in trouble. The town is built on high ground, but not high enough to escape full-fledged flooding. Then, there's the havoc it would cause in the mine. The water tables will be lifting and the drainage systems are already taxed to their limit."

"Oh."

They were nearly at the Dovecote now. Because of the mud and standing water, Gideon couldn't get to the door without miring the wheels in the muck, so he stopped on the matted grass next to the boards that had been laid down to give the women a walkway.

"I'll let you out here, if that's okay."

"Yes, that's fine. Thank you."

She waited until the buggy had come to a complete stop. Then, before Gideon could make any motions to come help her, she gathered her skirts and jumped to the ground. She was reaching for the basket when Gideon asked, "Would you like to come with me?"

"With you?" she echoed blankly.

"I'll be riding along the river road, then maybe head to the canyon and test out the roads. If we start to mire in the mud, then I'll know we can't get a heavy wagon through. I wouldn't mind some company, if you're agreeable."

A soft "Oh!" escaped unbidden from her lips. Gathering her wits about her, she managed to offer, "I—I'd like that. I'll just…take the basket inside."

She hefted the basket from the buggy, then made her

way over the boards. Once at the Dovecote, she darted inside. After leaving the items on the table with a quick explanation to Iona, she hurried back outside again.

Gideon waited for her beside the buggy and helped her inside, then rounded to take his own place again.

"You're sure you have time for this? I don't want to interfere with your work preparing meals at the cook shack."

Lydia didn't have the heart to tell him that she'd been banished from the cook shack kitchen long ago. Her role in serving the miners was purely organizational. She could brew a pot of coffee or make a sandwich, but those were the extents of her culinary prowess.

"It will be fine."

"I promise to have you back within the hour."

She bit her tongue before admitting that the other women were handling all of the details for the meal. For some reason, she couldn't summon the courage to admit her inadequacies to Gideon. Instead, she offered a vague, "An hour won't put a crimp in my schedule."

"Good." He gathered the reins and urged the horse forward with a "Walk on."

Gideon couldn't have told anyone why he'd invited Lydia to come along with him. He couldn't have explained it himself. He only knew that, as soon as he'd seen her walking on the lane ahead of him, the tightness in his chest and the need to flee had eased.

Maybe, it was because he knew they would soon start sparring and his mind would be diverted from the problems in town.

Or maybe, just maybe, being with her felt…

Right.

He drove the buggy in a wide circle around the Dovecote until he could negotiate the turn to the river road. But he soon found that his concern over the swollen river became secondary to the woman beside him.

"Have any of the ladies contracted the measles?"

She shot him a quick look that he couldn't decipher, then said, "No. We've avoided the disease so far." One of her brows arched. "Perhaps because we're always being kept at arm's length from the rest of the camp inhabitants."

He couldn't help grinning. "See, there are advantages to being under guard."

She offered a soft *hmph*, which delighted him no end. He had to admit he would miss his interactions with Lydia Tomlinson once the women left the valley. And that was something he never would have thought possible.

His gaze strayed to the river again. They had less than a foot of bank left in most areas—which didn't bode well for the coming weeks. Yesterday, there had been nearly a yard. But even with the encroaching water, his mood didn't dim.

"It's rising fast, isn't it?" Lydia said quietly.

"It is."

"How much longer before the river reaches the top?"

"At this rate, only a few days." He squinted up at a sky as blue as a robin's egg. "What we need is a good old spring blizzard."

"Surely not. Spring seems to be here whether we're ready or not."

He shook his head. "I wouldn't be too sure. I've seen early thaws like this one disappear beneath a second bout of bitter weather."

"I'm sure that's another reason you have for getting us out of the valley as soon as possible."

He didn't rise to the bait. Although he didn't mind sparring, he wasn't in the mood to argue with Lydia. Not today.

"Truth be told, I'd much rather bring in some fresh supplies. Who knows how long we could be stranded if the river washes out the roads?"

Her mouth made a becoming O. Then, she turned her attention to the river again. "I hadn't noticed until now how close the road runs to the banks."

"We could do without this particular lane, for a time. But if we lost the one in the canyon…"

She eyed him consideringly. "How long have you been here? In Aspen Valley."

He knew the date well. He'd been home from the war less than a year before he'd had to leave Ohio. There had been too many triggers there. A veteran in uniform. Crowds. Noise.

"I joined the Pinkertons in the summer of sixty-six, and received this assignment in sixty-seven."

"So, you've seen about everything the weather can throw at you?"

"Just about." He shot her a side glance. "The avalanche was a first. We've had some slides before, but nothing like what happened in the pass. I've never seen so much snow come down at once. If I didn't know better, I would have thought that a charge had been set to trigger it."

"And I suppose that you and Batchwell would lay the blame for that on us women as well?"

"Nah. As talented as you ladies might be, I don't think any of you could be in two places at once."

Lydia seemed slightly flustered by his teasing, but she finally smiled.

"Have you enjoyed living in the mountains?"

He nodded. "Very much. It's…peaceful."

Something about his intonation must have given himself away because she continued to watch him, her eyes so clear and blue they could have rivaled the sky. "And you found yourself in need of peace?"

Oddly, he felt the need to tell her things that he'd rarely shared with anyone else. But as soon as the urge hit him, he pushed it away.

"You might say that."

Unfortunately, she didn't take the hint to drop the subject. Instead, she asked softly, "Was it the war that made you so…restless?"

Tell her.

After all, what could it hurt. She'd be gone soon.

But even then, he hesitated. There was something… *weak*…in confessing his troubles. And it bothered him that she might think less of him. So, he offered her a noncommittal, "I suppose you could say that."

"Did you see a lot of battle?"

For the first time, the mere mention of the war didn't hit him like a punch in the stomach. "A bit. I was part of a cavalry unit."

"Which accounts for your horsemanship."

The offhand comment caused a warmth to flicker in his chest.

"I suppose. But toward the end of the war, I was captured by the Rebs."

"How awful."

"I spent the rest of the conflict in a prisoner camp in Georgia until Uncle Billy Sherman came to our rescue."

Her eyes widened, and he knew that she'd pieced together the clues. To his infinite surprise, she didn't shrink from him as so many people had done—as if the stink of Andersonville still clung to his skin. Instead, she reached out to touch his arm, squeezing softly.

Such pretty hands. So small. So delicate.

"No wonder you have the urge to ride like the wind now and again."

The fact that she must have seen him charging out of

town on more than one occasion made him wonder if her bedroom in the Dovecote overlooked the road out of town.

"I can understand those feelings." Her tone dropped, becoming thoughtful. Rueful. "I've had them often enough myself—without the availability of a horse to give me a means of escape."

"And what would you be escaping from, Lydia?"

He drew the buggy to a halt beneath a copse of wild plum trees that would soon erupt in blossoms.

Gideon expected her to offer a rejoinder that would either change the subject or lighten the mood. Instead, she stared up, up, up to the tips of the mountains.

"My life before going to live with my aunts was... unpredictable."

When she didn't continue, he prompted, "In what way?"

She shrugged as if the truth were of no consequence, but then her hands drifted into her lap and her fingers laced tightly together. For a moment, she stared down at the interlocking digits as if they held the secrets to the world. Inexplicably, he knew why she'd instinctively understood how his own memories could haunt him. The past wouldn't let her go, either.

"My father enjoyed a...nomadic existence."

Which, translated, meant that she'd had no stable home.

"That must have been difficult for you."

"He was not...a good man."

Again, the comment seemed to indicate that there was so much she wasn't telling him. But before he could pry for more details, she pushed her shoulders back and tipped her chin. Then, she pretended to glance at the fob watch pinned to her bodice.

"Oh, my! Look at the time! I really should be getting back to the Dovecote."

And in that instant, Lydia-the-suffragist returned.

Gideon knew that he could ignore the statement and delve deeper into the matters surrounding her past. But in those few moments of honest conversation, he'd felt the kinship of another soul haunted by past events. He wouldn't violate that honesty.

Or he'd scare her away.

"I'd better get you back, then."

She seemed to sag ever so slightly in relief. "Thank you, Gideon."

Chapter Six

A few minutes later, Lydia stood in her room, watching through her window as Gideon drove the buggy along the road leading up through the foothills—presumably to check on the canyon.

What on earth had she been thinking when she'd alluded to her childhood? In that brief unguarded moment, she'd nearly made a horrible mistake. A horrible, horrible mistake.

She'd taken great care over the years to erase the evidence of her early years. To Lydia, the moment that she'd been led into her aunts' home had been a moment of rebirth, and since then, she'd refused to think of that grubby little urchin she'd once been. Those early years had held nothing but deprivation and pain and guilt. Nothing could come from dwelling on her childhood. Instead, she'd focused her sights on the future, determined to make something of herself.

But when Gideon had been so boldly honest with her...

She'd felt compelled to reciprocate.

Whirling away from the window, she strode to the mirror where she began repairing the windblown tresses that had escaped the careful curls, the strict plaits. She looked a sight. It was a wonder that Gideon had asked her to join him at all.

Her fingers abandoned the pins and she returned to the window again. Gideon must have ridden into the trees bordering the pass, because she couldn't see him anymore.

You need to stay away from him. This infatuation has got to stop.

So why couldn't she turn away? Why did she draw the chair close to the window and rest her folded arms on the sill?

If he ever knew about her father...

No!

Her eyes squeezed shut for a moment as she tried to block out the reaction he would surely have: astonishment, suspicion, then disgust. Not only for the things that Clinton Tomlinson had done, but for those Lydia had done as well.

She supposed, in her defense, she could insist that she'd been a child, that her father would have brooked no disobedience to his orders.

But that didn't negate the fact that she'd known the difference between right and wrong. And as Clinton Tomlinson and his outlaw friends had become the scourge of the territories—robbing banks, rustling cattle, terrorizing farmers and businessmen—she'd been there with him.

And Gideon Gault, ex-cavalryman, veteran and Pinkerton must never find out.

Leaning her forehead against the glass, she closed her eyes. *Please, Lord. Please.*

Her prayer faltered. She didn't know what she was praying for. A successful protest? Gideon's understanding? Her future goals? Somehow, in the last few days, everything had become muddled, seemingly at cross-purposes. Yes, the protest still lay in the forefront of her mind, but thoughts of Gideon seemed to be crowding into her brain as well, making her feel confused and unfocused and...

Filled with a strange anticipation for her next meeting with Gideon.

Her eyes squeezed closed again and, since she had no clearer idea of direction than she'd had moments before, she whispered, "Please, Lord. Show me the way."

Gideon stared at the quarantine list in his hands, then glanced up at Charles Wanlass in disbelief, wondering how things could have changed so much in twenty-four hours.

"You're sure this is correct?"

Charles leaned back in his chair and nodded.

The man looked thoroughly at home in the small inner office located a dozen yards from the main entrance of the mine where the two main tunnels split in opposite directions.

"One of the women sent it to me this morning before the shift change."

"There's got to be...sixty men on this list."

"Sixty-three, to be exact."

"How are you managing to get anything done?"

Charles shrugged. "We're struggling. Production is down and some of the crews are incomplete."

Which meant that Batchwell would soon be on the warpath. Nothing sent the man into a panic more than lost revenue.

"What are you doing about it?"

Charles rubbed the bridge of his nose and seemed to stare absentmindedly at a map of the mine pinned on the opposite wall. Gideon knew from experience that when Charles adopted that far-off expression, he was often pondering another blast.

"Do? What can I do? I don't have the men to replace them and we're already spread too thin to alter the shifts."

Gideon had always thought that Charles would be a fine administrator. Like Jonah Ramsey, he had strong leadership skills and an ability to build a rapport with the men. But Charles had once stated that he loved the unpredictable nature of his job as blasting foreman. Gideon wondered if he'd change his mind now that he had a family.

"To be quite honest, I'm not too concerned," Charles continued. "We've had a record-breaking winter and we've got tons of ore stockpiled and ready for shipment. Right now, I'm thinking about what's best for my men, and if that means we have a few slow weeks, the mine and the silver will still be there when we're back to full force."

Gideon had never heard anything so astonishing coming out of Charles's mouth. The man actually seemed… *content* with a drop in productivity.

"Does Batchwell know?"

"Not yet."

Again, Charles seemed unfazed with the fact that Ezra Batchwell would soon have to be informed that his beloved mine was struggling. Gideon didn't even want to think about that conversation.

"When are you going to tell him?"

Charles's grin was slow and all-knowing. "Not until Willow has a chance to feed him."

At the mention of food, Gideon pulled his watch from his pocket and glanced at the face. Nearly two. If he hurried, he could probably get a quick shave and haircut before he went to the Dovecote.

He snorted to himself, wondering why he felt the need to be so particular about his appearance. Then again, he couldn't go to the Dovecote looking like a shaggy bear.

He was only being polite by ensuring that the mail-order brides would feel more comfortable around him.

Yeah, sure. It's the brides you're concerned about.

Shoving that thought aside, Gideon dropped the list onto the desk.

"I've got to go."

Charles's brows rose. "Oh? Where you headed?"

Gideon rued the heat that rose in his neck. "The women have invited me to come to the Dovecote for a meal."

"Have they now?"

Charles's tone was particularly bland, causing Gideon to bristle.

"They want to ask me some questions about their upcoming move."

The explanation didn't seem to alter the amusement glittering from his friend's gray eyes. But Charles's only response was, "Tell them 'hello' from me."

Deciding that a hasty retreat was in order, Gideon turned on his heel and strode from the office, heading for the beckoning sunshine at the end of the tunnel. With each step, he vowed that this strange new preoccupation with Lydia Tomlinson had to stop.

But that didn't keep him from heading straight for the barbershop.

Lydia paced the length of the Dovecote's keeping room, checking one more time that everything was in place.

"The roast is in the warming oven," Iona said, not for the first time. "Everything else is already on the table or the cooktop. You don't have to fix anything."

"What about the coffee?"

"It's made and being kept warm in the pots on the range."

Iona patiently continued to coach Lydia even as the older woman tied her bonnet strings under her chin.

"Relax. The man won't be here for another quarter hour."

Lydia pressed a hand against her waist in an attempt to still the stampede of butterflies that swirled in her stomach.

"Someone else should do this. He'll see right through me."

Iona reached to pat her arm. "We've been through this already. You've had the most interaction with Gideon Gault over the past few months, so you need to be the person to entertain him."

"But that's the problem. I don't know how to...*entertain* anyone, least of all a man."

Lydia didn't miss the amused twitch of her friend's lips.

"Then I'd say it's past time you learned."

Lydia scowled. Clearly, she'd get no help from this quarter.

Iona must have realized that her panic was real because she cupped Lydia's shoulders until Lydia met her gaze head-on.

"You and Gideon Gault will be sharing a meal, nothing more, nothing less. You'll talk, you'll eat, you'll ply him with food."

"That's the problem. I don't know how to sustain such... pleasantries. Not with him. With anyone else, I could sit and chat all day. But with Mr. Gault—" She grimaced. "We invariably slip into an argument."

"There's nothing wrong with a spirited discussion. My dearly departed Henry and I used to indulge in a few quick-witted debates. Just keep the topics as benign as possible."

"Such as?"

"The weather. The daily workings of the mine..." Even Iona seemed to scramble for ideas. "Literature. Art."

"Art? You expect me to converse a half hour or more with Mr. Gault about art? I don't know anything about art—and the man is bound to think that I've lost my senses. What did you and Mr. Bottoms talk about?"

Iona's cheeks grew pink. She and Phineas Bottoms had clearly developed a rapport because they were now meeting several times a day.

"Plants, for the most part."

"Plants?"

Iona needlessly fiddled with her sleeves. "Yes. I discovered he's an avid gardener. He's been thinking of cultivating a wide array of local wildflowers and shrubbery in the plots surrounding his cottage."

Lydia couldn't prevent a small smile. "So, the two of you are getting along?"

"Oh, well… I…" Iona finally met Lydia's gaze. "Yes. I do believe we are."

"Did you have a chance to ask how he felt about the women's efforts or mention our cause?"

Iona shook her head. "The time never seemed right. But we've arranged to meet in the private dining room for breakfast tomorrow. Phineas is going to bring the schematics for his garden."

"Marvelous."

As the word left her mouth, Lydia discovered that she was more pleased by the way Iona's voice softened when she spoke of Phineas than with the opportunity to further their agenda. Lydia knew that her friend dreaded the moment she would have to leave the valley. She'd originally been on her way to live with her sister's family in California. Although Iona looked forward to seeing her sister Clarice, she dreaded becoming a burden on Clarice's large family and her demanding husband. Like so many of the other girls, Iona had begun to regard Bachelor Bottoms as home. She'd found a purpose here. If the rules were changed, she would like to stay.

"Well, I don't suppose I can spend the afternoon talking about gardening with Mr. Gault."

Iona's serious expression cracked and she laughed. "I think you're right. If all else fails, ask the man about himself. In my experience, most men love to talk about themselves—especially in regards to their jobs. You might be able to garner some information that we can use." She squeezed Lydia's hands. "Regardless, help him relax so he'll be off guard."

Off guard. According to the report Lydia had received from Hannah a few minutes ago, Gideon had been snooping around the "quarantine" areas again. It was only a matter of time before he uncovered their ruse. The threat he posed had to be removed, and the only way to do that would be to drug him, restrain him, then keep him out of the way for the next day or two.

The butterflies in her stomach became a stampede of buffalo. Although she'd been fine throughout the planning stages of this latest escapade, she was discovering that putting those plans into action wasn't quite so simple.

"I don't think I can do this," she whispered. "It's one thing to keep the man busy for an hour or so, but I've got to get him to drink the sleeping draughts as well."

Iona patted her on the arm. "Come, now. You've never shrunk from a difficult task before. You've always been one to take your challenges head-on."

Yes, but this was Gideon Gault they were talking about. And the man had the ability to knock her equilibrium on its ear.

"There's nothing to it. You'll feed him a good meal and get as much information from him as you can. Then, when you feel the time is right, you'll offer him some hot coffee. The sleeping powder has been dissolved into the smaller pot, so make sure that you get him to drink some."

Lydia nodded. None of them had been confident that they could kidnap Mr. Gault through force, so they'd decided that putting him to sleep would be the best alternative.

If Lydia had been given her druthers, she would give the man the brew as soon as he walked through the door. But the other women had been insistent that she ply him for as much information as she could. Therefore, they'd made two pots. One with the sleeping powders and the other without.

She stomped back to the kitchen alcove to peek inside the oven—not that she had the slightest clue what she was meant to see, or what she would do if something was amiss. Thankfully, the aromas that swirled in the escaping steam assured her that nothing was burning.

Yet.

Her hand pressed over her stomach again, and she forced herself to breathe as deeply as she could. Unfortunately, vanity had played a part in her ablutions and she'd tightened her corset to the point where she could barely breathe.

"He's going to be suspicious as soon as he sees that everyone is gone," Lydia grumbled one last time. To her dismay, the other girls had insisted that an intimate meal for two would encourage Gideon to speak more freely. Lydia had tried her best to sink that idea, but the women had overruled her.

"Nonsense. You'll tell him that the women were making advance preparations in the cook shack and must have been delayed."

"But the table is set for two."

Iona took her by the shoulders.

"Be charming. If you're charming, he will assume that all the fuss being made is of a personal nature."

"That's what I'm afraid of," Lydia muttered.

"You may have vowed to live your life free of romantic entanglements, but that doesn't mean you have to completely ignore the male species. Who knows? You might even change your mind."

Lydia shot her friend a pithy look. "I doubt that will happen. Even if I should decide to abandon my spinsterhood, it wouldn't be for the likes of Gideon Gault."

Iona's eyes seemed to twinkle. And as she released Lydia to walk to the door, Lydia thought she heard her friend offer a blithe "We'll see. Things may surprise you. You may even find the afternoon enjoyable."

"Enjoyable," Lydia grumbled under her breath as Iona slipped outside and hurried away. "I'll be content if I can make it through the hour without throttling the man."

In the past, Gideon had proven to be too quick-witted for her to maintain her composure around him. If she began asking personal questions of him, it was only a matter of time before he decided to do the same.

No, no, no!

The last thing she needed was Gideon Gault getting a whiff of her past.

Her stomach seesawed and the stampede of nerves intensified even more.

"Do not let him bait you with personal questions," she whispered to herself. "You must remain calm, cool and completely collected. Keep the focus on him, only him."

Because if he started poking into her own background…

She was in big trouble.

Nerves skittered through his system as Gideon strode toward the Dovecote. Even as his gaze swept the yard, took in the water levels encroaching toward the dormitory and the makeshift boardwalk that led to the front door, inwardly, his nerves were jangling.

Knowing that he would be eating with a passel of women, he'd taken more pains with his appearance than usual. At the barbershop, Stan Fuller had shaved Gideon's jaw, trimmed his hair, and slicked the strands back with pomade. Telling himself that his Pinkerton uniform had been dusty and splattered with mud, Gideon had changed into a clean pair of wool trousers, a crisp linen shirt, string tie, a patterned vest and a black wool suitcoat—an ensemble usually saved for holidays and funerals. All the while, he'd wondered why he'd gone to such efforts. It wasn't as if he were trying to impress the women. The ladies in the Dovecote had made it clear that, as the head of the Pinkertons who'd been tasked with guarding them, they didn't like him much. Nevertheless…

He hadn't wanted to show up for Lydia's invitation looking like a grizzled fur trapper who'd been holed up in a cave for the winter.

Mindful of the boots he'd polished before leaving, Gideon took great care traversing the boards which formed a makeshift walkway. Then, once at the door, he slid his watch from his vest pocket.

Three on the nose.

He cleared his throat and wiped his hands on his trousers. If Gideon hadn't known any better, he would have thought he was courting. His heart was knocking against his ribs, and his pulse beat an uneven rhythm. Even his palms were sweating. For two cents, he'd be willing to turn on his heel and stride away again. It would be an easy enough matter to plead an emergency.

But when he imagined his next encounter with Lydia Tomlinson, he could envision her all-knowing look. He had no doubts that she would somehow divine the deceit.

How was it possible that one woman was able to get beneath his skin so completely?

Gideon quickly rapped on the door, afraid he'd talk himself out of the appointed meal if he didn't.

Just as quickly, the door opened and there stood Lydia, all pretty and smart and ready to do battle. Except, contrary to what he'd expected, she didn't immediately begin a verbal fencing match. Instead, her cheeks bloomed with a delicate pink that matched the print on her day dress and she stammered, "G-Gideon… I mean, Mr. Gault."

She bit her lip and he waited for her to admit him, but she didn't seem inclined to move.

"Have I come too early?"

Maybe his watch was fast or slow. Sometimes he forgot to wind it, and then he would have to go into the mine offices to check the official timepiece kept on the telegraph operator's desk.

"No! You're right on time."

The pink in her cheeks deepened, but she stepped aside, making a sweeping gesture with her hand.

"Come in, come in. May I take your coat?"

Too late, she seemed to realize that he hadn't worn a coat.

"Your hat, I mean. May I take your hat?"

He handed it to her, then surreptitiously smoothed his hair with his palms when she turned to hang it on the hall tree.

"Something smells good," he offered, hoping to prevent an awkward silence from settling around them.

"Elk roast, freshly baked biscuits, as well as some precious jams and pickles supplied by the other ladies."

His gaze swept over the room.

"Where are the other ladies?"

Lydia's eyes grew suddenly wide. "They…they had to…" She waved a hand in front of her in an incomprehensible gesture. "They'll be here soon. Problems in the… in the cook shack."

"Anything I need to know about?"

"No! Oh, no." She gave a brittle laugh. "Merely checking the roasts…that the men will eat…in the cook shack. Later. And then, a few of the brides are helping with the quarantine."

At that, his brow creased. "Yes, I encountered some of the overenthusiastic guards earlier today. Greta seemed especially fierce."

Lydia offered a laugh. "She does take her job seriously. But I suppose that she's eager to ensure the community's well-being." She moved to the table. "Sit, sit. I'll bring the food over."

Gideon noted the seat she'd indicated, then took in the fact that there were only two place settings. Inexplicably, his palms grew sweaty again.

She continued talking as she moved to the oven. "It's a lovely day, isn't it? If we have much more weather like this, the miners will be wanting picnics rather than meals at the cook shack. Ouch!"

He dragged his attention back to where Lydia was trying to wrestle a large pan out of the oven.

"Here, let me do that. It's got to be heavy."

He hurried to take a set of pot holders from her hands. She resisted for a moment. "I'm perfectly capable of—"

"I know you're capable, Lydia. I'd like to help."

That remark seemed to knock the wind out of her sails.

"Thank you. I have a platter ready, so you can set the pan on top of the range, then I'll transfer everything to the plate."

Gideon did as she'd asked. Then, rather than returning to the table, he lingered by the stove.

"What about the biscuits?" he asked, referring to the pan that still sat in the oven.

She glanced at them, then shook her head. "I think they need another minute or two."

In Gideon's opinion, they were already golden brown, but he supposed she knew more than he did.

"Anything else that I can help you with?"

She looked up at him with those blue, blue eyes. And for a moment, he thought he saw something within them that he'd never seen before. An uncertainty, a…vulnerability.

He held that gaze for a beat, then another, and another. Her lips parted as if to ask something. Then, at the last moment, she turned away, seeming slightly embarrassed by that hint of honesty.

Gideon suddenly realized that he didn't know Lydia nearly as well as he'd thought. Even a day earlier, had he been asked, he would have been confident that he'd pigeon-holed Lydia into the proper slot in his brain: opinionated, headstrong suffragist. But he was beginning to believe that he'd merely scratched the surface.

Had he been overconfident in his assessment of her? Could it be that the woman he'd wrangled with from time to time was only a veneer? If he were to poke and prod, what else would he discover? Deep down, there had to be a reason why she was so ardent in her pursuit of equality and emancipation.

What was she hiding?

Or more to the point…

What was she hiding from him?

As if sensing his regard, Lydia focused her attention on the roasting pan. She lifted the lid, allowing the fragrant, savory steam to waft into the air. Using two forks, she transferred the meat to the platter. Then she began ladling out chunks of carrots, onions and potatoes.

Knowing that the hint of intimacy he'd sensed had dissipated along with the steam, Gideon allowed himself to be diverted from anything too personal.

For now.

"I thought you said the potatoes were all gone?" he remarked as casually as he could, remembering her comments when she'd brought him breakfast the previous day.

"I forgot we had a small bag of them here at the Dovecote, so these truly are the last of them."

His stomach rumbled appreciatively when he noted the caramelized edges. In Andersonville, he and the other men had endured unspeakable hunger. At times, the need for food had outweighed all other thoughts. When he'd finally been released, and had made his way back home, Gideon had been consumed with cravings for fresh fruits and vegetables.

And potatoes.

To him, no matter how far he roamed, roasted potatoes tasted like home.

"Gideon?"

Too late, he realized that he'd been focusing on images of the past.

"Sorry. What can I do for you?"

"Will you take the platter to the table?"

"Of course."

He carried the plate to the table and she followed him with a small gravy boat that she'd filled with the drippings.

Gideon waited by his chair as she fussed with the other items on the table, making sure there were spoons in the jam pots, forks in the pickles, a pitcher of cold water and a pot of hot coffee. Then finally, she seemed satisfied and eyed him quizzically. "Aren't you going to sit down?"

"After you."

"Oh!" It was a bare puff of sound, but he liked the note of pleasure it held.

She settled into the chair at the head of the table and placed her napkin in her lap. He followed suit, sitting to her right.

"Would you say grace?"

He nodded and bowed his head. "Dear Lord Above, for these bounties and all our blessings we are truly grateful. Amen."

Lydia began filling his plate with food, tender slices of roast elk, vegetables, pickled beans, cucumbers and carrots.

"Thank you."

He regarded his plate, detecting a slight hint of scorching in the air, but everything looked delicious, so he had to be mistaken.

"Would you like some jam for your—oh!"

She suddenly bounded to her feet and raced to the range, flinging open the door. A puff of black smoke billowed free.

Chapter Seven

"Oh, no! No, no, no!" Lydia whispered under her breath. She reached to grasp the pan, then yelped in pain, her fingers flying to her mouth.

Gideon jumped to his feet. After grasping a pair of dish towels from the counter, he quickly took the biscuits from the range and set them on top.

"They're ruined," Lydia mourned.

Gideon opened his mouth to offer some mollifying platitude, but there was no way to get around the truth other than a bald-faced lie.

"Yep. There's no saving them."

She stiffened to full height, her feathers clearly ruffled. But at the last minute, her frame seemed to sag and she laughed instead.

"At least you're honest," she muttered. Then she sighed. "Unfortunately, that means we're stuck with day-old bread."

"One of my favorite varieties."

She reached on tiptoe to grasp a plate on one of the upper shelves and Gideon couldn't help noting that when she lifted her arm, he was afforded the sight of her balanced on her tiptoes like a ballerina, her skirt lifting up, until he could see the delicate span of her ankles and a hint of lace from her petticoat.

"Here, let me."

Gideon easily grasped the plate which held a loaf covered with a dishcloth. "Do you want to take it straight to the table?"

"Yes."

By the time he was seated again, Lydia had retrieved a knife, and she cut thick slices of bread.

"Take one of the inner pieces where they're soft."

He did as he was told, slathering it liberally with butter and then jam.

"That's Iona's cherry-berry jam. It's really delicious."

"And which one is yours?" he asked as he gestured to the various pots.

She seemed to flush and he wondered at her embarrassment.

"I'm afraid we used the last of mine."

She offered him a dazzling smile that left him feeling even more suspicious, so he decided to test the subject. "I imagine that you, of all people, concoct jams with entirely unusual flavors. What kinds do you make?"

Sure enough, the woman regarded him with the blank stare of a hare being sighted by its prey. He could nearly see her squirm.

"Strawberry with…apple and…and thyme."

Aha. So, the indomitable Lydia Tomlinson had never made jam in her life, but she wasn't willing to admit it. Did that mean there were other chinks to her armor?

"This roast is delicious. What sorts of spices did you use?"

Again, her eyes remained wide and blank. Even so, he could nearly see the cogs churning in her head. "Salt."

"Mmm-hmm. What else?"

"Pepper."

"And?"

"And sage."

His taste buds were telling him that there wasn't a speck of sage in the dish.

"It's good. Really good." Gideon knew better than to prod her any further until he'd finished his meal.

"Coffee?" she asked, her hand hovering near a tall pot.

"Do you have milk?"

The request seemed to throw her. "Yes."

"Could I have that instead?"

She rose to retrieve a glass from the cupboard and filled it from a pitcher kept on a shelf in the pie safe.

"There you are."

"Thank you."

She took her seat again, bringing that same mix of lemon and gardenia that seemed to hover over her. Vaguely, he wondered if it came from a particular scent or if it was a mix of her soap and perfume combined.

"Where are you from, Lydia?"

She seemed startled by the question. "From?"

"Where were you born?"

She pushed a piece of carrot around her plate. "I was born in Virginia."

Southern.

The moment the thought pierced his head, Gideon thrust it aside. The war was over. He, of all people, should know that.

"But I've lived most of my life in Boston."

Northern.

"That's where you lived with your aunts?"

She seemed surprised that he'd remembered. "Yes. They took me in when I was twelve."

"Whom did you live with before that time?"

He meant the question to be little more than polite conversation, but Lydia seemed to freeze. Then, she carefully poured coffee into an elegant porcelain cup. She only answered after she'd taken a sip.

"Before then, I lived with my father who…traveled quite a bit. When it became apparent that the lifestyle wasn't conducive to my well-being—" she shrugged "—I was sent to live with my mother's sisters."

"That must have been hard for your father."

Lydia held her cup with both hands. She took another hasty sip, coughed, then admitted, "By that time, my father was…gone."

Realizing he'd strayed into what seemed to be painful territory, Gideon altered the gist of the conversation.

"Tell me about them. Your aunts."

A spark of light returned to those blue, blue eyes, and she smiled. "Aunt Rosie and Aunt Florence are such dears. They recently retired from a prestigious finishing school. Aunt Rosie taught art and rhetoric, Aunt Florence literature and mathematics."

His brows rose. "That must be a rigorous school."

Lydia seemed to bristle. "For women, you mean."

"For anyone."

That clarification seemed to mollify her.

"Did you go to college, Mr. Gault?"

Gideon reluctantly nodded. "I spent two years at West Point before the war broke out."

"Oh."

Again, they'd hit a dead end. Try as they might, they couldn't seem to find a place to land without hitting unseen emotional impediments. Not wanting to regress into their usual verbal battlefield, Gideon tried to steer away from anything personal at all. He regaled her with funny tales about Creakle and Smalls, and the latest news about the twins that Willow and Charles had adopted.

All too soon, even that wellspring ran dry. Unfortunately, with each minute that passed, Gideon's enjoyment over spending time in Lydia's company began to shift into a vague suspicion. The table that had been set for two, the continued absence of the other women, the savory meal and Lydia's attempts to steer him away from the subject of cooking and anything at all related to her past, were enough to inform him that he'd been brought here for a reason.

But what?

For the life of him, he couldn't fathom what that purpose might be. If he hadn't known better, he would think that Lydia was attempting to "exert her feminine wiles" in order to sway his opinion about allowing the women to live in the mining camp. But so far, she hadn't brought the subject up at all.

Then again, he was probably the last person on earth she would ever try to woo into joining her side.

Once his stomach was full, he leaned back in his seat and laced his hands over his satisfied belly.

"That was a delicious meal, Lydia. You're a fine cook."

Again, a hint of color touched her cheeks. Unlike Gideon, she'd merely toyed with her food, pushing it from one side of the plate to the other.

"The other women seem to be taking longer than you'd thought."

"Coffee?" She reached for the pot, then grimaced. "It's probably cold by now. I'll heat this one up and get the other one."

She jumped to her feet and hurried to the range where she set the pot on one of the burners, then used a dish towel to carry a smaller one to the table.

After such a delicious meal, Gideon didn't have the heart to tell her that he rarely drank coffee. His years in the Army had cured him of that particular predilection. Too many hours in the saddle augmented with strong black coffee to keep him awake, and ersatz substitutes made from toasted grains or beans in Andersonville had put him off the dark brew. If he had his way, he much preferred a tall glass of milk or cold spring water.

"What sorts of questions did they have?"

Lydia regarded him blankly. "Questions?"

"You said the women had questions about the journey. That's why you invited me here."

"Oh, yes. I... I'd really better let them ask you. They should be back at any moment." She went to pour more coffee into his mug, only to discover that it was still full. "Would you like me to get you a new cup? O-or I could dump this one out."

He shook his head. "No thanks. I'm fine. Really. I'm not much of a coffee drinker."

Once again, she seemed to blink at him like a startled hare.

"W-would you like some cocoa?"

"No. But thank you."

"Tea?"

"I'm not much for hot drinks once the weather gets warm."

"Oh."

She set the coffeepot back on the range, then returned to sink into her chair. Her eyes grew curiously guarded and she slumped in her chair as if he'd just kicked her favorite puppy.

"I probably won't be able to stay much longer. I've got an errand that I need to run before I head back to the mines."

He thought of the light he'd seen two nights ago and

the warm ashes he'd found the following morning. Even though he knew the errand was probably useless, he couldn't help thinking that he should sweep the area, one last time, and see if he could pick out a trail. If he could assure himself that the person responsible had headed away from the mine, maybe he could put his suspicions to rest.

"Did you tell the girls they should start packing?"

"Yes."

Since she didn't elaborate, he prodded, "So have they? Started packing?"

"No. Not yet. They wanted to talk to you first."

"I'll try to drop by later this evening if I can. In the meantime, warn the women that they won't be able to take everything with them at first. They'll have to pack their trunks, label them, then store them here in the Dovecote. Tell them they can only take one small bag or trunk with their most necessary items. As soon as the weather clears and it's easier for us to get to one of the railheads, we'll ship the rest of their belongings to them."

Something in his words seemed to bring the starch back into her posture.

"But you can't do that! If they do as you ask, they could arrive at their destinations with little more than the clothing on their backs!"

"I know it's inconvenient for them, but—"

"Inconvenient? It's impossible! These women have no guarantees that the men they've agreed to marry will still be at those destinations, or if they've found other brides, or if they've changed their minds about marrying them at all! If you keep their things, they'll be marooned at these far-flung outposts until the rest of their belongings arrive!"

"I understand that. Honestly, I do. But you don't seem to realize the difficulty we'll have getting the women through the pass and on their way. To add hundreds of trunks to that endeavor—"

"Hundreds of trunks," she scoffed.

"Yes, *hundreds*. We have over fifty women, two families, the railway crew and several farmers and salesmen to evacuate. I'd say my estimation is far too conservative. If each one of those people had only two trunks, that's well over a hundred trunks—and you know most of the women brought more than that on their trip to the territories."

Her mouth snapped shut.

"How many trunks did *you* bring, Lydia?"

"We weren't talking about me, per se. I would have an easier time waiting for my belongings—"

"How many, Lydia?"

She was the picture of resistance, lips tight, hands clasped in her lap. But she finally relented and mumbled, "Thirteen."

Sure that he hadn't heard right, he said, "How many?"

"Thirteen."

"Thirteen!"

"But I've given away a lot of clothing since then, and used up many of my original supplies. I'm sure I have less than a half dozen to worry about."

"A half dozen! At that rate, our estimate has shot up to nearly three hundred trunks."

"Not everyone will have that many."

"But some will have more."

She reluctantly conceded that point.

"Even you would have to admit that this mining community doesn't have enough teams and wagons to haul that much baggage out of the valley, let alone the resources to get through a pass that will be choked with mud and melting snow."

"You could let some of the women stay. For good."

Gideon scrubbed his face with his hands. "We've been over and over that argument. Ezra Batchwell won't allow it. Not now, not ever."

"But isn't there some way that we could force him to see reason? Think of the community this could become. Instead of a sterile, joyless, male-only, bachelor-laden... *hovel*—"

"Oh, come on now!"

"Yes, hovel. Even you have to admit that before the women came, the cook shack, the Miners' Hall—even the Meeting House—were caked in mud and dust and grime."

She had a point there.

"Since the women have been in Bachelor Bottoms, we've brought cleanliness, and order, and...and *beauty*. Even more than that, we've brought a measure of civility that has encouraged the men to wipe their feet and use their napkins, and...and..."

If Gideon hadn't known better, he would have thought that Lydia's voice had grown slightly choked at the end.

"Be that as it may," Gideon said slowly, gently. "Ezra Batchwell will not change his mind. Many before you have tried, and I would wager that many after you will do the same. But the man is adamant in keeping his rules."

"Why?"

"Why what?"

"Why does the man hate us so much?"

Gideon sighed. "It's not that he hates you or any of the other women."

She snorted and he had to admit that the ladies had plenty of evidence to the contrary.

"He simply loves his mine more. And anything he perceives could interfere with the workings of the mine is forbidden as far as he's concerned."

"But there has to be a way to alter his way of thinking."

Gideon searched his words carefully before saying, "How? By fixing him a fancy dinner and charming him with your feminine companionship?"

She blanched, giving Gideon proof that this meal had been a setup from the very beginning. Lydia hadn't invited him to speak with the other women. She hadn't even invited him for personal reasons. This had been an attempt to butter him up and sway him into joining the women's protest.

A shard of disappointment sank deep into his chest, but he pushed it away. He had to remember that this had been a business meeting, pure and simple. He was more than capable of keeping things on a formal footing.

Pushing his chair back, he strode across the room and swept his hat from the hall tree.

"You and your women are fighting a war that can't be won, Lydia. You can bat your eyes and coo and sashay, but it won't do any good. Even though the lot of you have half the camp twined around your little fingers." He pointed his hat in her direction. "But it won't work. Batchwell would be willing to fire all of us and start from scratch if it would keep his precious mine the way it is."

With that, he headed out the door. And this time, it was his turn to slam it behind him.

Lydia fought the urge to lay her head down on the table and cry.

She never cried. Never.

"Is the coast clear?"

She looked up to find Willow Wanlass poking her head through the door that led into the rear apartment where Sumner Ramsey had once slept and held her medical offices.

"Yes, he's gone." Lydia's mood brightened ever so slightly. "Did you bring the twins with you?"

"Yes. But I daren't bring them any farther than the back door. Charles put wheels on their little sledge so that I could pull them around town, but I don't want to track mud into the Dovecote." She eyed Lydia with concern. "I take it from your expression that things didn't go well with Gideon."

Lydia shook her head. "The man doesn't drink coffee. In all this time, why didn't I notice the man didn't drink coffee?"

She wasn't sure, but she thought that Willow disguised a giggle behind an abrupt cough.

"Fetch your bonnet and wrap and come with me. I've had an idea."

Lydia's brows rose, but she moved to gather her things. "What do you have in mind?"

Willow held the door wide for her.

"I think it's time we stopped focusing our attention on the miners and the Pinkertons and bearded the lion in his own den."

"What lion?" Lydia asked morosely as she pinned her bonnet to her head.

"The great man himself. Ezra Batchwell."

The sky hung above them like a blue bowl with nary a cloud in sight as Lydia and Willow climbed the lane leading to the spot high above the miners' row houses where Batchwell and Bottoms had constructed their own private residences.

"I think, if I were asked which of these two houses I would prefer for myself, I would take Mr. Bottoms's cottage," Willow remarked as they passed the first of the buildings.

Lydia had never been this close to either building so she paused to take them both in.

According to what she'd been told, the previous summer, the owners of the mine had hired crews with the specific purpose of erecting their private residences. Not surprisingly, the men had drawn upon memories of their birthplaces in Scotland to inspire their designs.

Phineas Bottoms's cottage had been the first structure to be finished—and not surprisingly. His was a modest two-story dwelling with thick rock walls and a slate roof. If Lydia hadn't known better, she might have thought that the house had been plucked from the wilds of the Highlands and had been transported magically to the Uinta Mountains.

"Really? I would have thought that with your little family, you would want something bigger, like Mr. Batchwell's mansion."

Willow shook her head. "Too many floors to scrub."

Lydia laughed and supposed that Willow had a point. While Phineas Bottoms's house seemed quaint and compact, Batchwell's had been constructed to impress. She could count three full stories—and if the upper garret windows were to be believed, there could be another partial floor above that. The walls were made of imported limestone blocks with stout, square columns, and heavy carved pediments over arched windows. It reminded Lydia of the stately manor houses described by some of her favorite British novelists—and she wouldn't have been surprised to see Mr. Rochester or Mr. Darcy stride from the heavy doors to a waiting carriage in the circular drive.

"Iona said that Mr. Bottoms intends to plant a cottage garden."

Willow's features brightened at the prospect. "Won't that be lovely? I must tell him I have some seeds I brought with me from England. I'd be more than happy to give him some." Her features clouded. "Especially since Charles and I won't know where we'll be living for a while."

Lydia grasped her friend's hand and squeezed. For the time being, Charles was being allowed to work in the mine as a temporary consultant. But everyone suspected that as soon as the women were forced to leave, Willow would be among them. Charles had insisted that he would get a new job if he and his family couldn't live together. But since Jonah had circumvented the rules by living off company property on a piece of land he'd originally homesteaded, Charles was hoping to do the same. It was rumored that there were still parcels available to the north, but until Charles could make a trip to the land offices in Ogden, the Wanlasses' plans were up in the air.

As they passed Bottoms's untidy, unfinished garden and moved closer to Batchwell's property, she could see that his yard had already been planted with formal trees and shrubbery surrounded by an ornate cast iron fence. The entire effect seemed less grandiose in her opinion than sad. Mr. Batchwell seemed intent on closing himself off from Bachelor Bottoms. If he only knew how warm and welcoming the community could be.

When Willow paused to unlatch the gate, Lydia stared up, up, up, her eyes widening slightly when she noted that intricately carved gargoyles had been placed at each of the four corners of the copper roof.

"Those things give me the shivers," Willow muttered, noting Lydia's gaze. "According to Charles, they're supposed to represent the four winds. In my opinion, they look like the horrible little beasties of the forest that my mother threatened me with whenever I grew naughty. I'm not usually superstitious, but you won't catch me up here after dark."

Lydia laughed. "You have to admit the place is im-
pressive."

She didn't miss Willow's instinctive shudder. "Wait.
You haven't seen the inside yet."

Lydia was surprised that Willow had been allowed this
far up the hill without a Pinkerton guard, let alone inside
Mr. Batchwell's home. But then she supposed, as a married
woman, Willow was given certain allowances.

"Why on earth did you volunteer to feed the man?"

Willow shrugged. "I wanted to help with the protest
in some way, and as the lay pastor's wife, it seemed like
a logical way to foster a little goodwill with him. With
the new tunnel opening up, manpower being strained to
the limit—and a mysterious measles epidemic sweeping
through town—Charles needs everyone in the mine that
he can find." Her eyes twinkled. "Besides, I was the only
person who was willing to do it."

She pulled the cart to one of the side doors, then tugged
on a chain. From deep inside, Lydia heard a bell ringing.

"I thought he'd broken his leg," Lydia whispered as the
sounds of footfalls approached the door.

"Oh, he did. But he has a personal servant who waits
on him. A kind of butler and valet combined."

"And his servant can't cook?"

"Apparently not." Willow kept her voice low as well.
"Batchwell wouldn't even let the man leave long enough to
come down to the cook shack to retrieve his meals. From
what I've heard, Mr. Batchwell runs the poor man ragged."

The door suddenly opened, revealing a tall, taciturn
man with a hooked beak of a nose and a fringe of dark
hair that circled around the back of his head.

"Hello, Boris."

"Mrs. Wanlass."

He peered down, down, down his nose to regard Lydia with the suspicion of royalty being confronted with a peasant.

"This is Miss Tomlinson. She's come to help me today."

Willow bent to scoop baby Eva from the wagon and handed her to Lydia, then lifted Adam into her arms as well. Then, she retrieved a basket from where it had been perched on the little bench seat of the converted sledge.

"May we come in?"

At the sight of the babies, Boris's lips thinned to the point of disappearing altogether.

"I don't think that Mr. Batchwell would approve of children in his—"

"As I stated, I couldn't find anyone else to watch them." Her eyes narrowed in a silent challenge that Lydia wouldn't have believed possible in her friend mere weeks before. "He does require a hot meal, doesn't he?"

"Yes, madam. But—"

"Then you'd best let me cook it." Before Lydia could credit what she was seeing, Willow brazenly pushed past the man and entered the house. "Come along, Lydia."

Boris sputtered in protest, but a high-pitched bell came from somewhere inside the house—and judging by the way the man snapped to attention, Lydia surmised it was a summons from the master himself.

"The kitchen is—"

"I know where everything is, thank you, Boris. While you're tending to Mr. Batchwell, you may as well help him move from the bed to the chair. He'll want to eat sitting up and I promised him that I'd change his linens and take them back to the company laundry."

Boris's lips moved silently—and it was clear he wanted to protest his imprisonment—but before he could speak, the bell rang again.

After huffing in irritation, the man disappeared down

a long marble corridor. Only when he was out of earshot did Willow giggle.

"He really is a nice man. But he's a bit puffed up around strangers."

"And women."

Willow conceded that point with a grin. "Come on. This way."

Chapter Eight

Willow led the way down a shorter hall, then through a door that led into an enormous kitchen. Lydia's mouth gaped when she took in the high ceilings, gleaming tile walls, multiple ranges and a preparation table that could have seated most of the brides at once.

"I know what you're thinking," Willow said. She went to the far corner where she spread out a blanket, then laid Adam on his back. Within a few seconds, she had the baby divested of his hat and outer coverings. Through it all, the infant gazed up at her with sleepy adoration. "This place is grand." While Lydia held Eva, Willow followed suit with the smaller twin's hat and knitted sacque. "But it's cold. Not physically cold, mind you, just...sterile."

Gazing around her, Lydia could see that her friend had a point. The white marble walls, gleaming tile and chrome-adorned ranges were shiny and bright, but hard and un-yielding.

Much like Mr. Batchwell.

"The larder is over there. Charles stocked it with meat and staples this morning, along with several loaves of bread from the baking we did in the cook shack. It will take me a few minutes to warm everything up and make a tray." Willow's gaze sparkled with amusement. "If you wouldn't mind helping me change the linens on Mr. Batchwell's bed in a few minutes…"

Lydia moved to hand Willow the baby, but her friend shook her head.

"Adam has been a little fussy today. We'll take her with us so he'll fall asleep."

Lydia glanced down at the baby in question, but he seemed fine to her. His eyes were nearly closed and he unconsciously tried to shove his fist into his mouth.

"I think Eva would benefit from being held for a little while longer."

Lydia heard Boris's footsteps in the hall.

"But how are we going to—"

Then it dawned on her. Willow had spoken of a grand plan, and now she was doing her best to arrange for Eva to be taken to Mr. Batchwell's room.

Aha.

"I think you're right, Willow. Eva could benefit from being held."

Boris stepped inside. "Mr. Batchwell would like tea with his meal rather than coffee."

"Of course."

In an exaggerated show of concern, Willow's brow creased and she eyed Boris up and down.

Lydia had to bite her lip to keep from grinning. Willow had a slight build, guileless blue eyes and a coronet of red-gold braids—and in that moment, she could have been the embodiment of innocence. Knowing she was up to something, Lydia unconsciously rocked the baby and decided to enjoy the show.

"Mr. Boris, are you feeling quite well?" Willow asked.

He glared, and Lydia wondered if Mr. Batchwell's grumpiness was contagious.

"The name is Boris Vladivostok, not *Mr.* Boris."

"But are you feeling well?"

He glanced down, a hand smoothing over his somber suit jacket as if he were looking for the source of her concern.

"Madam?"

"It's simply that we've had a wave of measles in the valley and you're looking a touch…pale." She turned to Lydia. "Don't you think so?"

Lydia nodded solemnly. "Mmm. He does look peaked. When was the last time you ate?"

"This morning," the man offered defensively. "I had my usual breakfast."

Willow stepped closer to Lydia. She lowered her voice, but not so much that Boris couldn't hear them.

"I don't see any spots."

"Nooo. But there's definitely something wrong."

"Perhaps some sun would do him good."

"It couldn't hurt."

"At the very least, a brisk walk would bring the color back to his cheeks."

"I agree."

As their conversation continued, Boris's expression lost some of its severity. Indeed, he began to adopt the look of a drowning man being thrown a lifeline.

"Boris, Miss Lydia and I will be here for at least thirty—"

"An hour," Lydia inserted quickly.

"An *hour.* Maybe two. I'm sure Mr. Batchwell will be eating most of that time."

"At least."

"If you'd like to take a walk—"

"Get something to eat in the cook shack—"

"Drop by the barber's—"

"Or the company store—"

"We can take care of things here."

Clearly, they'd underestimated the degree of the man's cabin fever because he muttered a quick, "Thank you, ladies!" Then he turned on his heel and strode toward the rear staircase. A few minutes later, he clattered back down, wearing his hat and coat.

"I'll be back in an hour!"

"No rush."

The man dodged out the rear door, slamming it behind him.

As soon as he was gone, Lydia giggled. "For a pastor's wife, you are positively wicked."

Gideon swung from his saddle and tied the reins to a nearby branch. Then, taking care to stay on the matted grass, he surveyed the area near the riverbanks.

When he'd come to this spot once before, he'd been more intent on assuring himself that the fire he'd seen had actually existed, but this time, he took greater care examining the area around it.

He'd done enough scouting work during the war that he could read the scene at a glance. There were boot prints still pressed into the mud. Large. Male. To one side, on the grassy verge, he found a patch of grass that had been pressed more firmly into the earth than the rest. A logical spot for a bedroll. In the fire pit, he could see the remnants of a log, so the flames had been extinguished in a hurry, rather than being allowed to burn themselves out.

Crouching next to one of the boot prints, Gideon found no special markings. The soles were misshapen from the slickness of the mud, so Gideon would wager the man was tall, heavy or both.

He slowly circled the area to see what else the campsite could tell him. On the far side, he found evidence of a horse, one that had been well-shod. Nearby, Gideon found what looked like the remains of crumpled butcher paper—a fact that set his teeth on edge. The garbage could have easily been burned, but the man who'd been here had seen fit to befoul the pristine wilderness instead. To Gideon, that spoke volumes about the person's character.

After making a complete circuit of the area, Gideon found the beginnings of the man's trail away from the riverbank, so he retrieved his horse and swung into the saddle. Just as he'd supposed, the stranger had been heading toward the mouth of the canyon and Aspen Valley. Judging by the size and space of the hoof marks, there had been no rush. Instead, the horse had been kept to a slow, leisurely walk until…

The road curved away from the river, hugging the side of the mountainside. In this spot, the shade had caused a thick sheet of ice to layer the track. Runoff from the upper slopes had drained and frozen, drained and frozen, obscuring signs of someone having been through the area.

Since the spot also led to side trails that led into the trapping areas of the local mountain men, Gideon spent a fruitless hour looking for tracks, all without success. But even as his brain urged him to abandon the search and head back to town, he hesitated.

Logically, he knew that the evidence of an encampment could be completely benign—and he reassured himself for the hundredth time that the fire could have been from one of the trappers or an eager homesteader wanting to find his claim as soon as the pass cleared.

But his gut didn't seem mollified by the idea.

None of the trappers he knew would leave a fire pit behind, let alone scraps of paper. They would bury the ashes and leave the area as pristine as when they'd found it. And a homesteader…

Gideon had never known a homesteader that would pass through the area without stopping in Aspen Valley to have a look around or introduce himself.

He took his watch from his pocket and glanced at it one last time. He had at least another hour before he was needed back in town.

It wouldn't hurt to backtrack and have another look.

Willow carefully carried a tray of food up the back staircase while Lydia followed behind her with the basket of linens and Eva.

"Are you sure it's a good idea to bring the baby upstairs with us?" Lydia whispered.

When they'd persuaded Boris to go to town, Lydia had agreed with Willow's idea to bring the infant up to Batchwell's private rooms. Ever since the twins had been found in Charles's row house, Lydia had seen the way that the youngsters caused eyes to gravitate their way, voices to drop to a murmur, and even the most hardhearted miner to smile and speak gibberish.

Not that Lydia had expected Batchwell to take one glance at Eva and become…*human*. But she had thought the infant might have the ability to mellow his mood.

Unfortunately, in the time it had taken Adam to fall asleep, Eva had grown tired and fractious. She whimpered against Lydia's shoulder, one hand flailing piteously.

Nevertheless, Willow seemed completely unfazed. "I timed things this way."

Lydia didn't have the slightest idea what that remark meant, but she dutifully followed her friend down a long hallway to the front of the house.

Juggling the tray, Willow opened a pair of double doors and stepped inside.

The room laid out before Lydia could have graced any palace. Gleaming mahogany floors had been scattered with intricately patterned Oriental carpets. The walls were covered in gold damask silk, and heavy draperies framed the windows. The fireplace on the opposite wall was so large, an entire side of beef could have been roasted inside of it. And the mantel…

For a confirmed bachelor, Ezra Batchwell had a fanciful side. The woodwork surrounding the roaring blaze had been festooned with vaulting stags, woodland animals and the carved busts of what Lydia could only assume were representations of Mother Nature.

"Good afternoon, Mr. Batchwell."

The man sat in a tufted chair near the fire rail. His foot, splinted and swathed in bandages, had been propped on a gout stool laden with pillows.

"Where's Boris?" he grunted peremptorily.

"We sent him into town."

Batchwell thumped the end of his walking stick on the ground, causing Eva to start in Lydia's arms.

"But I need him here!" Batchwell roared, his heavy eyebrows poised thunderously over dark eyes.

"He needed a breath of fresh air, and we were happy to provide him with it."

"I'm the master of this house!" He punctuated his shout with another bang of his walking stick.

Eva reared back, then began to cry, her sobs growing more and more frantic. She seemed to search the room for her mother, but for once, Willow didn't respond.

"Now, look what you've done, Mr. Batchwell."

Lydia's jaw nearly dropped. Willow—shy, reticent

Willow—had scolded Mr. Batchwell like a seasoned schoolmarm.

"Why is that…*thing*…in my house?"

Lydia couldn't tell who grew louder, Eva or Mr. Batchwell.

"That *thing* is a baby, Mr. Batchwell." Willow set the tray on a small round table near the window. "You know full well she's my daughter. Her name is Eva."

She cut her eyes toward Lydia, and surprisingly, Willow seemed to be indicating that Lydia should hand the child to Mr. Batchwell.

"Lydia, could you help me with this table please? It's too far away for Mr. Batchwell to reach."

Again, Willow gestured ever so subtly in Mr. Batchwell's direction. Lydia prayed that the woman knew what she was doing.

"Yes, of course."

Without giving the man an opportunity to refuse, Lydia placed the squalling infant in Mr. Batchwell's arms.

To his credit, the man reacted instinctively, his arms closing around the baby, but his expression couldn't have been more thunderstruck if Lydia had dropped a bucket of ice into his lap.

Then, the most amazing thing happened. The baby stopped crying. She regarded Batchwell with wide tear-laden eyes, seemingly mesmerized by the curly tuft of hair surrounding his balding pate and the wiry mutton-chop whiskers.

For a moment, Batchwell didn't seem to know how to respond. He continued to gaze at the baby with a thunderous scowl, but when Eva offered him a watery smile, he sank deeper into his chair.

Lydia and Willow lifted the table, carrying it to a point

near Batchwell's elbow. Then, when the man seemed to be held in a trance, Willow gestured to the bed.

"Could you help me with the linens?"

Lydia and Willow made quick work of changing the sheets—and even here, Lydia could see evidence of Willow's feminine touch. A length of crocheted lace had been tacked to the hem of the newly laundered linens, and several threadbare spots had been darned so skillfully that the work was hardly visible. Having seen Willow's needlework before, Lydia knew that her friend was probably responsible.

"If we get another sunny day, I'd like to air your blankets and pillows outside on the line, Mr. Batchwell."

The man grunted, but made no other reply. Instead, he'd moved the baby to the crook of one arm and dunked his sandwich into his soup with the other. Taking absent-minded bites, he continued to stare down at Eva as if she were a curious oddity.

"If you can handle things here, we'll clean up in the kitchen, then come back to fetch the baby."

Again, a grunt.

Willow grabbed Lydia's hand, pulling her into the hall where the two of them hurried out of earshot before bursting into laughter.

"'*Wicked*' isn't the only word that should be used to describe you, Willow. I believe I should add *ingenious* as well."

Willow beamed. "I'd hoped something like that might happen. Come on. Let's clean up like we said, then come retrieve her. Her good mood will only last so long."

"Gideon! We've got a rider coming into town!"

Gideon looked up from where he and Smalls had been examining the condition of the wagons needed to haul the ore out of the valley. Since the coming of the railroad, the wagons had been used more for transportation than freight. Now, they would all have to be returned to service and reinforced for the long haul of the precious metal.

"Who is it?"

Winslow shrugged. "No one seems to know him. He's not from around these parts."

Gideon's thoughts immediately skittered toward the encampment he'd examined. He'd spent the better part of an hour trying to pick up the trail, but hadn't had much success. With so much ice on the road and the melting snow, the hoof prints had seemed to disappear into thin air.

Even so, the news that a rider had arrived from the outside world didn't offer him any comfort. If this was the person who'd camped in the canyon—and he'd come to Aspen Valley on official business—why had it taken him so long to show up?

"I'll be back," he said to Smalls.

The huge man nodded, but he must have sensed Gideon's unease, because he followed him out of the wagon shed and onto the main thoroughfare.

Gideon crossed the road to the Pinkerton offices, then stood at the edge of the boardwalk. As the horse and rider ambled toward him, he took the time to study the man. Dusty black hat, blue jacket, black holster. The fact that he was wearing a Pinkerton uniform should have allayed Gideon's suspicion, but the prickling at the back of his nape merely intensified. Gideon knew every detective from here to Denver, and there was nothing familiar about this man's face. That didn't mean that someone couldn't have been hired. It simply meant...

Who knew what it meant? Gideon's normal routines had been upended and turned inside out since the avalanche and he couldn't seem to get himself back into a proper working mode.

The rider came to a halt a few feet away. Touching a finger to his hat, he offered, "Howdy." He grinned. "Seems the pass is finally clear enough for me to come find you boys."

He swung to the ground, then looped a pair of bulging saddlebags over his shoulder. His boots squelched in the mud as he tied the reins to the hitching ring on one of the main supports.

"The name's Jubal Eddington."

He held out a gloved hand and Gideon shook it. All the time, his gaze scanned the man's face. No. He didn't know him. He was older than most Pinkertons in these parts, probably in his midsixties. When he lifted his hat to swipe at the sweat on his brow, Gideon could see that his hairline had receded and turned to gray.

"I've got some correspondence for you from the offices in Denver and Ogden. Then, the railway company asked me to deliver a few things since I was headed this way."

Gideon jerked a finger behind him. "Come on in. I'll have one of my men round up something for you to eat while I go through everything. I might need you to take a reply back. You'll probably want to stay the night, so we'll find a cot for you upstairs."

"Thanks, but I've been told to head right back."

"You're sure? It'll be completely dark in an hour or so."

"I'm sure."

Again, Gideon studied him. He found no reason not to take the man's words at face value. But the stranger's eagerness to leave rankled. He'd have to make camp as soon as darkness fell anyway. Why not sleep in a comfortable bed rather than the mud?

"Have a seat."

The man sank into the chair in front of Gideon's desk just as Lester Dobbs burst through the door.

"Dobbs, this is Jubal Eddington. He's brought us some things from the Ogden office."

Eddington tossed the saddlebags onto the desk and Gideon began removing the letters, packets and papers that had been stuffed inside. Automatically, he sorted them— Pinkerton business, mine business, personal correspondence to various residents and miscellaneous items that would need to be examined to assess their import.

"Looks like this is going to take a while. Dobbs, why don't you take Mr. Eddington to the cook shack and scrounge up something for him to eat? Once you're done, I'll have a better idea of whether or not I'll need to send a response back."

Eddington seemed reluctant, but Dobbs, ever solicitous, held open the door.

"Sure thing, boss. Mr. Eddington, you're in for a treat. The ladies have been cooking a hearty ham and bean soup tonight with thick slabs of corn bread for dunking. It's been windy today, so after your long ride up the canyon, it will warm you from the inside out."

Eddington rose and trailed behind Dobbs like an obedient puppy, but it was only when the door was closed that Gideon was able to concentrate on the piles laid out on his desk. Once again, he went through the stack he'd designated as mining business. In these, the envelopes had clearly been directed to Batchwell, Bottoms or Jonah Ramsey. When he found one addressed to himself, Gideon slid it over to the Pinkerton pile.

In the personal stack, he riffled through them, noting that most of the letters had been addressed to his men, no doubt from their wives or sweethearts. He placed those on the far corner of his desk where his fellow detectives could help themselves. There was also a thick envelope that held more loose papers inside, which he set at his elbow. The others—addressed to a few of the women—he set near the far edge. He'd take those to the evening Devotional. No doubt, the women would want to read them as soon as possible.

Next, he addressed the Pinkerton correspondence. The first few envelopes contained the usual reports and information bulletins from offices all over the country. There was an updated payroll chart that was supposed to have taken effect in January. Gideon smiled. A little bonus was in store for his crew. They'd be pleased to hear that. An enclosed announcement proclaimed that there would be a new office opening in the southern part of the territory, job openings in Colorado and Texas, and a supervisor position available this summer in San Francisco. Such news often brought a change to Gideon's staff when some of the men decided to move on to postings where they could bring their wives and families.

The thought brought a niggling to his conscience when he realized that Lydia had hoped to make Aspen Valley such a community. Gideon knew that Isaac Clemente would welcome such a change. He used all of his leave time to visit his wife Anna and their two sons, who had taken up residence in Ogden, forty miles away. Usually, it was only a half day's journey by passenger train to get there. But with the railroad unable to come into town for the next few months, Gideon was sure the man was chomping at the bit to find a way to visit them. If Anna and the boys were able to live here…

Stop it.

He reached for another envelope and tore it open. But he'd only read a few of the lines when the prickling suspicion he'd felt for days now spread through his whole body, causing his nerve ends to jangle. His eyes raced to read the missive even as his brain sluggishly tried to assimilate the information.

Beware of a possible plot to steal the current cache of silver...credible evidence...remain alert...anticipate large opposing force...take every precaution...

The door opened and Gideon quickly swept the letter into the lap drawer when Eddington appeared.

"Finished already?"

Eddington shook his head. "The women are still setting things up, so they told me to come back after something called...evening Devotional."

"That's right. We usually meet before the meal, but if you're hungry..."

"No. I can wait and eat with the rest of your men." The man's gaze slid over Gideon's blotter, noting the different piles. "It looks like you're still busy. Do you mind if I wash up in the meantime?"

Gideon shook his head. "There's water kept warm on a box heater in that back room there. Privy's outdoors."

"Thanks."

Once again, Gideon waited until the man's footfalls had disappeared. But rather than removing the letter from his desk, he removed a key instead. He carefully twisted the lock, then scooped the rest of the Pinkerton correspondence into the drawer beside it and locked that as well before slipping the key into his tunic pocket.

His gaze fell on the last pile of miscellaneous correspondence. Sorting through them, he found five thick envelopes addressed to Lydia Tomlinson, a package for Dr. Sumner Havisham, a flier for scenic railway tours and a packet of folded Wanted posters. Gideon and other lawmen in the area were to be on the lookout for the John Kinney Gang, the Jesse Evans Gang...

A brief glance at the pictures provided and the information that the outlaws worked several hundred miles south of town had Gideon setting the posters to the side. But when he moved on to the next one he froze.

The fairly recognizable sketch of a woman stared back at him along with the caption:

Wanted!
Lydia Angelica Tomlinson, age twenty-three.
Bank Robbery and Cattle Rustling!

Chapter Nine

Lydia and Willow were able to wash the dishes and stow the leftovers in the larder in record time. Through it all, they kept their ears cocked for the sound of Mr. Batchwell's bell or Eva's cry. But the silence continued. Finally, as Willow loaded a sleeping Adam back into the wagon, Lydia volunteered to retrieve Eva.

She crept up the stairs, wondering what she would find once she rounded the corner into the bedroom. But the sight that met her eyes was inexplicably tender. Eva lay fast asleep in the crook of Batchwell's arm while his own head lolled against the wing of the chair. With his features slackened in slumber, the man didn't look nearly so fierce. Instead, he seemed completely benign, grandfatherly...*kind*.

Not wanting to disturb him, Lydia carefully lifted the baby into her arms. Eva started, but didn't open her eyes. Within seconds, she'd settled back asleep, her mouth pursing in a sucking motion for a moment before relaxing.

Lydia reached for a quilt that had been folded at the foot of the bed and settled it as best as she could over Mr. Batchwell's lap and shoulders. Then, not quite sure why she felt compelled to do so—only that his drooping head and slack jaw reminded her of Aunt Rosie when she fell asleep in front of the fire—Lydia leaned over to squeeze the man's shoulder.

"Sweet dreams, Mr. Batchwell."

Gideon sat on the far side of the cook shack, his plate untouched. In truth, he hadn't been hungry—not after the meal that Lydia had given him mere hours ago. Gathering the food had been a ruse to give him a reason for being here with the other men. Even better, it gave him a vantage point where he could watch the newly arrived messenger eating at a table with Dobbs, Winslow and three miners.

"You look like you've got the weight of the world on your shoulders."

Gideon glanced up to see Charles Wanlass holding an enamelware cup and a plate of gingerbread cookies.

"Mind if I sit here?"

Gideon nudged the chair with his toe.

"Go right ahead."

Charles settled into his place, then took a sip from his mug. Judging by the dust coating his clothing, he and his blasting crew had been working hard in the mine.

"You're not eating at home tonight?"

Gideon would have thought that, after giving his sermon at the evening Devotional, Charles would have gone home to Willow and the children.

"She's been taking meals up to Mr. Batchwell, so she told me we'd push our own meal back an hour or so." He gestured to the cookies. "Still, I couldn't resist a cuppa and a little something to tide me over."

Knowing how hard Charles worked, the man had to be starving. It was a testament to his new family that he was willing to wait until they could all be together.

"How are things going below ground?" Gideon asked.

"Good. Really good. My crew blasted another section

of the rock face away this morning, lengthening the tunnel. That new seam of silver seems to get bigger the deeper we go. That should mollify Batchwell a bit."

Despite his best efforts, Gideon's attention was split. Over and over again, he kept studying the messenger. Try as he might, he couldn't help thinking that something was…off about the man. Granted, he wore the uniform well and seemed to know all the right things to say. He hadn't gone to Devotional with everyone else, but a man couldn't be faulted for that. When Gideon had hung back to watch him, Eddington had done little more than take a slow walk around the camp. There'd been nothing suspicious in his actions, but…

What was it?

Maybe it wasn't the man at all, but the information he'd brought with him. That Wanted poster of Lydia.

It couldn't be genuine, could it?

"Hey, Charles. You've spent some time with Lydia Tomlinson, haven't you?"

Charles eyed him with quiet gray eyes over the top of his mug. "Some. She's a good friend of Willow's, so she's been at the house quite often."

"What do you make of her?"

The other man shrugged. "She's smart, quick-witted, spirited."

"But what do you think of her character?"

Charles sipped, then set his tea on the table. He took a cookie, then nudged the plate in Gideon's direction. Absently, Gideon took one of the gingerbread men, biting an arm off with more ferocity than was necessary.

"She appears to be a woman of exceptional character— kind, friendly, loyal. Why do you ask?"

In his mind's eye, Gideon could see the primitive drawing from the wanted poster. The sketch hadn't been exact, but it had looked enough like Lydia to give it credence. Even so, he couldn't seem to reconcile the poster with the woman who had entertained him for lunch.

"Do you think Lydia could be capable of deceit?"

This time, Charles's eyes narrowed.

"Anyone is capable of deceit. But I've seen no evidence of it with Lydia. Why do you ask?"

Gideon opened his mouth to explain, but he couldn't bring himself to mention the poster—and that fact was more disturbing than anything he'd experienced so far. If the woman was a fugitive, he should be marching into town, finding Lydia and placing her in the company jail until law enforcement could make the trip to retrieve her. But a part of him, some untapped corner of his being, balked at the thought. Granted, he and Lydia tended to make more sparks than poetry when they were together, but he couldn't bring himself to believe that she rode through the territories robbing banks.

"Gideon? Gideon!"

He started, realizing that Charles had been speaking and Gideon hadn't heard a word. Even worse, Gideon had been unconsciously plowing his way through the cookies to the point where the plate was empty and he held a headless gingerbread man in his grip.

"Would you like me to get you another plate of cookies?" Charles asked wryly.

"No, I—" He trailed into silence again, his gaze swinging back to the messenger.

"Who's the fellow you keep watching?"

"He's from the Pinkerton office in Ogden. He managed to make it through the pass with some correspondence."

"And?"

As usual, Charles was too astute.

"I don't know. Maybe it's my natural suspiciousness

being reawakened by contact with the outside world. We've got a mountain of ore to transport, no railway lines, a restless population and an epidemic of measles spreading through the valley. But even with all that going on, my gut keeps telling me that something else is wrong."

He glanced at his friend again, sure that Charles would offer some pastor-like platitudes to reassure Gideon that he was overreacting. Instead, he found Charles studying the messenger as well.

"He looks like one of your detectives. Although he seems a little old for a Pinkerton around these parts."

Exactly.

Charles met Gideon's gaze. "With everything on your plate, it's only natural you should worry—especially now. We're all a little antsy after three months holed up in the valley, the stockpile of silver at its highest, added overtime, and, let's face it, the future of the women hanging in the balance. But if there's one thing I've learned to trust, it's that gut of yours. If it's telling you that something is off, I'd give heed to it." He rose to his feet. "And you let me know if there's anything I can do to help."

After walking Willow to the row house she shared with Charles and spending a few moments with the twins who were now awake and ready to play, Lydia finally took her leave and wandered in the direction of the cook shack. She needed to check in with the other women, apprise them of the fact that she'd failed in her attempts to capture Gideon Gault, and discover how many more miners had been "apprehended" in her absence.

But for some reason, she found herself loath to join them. Apparently, the shrinking Pinkerton crew had relaxed the guarding of the women more than ever because she hadn't seen hide nor hair of any of the detectives in hours—except Gideon, of course. She supposed that she should be celebrating the fact that, for the first time in months, she'd spent an entire day without the irritating company of a guard challenging her every move. She'd been able to do what she wanted, when she'd had a mind to do it. These were the freedoms the women had been fighting for since they'd arrived and Batchwell had ordered the annoying supervision. Lydia knew she should kick up her heels and shout to the stars that were beginning to peek through the dusky sky.

Instead, she felt…

Melancholy.

Things had been so much simpler when she'd begun her cross-country journey. She'd been filled with anticipation at the adventures she would have in striking out on her own, and she'd gloried in her goal to spread hope and purpose through her speaking circuit up and down the Western coast.

Now, all that seemed a lifetime away—as if it had been part of someone else's existence.

How had that happened?

She still firmly believed that all women should be allowed to pursue their dreams, that they should have doorways to education and employment opened to them, that they should be given the same rights as men in owning property and being allowed to control their own money. And if wronged, they should have the same avenues to pursue redress through the courts or the ballot box.

But what had once been such a concrete goal seemed abstract to her now, as if she were swatting at flies that flitted out of her reach.

Where here, in Bachelor Bottoms, everything seemed so *real.*

She was fighting for her friends, for a way of life that

Lydia had always shunned for herself: homes, husbands, children. The opportunity to live together as a family.

Family.

Lydia didn't know if she even fully understood the concept. Her aunts were her family. They'd loved and cared for Lydia as if she'd been their own. But they were hardly conventional. They sometimes looked down their noses on women who'd "settled for the stereotype life," as they put it.

But when Lydia thought of the love she'd seen between Jonah and Sumner, Charles and Willow—and yes, even the emotions she saw blossoming between Iona and Phineas—*settling* seemed an inappropriate word. In Lydia's opinion, these women seemed to have found something precious and nurturing and…

Glorious.

"So pensive."

Lydia started, whirling to see Sumner stepping out of the infirmary. Lydia blinked, thinking that her thoughts had triggered some kind of walking dream, but when Sumner grinned at her, she realized her friend was here in the flesh.

"You gave me a fright," Lydia admitted, folding her arms. Now that night was falling, the air grew chilly and she hadn't thought to bring a wrap with her. "I was just thinking about you."

"Good thoughts, I hope," Sumner said with a smile, approaching the spot where Lydia had unconsciously paused on the edge of the boardwalk.

"Of course. What are you doing here?"

"Charles sent word to me of the…measles epidemic." Her tone bubbled with suppressed mirth. "My goodness. When you stage a protest, you go all out, don't you?"

Lydia hoped the deepening shadows hid the blush that she could feel rising like a tide of heat into her cheeks.

"We were hoping it would buy us more time."

Sumner gestured to a nearby bench. "Well, it delayed Jonah's return for a few days, anyway," she said as they settled onto the hard wooden seat. "He's been chafing against my orders for him to stay at home, and I've been expecting him to revolt at any minute, saddle up his horse and ride back to the mine. Especially now that the fever's long gone." She laughed. "I left him stewing with guilt, sure that he's responsible for the entire workforce being ravaged with illness."

Lydia snorted. "Hardly. We've only got about sixty men so far."

"I believe the total is substantially more by now."

"Really?"

Lydia's tone was filled with such obvious delight that Sumner laughed.

"As for your…*epidemic*, hopefully, my visit will give it credence, but I wouldn't plan on the situation lasting much more than a day or two. Despite his guilty conscience at infecting his coworkers, Jonah will soon feel that his duty to the mine outweighs the need to recuperate at home." She waved toward the infirmary. "And I wouldn't think that your willing captives will last much longer than that. Right now, they're enjoying an unaccustomed holiday and having the other girls dote on them. But they're miners to the bone and they'll be itching to get back to work."

Lydia nodded, knowing that her failure to capture Gideon Gault still remained the largest obstacle to their efforts.

"Tomorrow," she promised. "Come what may, we'll go into the final phase of our plans."

"Anything I can do to help?"

"Keep Jonah at home."

"I'll do my best."

A comfortable silence spooled between them for a moment. Then, knowing that her friend might be the only person who could help Lydia sift through her confusing emotions, she asked, "Have you ever felt as if you somehow veered off the path you'd set for yourself? So much so that you find yourself…lost?"

It felt strange, confiding such thoughts with another person. As much as she loved her aunts, they weren't women to suffer any sign of weakness or vulnerability. Their mantra had always been: forge forward at all costs.

But Lydia wasn't quite sure what *forward* meant anymore.

Sumner took her hand, squeezing it.

"Right now, I'm living the other path."

When Lydia looked at her questioningly, she explained, "I probably never told you, but my father was not…a loving man. At least not to me."

Lydia's brows rose.

"When he discovered my mother had given birth to a girl rather than a boy, he didn't even bother to choose a new name. I became Sumner Edmund Havisham."

"Really?"

"Mmm-hmm. Despite that male moniker, my father believed that, as a female, I should adhere to the strict parameters outlined by society—which was, in effect, be seen, but not heard. I was to learn the arts of housekeeping and embroidery and nothing more. When I announced that I intended to become a doctor, he was livid. For a time, he tried to force me to comply to his narrow rules."

Lydia had known that Sumner had become a doctor through the sweat of her own brow, but she'd had no idea the opposition her friend had encountered at home.

"What happened?"

Sumner squeezed her hand again. "He disowned me. By that time, he had his precious son through my stepbrother. I, on the other hand, was considered a disgrace and a stain against the family name because of my chosen profession. That's how I ended up here, in Aspen Valley."

"Thereby incurring the wrath and disapproval of a whole new set of men."

Sumner laughed. "Oh, yes. My gender was a most unwelcome surprise. And I will admit, that I came into the situation with a giant chip on my shoulder. I felt I had to prove my worth at every turn until…" She seemed to focus on a spot several yards away, but Lydia knew that Sumner was plumbing her memories. "Until I learned that the path I'd been searching for all along was love. It's the reason why I became a doctor. Even more importantly, it's why I finally opened my eyes to happiness and what my heart yearned for the most. Acceptance."

The word pinged in Lydia's heart, the effects radiating throughout her soul.

Acceptance.

Wasn't that at the core of what she fought for as well? For women to be accepted with dignity and respect for the talents and desires that God Himself had given them?

And yes. That was what Lydia yearned to experience. Acceptance. Not simply from the world at large acknowledging that her gender had untapped potential to offer, but also from one man in particular.

Gideon Gault.

If he knew her, *really* knew her, he would never accept her. How could he? The Pinkertons might be a private agency; their men might be described as detectives. But here in Aspen Valley, they were the law enforcers. Gideon had spent years developing a reputation with the mine. He was known by all to be fair, honest and loyal. He'd earned the trust of his employers, the miners and the men. If he knew even an inkling of Lydia's true background, he would have nothing to do with her.

"Lydia?"

Too late, she realized she'd lapsed into silence and now Sumner was eyeing her with open concern.

"Is something wrong?"

"No, I—" Lydia broke off, realizing that she owed Sumner more of an answer. She laced her fingers in her lap. "I suppose I find myself at a crossroads of sorts, and I'm not quite sure which path to take."

Sumner reached over to shake one of Lydia's hands free, then held it in her own capable palm. "When the time comes to make a decision…follow your heart."

Gideon had been subtly following Eddington as he left the cook shack, took a lazy circuit around town, then headed inside the Pinkerton building, presumably to sleep in the cot that had been set aside for him. But even though Gideon's body thrummed tiredly, he knew it would be useless to turn in himself. He didn't sleep much anymore. Unless he drove himself to exhaustion, he'd lie in bed with his memories circling through his head like a worn-out carousel. The more he thought, the darker the images became, and then the nightmares were soon to follow.

For that reason, he'd become a haunt himself, roaming around town until well past midnight, or riding his horse out of town in an effort to flee the past.

As he sat on the bench outside the barbershop, whittling a piece of wood with his penknife, he saw Lydia appear from the direction of the Wanlass home. He'd been about to stand and approach her when Sumner stepped from the infirmary.

The two of them soon settled into conversation, and not wanting to appear as if he were spying on them, Gideon stayed in the shadows. Watching.

When had things changed between Lydia and him? There had been a point when they'd only had to share the same room for his body to flood with exasperation. From the very beginning, she'd had an uncanny knack of riling up his emotions. He'd gone from antagonism to irritation to anticipation. And now, he had only to look at her to feel a certain…peace.

How had that come about? How had they settled into this odd place where he spent most of his time unconsciously seeking her out, only to have his heart flip-flop in anticipation once he'd found her?

Did she feel it too?

His brow creased when he noted the serious nature of her conversation with the good doctor. Briefly, he wondered if she were conversing with Sumner about a medical complaint—did she worry that she'd contracted the measles?

As soon as the thought appeared, he pushed it away. Judging by the way she'd been charging around town with her usual spirit and flair for the dramatic, she didn't need the doctor's medical advice.

Which meant she'd approached her friend on another matter.

Maybe an affair of the heart?

Stop it!

Just because he'd begun to follow her every move like a young lad in the throes of puppy love didn't mean that she felt anything of the kind herself. Lydia was a woman of the world, highly educated, driven and a self-proclaimed suffragist. She wouldn't think along those lines. Men were superfluous for women of her ilk. She longed to take the stage and flood the theater with fiery discourse in order to change the world for women. And Gideon had to grudgingly admit that he'd love to see her in her element. Although he'd never really thought much about women's suffrage, he could imagine the fire in her eyes and the high color in her cheeks once Lydia had been given a lectern and an audience.

But that would never happen here. Not in Aspen Valley. So, it was unlikely that Gideon would ever have a chance to hear one of her speeches.

"She's confused, you know."

Gideon looked up to find he wasn't alone in the darkness. Iona Skye had somehow approached and stood only a few feet away. Honestly, the situation with the women was becoming increasingly intolerable if they were able to wander around town so openly with nary a guard in sight. Gideon knew he should put his foot down, right now, march into the cook shack, and order his men to get these women under control and sequestered in the Dovecote.

But he didn't have the heart to do it. Not when they would be gone soon.

He pushed himself to his feet. "Would you like to sit down?"

Iona seemed surprised by the invitation. Obviously, she'd expected him to order her back inside with the other women.

"Thank you. It grew so warm in the cook shack that I came out for a breath of fresh air before things grew too cold."

She sat on the bench, arranging her skirts so that he could sit beside her. "It's a lovely night, isn't it?"

Gideon glanced up at the ever-darkening sky, at the stars glittering like chips of ice.

"Yes. It is."

Iona gestured above her. "This is one of the things that

first struck me upon my arrival in Aspen Valley. I spent most of my life in New York. There, the stars seemed much fainter and a million miles away. Here, it feels as if a body could reach up and snatch one of them from the sky."

"I know what you mean."

Silence spooled between them for a few moments. But Gideon found that the quiet wasn't uncomfortable. Quite the contrary, in fact.

"Do you care for her?"

Too late, he realized that his gaze had strayed to Lydia again. He opened his mouth to offer an immediate denial, but found he couldn't say the words. Mere days ago, he would have scoffed at the idea that he would have tender feelings for anyone, let alone the indomitable Lydia Tomlinson. Now...

"I don't know what I feel," he offered honestly. The fact that he'd shared such an intimate thought with anyone— let alone one of the mail-order brides who had been the bane of his existence since being stranded in the valley— should have shocked him to the core. But there was something about Iona, her proud bearing, the wise eyes, that reminded him of his own dearly departed mother. Somehow, he knew that his confession would be safe with her.

"I daresay she's experiencing a portion of the same confusion."

Gideon chanced another glance in Lydia's direction.

"You think so?"

"Yes. There seems to be a lot of that going around lately." Her tone was wry. "It's as if the spring thaws are sending all of our emotions topsy-turvy."

Gideon couldn't help but smile. "You sound like you're not immune to the situation."

"Definitely not. I am discovering that, contrary to what I'd always believed, there is no age limit to happiness or the Lord's blessings. Sometimes, such things come when we least expect them." She reached to pat his knee, much as his mother used to do when she wanted to emphasize a point. "Just remember that in the next few days, hmm?"

She stood and returned to the cook shack, leaving Gideon to wonder why he felt as if he'd been forewarned.

Chapter Ten

Lydia found herself lagging behind the other women as they left the cook shack and headed back to the Dovecote.

Nighttime had fallen in the past few hours. Without the sun to cast its rays, the air had grown chilly and the breeze had the ability to nip through their clothing and cause them to hurry.

Nevertheless, Lydia found herself unconsciously isolating herself from their chatter and seeking the silence of the evening.

She didn't realize how far away the women had become until a shape stepped out of an alley, blocking her way. Lydia gasped, realizing that one of the Pinkertons had stopped her.

No. Not one of *their* Pinkertons.

Although the gentleman wore the blue uniform, she didn't recognize his face. And after so many days and weeks and months at Bachelor Bottoms, Lydia knew everyone in the community.

She'd borrowed a shawl from one of the other women and her hand automatically reached to pull the wrap tighter to her neck. She'd heard a stranger had come to Aspen Valley with correspondence from the outside world. The news had spread like wildfire through the cook shack, so much so, that the place had been a-buzz by the time Lydia had returned to the kitchens to help. But since she'd spent the remainder of the evening in the preparation area, she hadn't seen the stranger.

Until now.

The man lifted his hat. "Miss Tomlinson."

His tone was polite. Respectful. But for some reason, the greeting unsettled her. The fact that he already knew her name was disconcerting, making her feel as if she were at a disadvantage in the conversation.

"Good evening." She didn't bother to ask for his own name in return. In her opinion, any man who would boldly confront a woman on the boardwalk at this time of night without having been properly introduced, strained the bounds of polite society, if not safety. Her aunts would have been appalled—and since they'd taught Lydia how to defend herself from impertinent gentlemen, he was fortunate he wasn't contending with the business end of a hatpin or the single shot derringer tucked into her corset.

"You ladies sure know how to cook. I don't think that I've tasted anything so delicious in…well, in a very long time."

She tipped her head in what she hoped was an imperious, dismissing manner. More than anything, she wanted to catch up to her friends. For the first time since coming to the area, she longed to see one of the guards who'd been overseeing their safety for last few months.

"If you'll excuse me…" she murmured, hoping he would realize she wasn't in a mood to converse.

"Of course, ma'am. I didn't mean to startle you. I simply wanted to offer my thanks."

"You're more than welcome. Good evening."

This time, she didn't bother to wait for him to move. She

stepped into the street in order to make her way around him, quickening her gait.

"Oh, and Miss Tomlinson, you be sure to have yourself a good nighty-night under the starlight bright."

Lydia stumbled, a tingling numbness settling into her fingertips and toes.

Have a good nighty-night under the starlight bright, Lydia Lou.

She whirled to confront the man, but just as quickly as he'd appeared, the stranger had disappeared.

Nighty-night under the starlight bright...

Images thundered through her brain. A rat-infested tenement...a revival tent...a camp under the stars...

And being afraid. So very afraid.

"Lydia?"

She jumped, whirling again, her hand automatically reaching overhead for the jeweled hatpin that Aunt Florence had designed with her own two hands. The steel shank was sturdier than most, and kept razor-sharp.

But when her eyes focused on the shadow approaching her, she wilted in relief.

Gideon.

His name burst from her lips and she couldn't help lurching toward him.

Gideon automatically grabbed her elbows, steadying her. "Is something wrong?"

"No. No, I—"

Nighty-night under the starlight bright...

Only one person had ever used that phrase with her. Even now, the words brought a rush of helplessness and fear. Because once he'd uttered the words, her father would offer a litany of empty promises.

One more job, Lydia Lou. Then we'll live in a big house with plenty of food and you can go to school...

"Lydia?" Gideon shook her slightly, drawing her attention back to the dark intensity of his gaze. "Has someone hurt you?"

"No. I—I fell behind the others and…"

She couldn't bring herself to tell him about her encounter with the stranger. As far as she knew, the man's choice of words could have been a coincidence.

But the thought rang hollow. The whole encounter—his stopping her on the boardwalk, engaging her in conversation, employing that oh, so familiar phrase—hadn't been a coincidence.

It had been a message.

"Lydia, where are your guards? I told a pair of men to accompany all of you home before they turned in for the night."

"They're with the other girls. I—it was my own fault. I didn't keep up with them and—" She found herself scouring Gideon's features, taking comfort in their familiarity. "Gideon," she asked hesitantly. "Will you walk me home?"

It would have been so easy for him to refuse—or to ask one of his men to come to her aid. But the man didn't even hesitate. Instead, he gripped her hand and pulled her forward.

"Of course."

To her relief, he didn't release her once they'd begun to walk down the lane. Instead, he wove their fingers together, making it clear to her that he didn't plan to leave any time soon.

"Can you tell me what's wrong?"

Lydia opened her mouth to talk about the stranger dressed in the Pinkerton uniform, but she found she couldn't think of a thing to say that wouldn't ruin everything. With a few well-chosen words, the man had stripped away years of training, education and confidence, leaving her feeling like…

A frightened little girl.

But she couldn't bring herself to lie and say that nothing was wrong, either. At this point, she didn't think she could summon enough bravado to make the assertion believable.

"Maybe later. But not right now."

To his credit, he seemed willing to follow her lead.

"Oh, I have something for you." He reached into his jacket pocket and retrieved several envelopes. "A messenger made it through the pass and brought mail for the mining officials and my own office. These were mixed in with them."

He paused long enough to hand them to her, but still kept ahold of her hand.

There was enough moonlight for her to make out the familiar, loopy scrawl. "My aunts!" She tucked the envelopes against her chest. Her eyes prickled with tears and an unaccustomed lump settled in her throat.

Just when she needed them most, her aunts had found a way to bolster her courage yet again.

"I thought I should bring them to you as soon as possible."

"Thank you! I'll read them as soon as I get to the Dovecote."

They settled into a companionable silence accompanied by little more than the crunch of their footfalls on the gravel and the chatter of the bare-limbed aspen trees swaying in the breeze. Lydia found the experience remarkable. Normally, she would feel compelled to fill the void of silence with conversation. But here, tonight, it felt right to remain quiet. In the stillness, she could concentrate on the warmth of his hand around hers, on the stray sweep of his thumb over her knuckles.

It wasn't until the Dovecote loomed into sight—big and bare and gleaming with lamplight—that she knew she had to speak.

"Thank you, Gideon."

"For what?"

"For bringing me home. For making me feel safe." She hesitated before adding, "For not pummeling me with questions or chiding me for being afraid of the dark."

He stopped, and with a slight tug, forced her to face him. "We're all afraid of the dark at some time or another."

She huffed in disbelief. "I doubt you've ever had that problem."

His features settled into an expression that appeared curiously…sad.

"You'd be surprised."

She remembered then that he had his own memories that sometimes came to haunt him.

"The war," she murmured.

"Sometimes, it feels like I've only stepped away from that life for a few moments and it will reach out to snatch me back."

His words echoed her own storm of emotions so completely, that she couldn't help whispering, "What do you do when you feel like that, Gideon?"

He squinted into the darkness. "I get on the back of my horse and ride."

She'd seen him on several occasions, leaning low over the neck of his gelding, galloping toward the foothills or along the river road. Each time, she'd wondered what had happened to drive him to ride as if someone pursued.

"Do you manage to escape the memories?"

A part of her wondered if his solution would work for her. Could she outrun the past? Could she drive back the sensation that no matter how much she learned, how much she progressed, how much she fought, she would never be able to erase the stain of her childhood from her soul?

That she would never be good enough to deserve someone like Gideon Gault?

Gideon shook his head, and she wished that the moonlight hadn't cast so much of his face in shadow.

"No. But sometimes the wind against your face and
the roll of the horse's gait can…help you gain a new perspective."

Somehow, Lydia didn't think that solution would work
too well for her. At this moment, if she were to saddle a
horse and ride out of town, she doubted she would be able
to stop. Now, more than ever, she wanted to escape. She
wanted to go back to being that naive woman who had
boarded a train with utmost confidence in her abilities.

Unfortunately, she'd committed herself to Bachelor Bottoms, to the mail-order brides, and to seeing their protest
through to the end. Only then would she be able to leave.
Hopefully, before her father could catch up to her.

Gideon reached to skim her cheek with the tip of his
finger, anchoring her back in the present, to this moment.

To him.

The caress continued, moving to her temple, her brow.

"Does it help? Having a new perspective?"

"Sometimes. Sometimes a good ride clears my head
and helps me think more clearly. At other times, it merely
helps me to sleep at night."

Lydia unconsciously squeezed his hand, knowing what
he meant. She'd had her own share of evenings where the
gnawing of her belly and the overwhelming sense of fear
were so real that the border between dreams and reality
had seemed to disappear.

They'd reached the porch by now, and Lydia reluctantly
stepped onto the stoop. For a moment, the lamplight cast
a buttery glow over Gideon's features. She inexplicably
clung to the tenderness she saw reflected there. And some-

thing more. An awareness that even though the two of them had thought they existed on opposite ends of the spectrum...

They were really more alike than either of them would have ever thought possible. Lydia wanted to invite him inside so that they could continue their conversation. But she had no idea if the rest of the brides had gone to bed or if they'd lingered in the keeping room for cups of tea and giggling confidences. A part of her didn't want to share Gideon with the other girls. Not yet.

"Good night, Gideon. Sleep well tonight. And thank you."

His finger traced her cheek again. "It was my pleasure, Lydia. I hope you know you can approach me any time you need help."

She nodded, knowing that he would come to her aid if requested, but also knowing that, where her father was concerned, she could never allow herself to ask. The mere thought of Gideon knowing that she had once ridden with the infamous Tommy Gang was something he must never know.

Astonishingly, he lifted her hand to his lips and placed a brief, fleeting kiss on her knuckles.

"Sleep well, Lydia," he murmured, echoing her own sentiment. Then he added, "Sweet dreams."

Then he released her and disappeared into the darkness.

For the first time in weeks, Gideon skipped his nightly visit to the livery. Instead, without really having any memory of how he'd come to be there, he let himself into the Pinkertons offices through the back door. Here, the men had added a few comfortable chairs, a box stove, and a cupboard to hold a few foodstuffs, plates, mugs and utensils.

When he entered, Dobbs looked up from where he'd been pouring coffee out of an old battered pot.

"Hey, boss. Would you like some?"

"Nah. Do we have any milk left?"

Dobbs pointed to a pitcher on the corner of the counter. "Winslow brought some fresh on his way back from the cook shack."

Gideon knew that the overture had been done more for him, rather than for the men to mix with their coffee, and he appreciated the gesture. It spoke to the fact that his group of detectives were friends as well as coworkers.

"Everything quiet?"

"Seems to be. I hope you don't mind, but I doubled the guard around the ore warehouse. There's something about knowing the canyon is completely passable that's had me feeling a little antsy lately."

Finally. Someone else was picking up on the same anxiousness that Gideon had been feeling for days.

"Tomorrow morning, I need to have a word with everyone. The Ogden office sent a letter warning me that they've heard some rumors about someone planning to steal the ore before we can get it shipped to Denver." He thought of the note still locked in his drawer. "I haven't had time to read it through, but once I have, we need to come up with some solid security measures, especially once we start hauling things out by wagon." He lowered his voice slightly. "Let everyone know we'll meet right after the morning Devotional, as soon as Mr. Eddington leaves for Ogden."

"Oh, he's gone."

"What?"

"He came back about twenty minutes ago, packed up his things, and headed out of town." Dobbs eyed Gideon over the rim of his mug. "I took the liberty of saddling a horse and trailing him to the mouth of the canyon."

A cold finger seemed to trace the length of Gideon's

spine. It didn't make sense for the man to leave now with the darkness and the cold settling in. But nothing about the man's arrival had really made any sense.

"Spread the word that we'll meet at first light. Before Devotional."

"You got it."

Dobbs set his empty mug on the counter, then left the room. The thud of his footfalls marked his progress upstairs.

Gideon waited until the sounds had faded away before pouring himself a glass of milk and heading into the front office. After lighting the lamp at his desk, he sank into his chair and reached for the key he'd tucked in his pocket. As he did so, he was struck by the sight of several deep gouges that had been etched into the wood around the lock.

Reaching for the lamp, Gideon held it up to the drawer. Someone had been trying to force the lock.

His fingers fumbled with the key, the hole seeming to be two sizes too small, before he finally managed to twist it into place. As soon as he was able, he jerked the drawer open, his shoulders sagging in relief when he found that the correspondence from the Pinkerton offices was right where he'd left it. Apparently, the stout, ugly desk that had been supplied to him by the mining company had been strong enough to prevent the attempted theft.

Gideon immediately dismissed the idea that one of his men or a miner could be responsible for the vandalism. Although he had no proof, he would guess that Eddington was to blame.

But why? If the man had wanted to tamper with the mail, he could have done so before delivering it.

Unless it had never occurred to the stranger that he could be handing Gideon a warning. Too late, Gideon realized that Eddington must have seen the way he'd swept the letter into his desk, locking it hurriedly away when the man had entered the offices unannounced.

The inconsistencies that Gideon had filed away—the man's age, his odd manner, the way he'd seemed to frighten Lydia—now seemed all the more telling. The fire Gideon had seen and the fact that no stranger had appeared in Aspen Valley for two more days heightened Gideon's sense of caution. He had the feeling that unseen forces were swirling around Aspen Valley like the beginnings of a whirlpool.

And if he didn't remain on guard, they could all be dragged down into events that could lead to untold harm.

Your father has escaped from prison and it is only a matter of time before he finds you.

Lydia's hands trembled as she finished pinning the last braid in place. As she stood in front of the mirror, eyeing her reflection in the harsh morning light, even *she* could see that she looked pale.

"Are you feeling all right?" Iona asked behind her.

"Yes. Yes, I'm fine."

But she wasn't fine. She'd spent the night poring over her aunts' letters, charting the progression of her guardians' emotions from the first note expressing their pride in her independence, to the worry that she hadn't informed them of her arrival, their frustration when the railway company had no information on the missing train, to their apprehension once the blocked pass had been discovered.

And then that final letter.

Your father and five members of his original gang have escaped from prison. From what we've been able to deduce, he is rounding up an army of old followers. He may seek retribution.

Lydia closed her eyes, then opened them again when the image of Clinton Tomlinson seemed to swim into view.

Some might think that her aunts were being overly dramatic. It would have been more logical for her father and the Tommy Gang, as they'd called themselves, to ride hard for Mexico.

But Lydia knew her father well. Once he felt he'd been slighted, he would demand retribution. She'd seen him knife a man for accidentally bumping into him on a crowded street. That being said, how much more vicious would his retribution be for the daughter who'd been responsible for sending him and his men to prison?

Iona laid a hand on Lydia's shoulder, causing her to start.

"Are you sure you're feeling well? I know for a fact you didn't sleep a wink last night." She hesitated before adding, "Did you receive bad news in those letters Mr. Gault gave you?"

"They were from my aunts. Actually, most of their news was good. They realized right away when I didn't telegraph them of my arrival that something had happened." She could picture Aunts Rosie and Florence—one of them tall and thin, the other short and stout—storming the railway offices demanding answers. The two of them would have been a formidable force. "From what I could gather, they insisted the railway company investigate matters. Then, when it became clear that the pass had been blocked by an avalanche, they begged them to send a rescue party."

"Which would have been nigh on impossible. If there had been any way to get through that canyon, Batchwell would have tossed all of us out on our ears."

Lydia nodded. "They wrote dozens of letters, willing themselves to believe I was still alive, having faith that their notes would get to me at some point." A portion of her anxiety coated the words. "And yet, even burdened with their own worries, they requested that the railway company give them the names of everyone on board so that they could notify their relatives of what had occurred."

Iona touched a hand to her lips. "Thank the Good Lord Above. I've been so worried about what my sister was thinking all this time."

"Which is why we need to be successful in our plans today. We only have a matter of days before we'll be able to contact our loved ones ourselves. And it's my goal that, when we do, we have a wealth of choices available to us for our future plans—including being able to stay in Bachelor Bottoms."

Lydia knew more than anyone that their time was swiftly running out. They had to see their protest through to the end before Clinton Tomlinson could throw a wrench into the works.

Straightening her shoulders, Lydia took a deep breath, then said, "Let's go."

She and Iona hurried downstairs where the rest of the women waited for them. Before speaking, Lydia did a quick head count. A small contingent of women had gone to the cook shack that morning to prepare the meals. There were already six women guarding the "quarantine" locations. That left…thirty-two women to help carry out their plan.

"Ladies…ladies!"

The chatter died down and all eyes turned in her direction.

"As you may have heard, a messenger from Ogden was able to make his way into the valley yesterday." A murmur rippled through the group at that information. "Among the items he brought were several letters from my aunts, which were forwarded through the railway company. I wanted to let you know that, through their efforts, our plight was discovered within a few days after the avalanche occurred. Soon thereafter, my aunts went to great lengths to contact your families so that they knew a rescue would be sent as soon as possible."

The group erupted. Lydia could only distinguish smattered phrases.

What a relief.

Praise be to the Lord!

After a moment, Lydia held up her hands until the group grew silent.

"Unfortunately, now that a messenger has confirmed our whereabouts—as well as the fact that the pass is negotiable—it's only a matter of time before we are either escorted from the valley or our rescue party appears."

Murmurs rose, then fell.

"That means that we are running out of time."

She saw that some of the women instinctively reached out to squeeze a hand or touch a shoulder.

"Ladies, this has been a trying few months for all of us. But I think that I can safely say we've all been enriched by the experience." She lifted her hands to gesture to the group at large. "We have made wonderful friendships."

"Hear, hear!"

"And we've all grown through the many acts of service that we've been able to render in the cook shack, the infirmary and the community at large."

Several of the women applauded, so she waited a moment before holding up her hands again.

"Last of all, for some of you, this experience has brought you something that you never expected to find. Love."

Her eyes scanned the group. There were those she knew of—Hannah and Greta, who had formed attachments with a pair of men from Wales; Stefania, a gentleman from Greece; Myra and Miriam, who had astoundingly fallen in love with a pair of brothers from a town in Virginia less than a half-dozen miles away from their own birthplace.

For each romance Lydia knew about, she was sure that more were being kept secret.

"I realize that so many of you are eager to return to the lives and futures that were interrupted. But I think that we are all agreed that our last act of service should be to our friends and this community that we have grown to love."

This time the applause was even louder.

Lydia took a calming breath. "So, ladies. Let's bow our heads and pray. And for this special prayer, let's all join hands."

Bit by bit, the women shifted into a circle, linking hands with one another.

"Dear Father, we are so very grateful for all that Thou has given us: our health, our safety, and our love for one another and this beautiful corner of Thy Kingdom. We thank Thee for the men of Aspen Valley who have kindly given us shelter and provided for our welfare. At this time, we ask for Thy special hand in our endeavors. If it be Thy will, please help us to bring a change to this valley so that this might be a proper home for all. One where families can flourish under Thy hand. For these and all Thy bounties, we are truly grateful. Amen."

"Amen!"

Lydia's eyes stung with tears as she surveyed the group of friends before her.

No. Not friends.

Sisters.

A tightness gripped her throat and she waited a moment before subtly clearing it. Then she smiled broadly and drew to military-like attention.

"All right, ladies. You've all been given a list of targets and objectives. If we're going to succeed, we need to work quietly, quickly and maintain the element of surprise. Are there any last questions?"

When no one raised a hand, she nodded.

"Don't forget to report your progress to Iona. She'll be stationed in the cook shack until midday when we begin phase two of our plan."

Iona waved. "I'll be eager to cross off all the items on our list or to fortify you with some strong tea."

The women laughed, then turned their attention back to Lydia.

"We can do this," Lydia said firmly. "We are strong and resourceful, and we're fighting for the most important cause on earth. Our families."

Again, a hand seemed to clutch her throat. Until her aunts had taken her in, Lydia hadn't known what that word meant. Her father had insisted that family meant shared blood and blind loyalty—even if such devotion meant abandoning one's values.

But when she'd been led up the walkway to her aunts' brownstone, Lydia had been given her first taste of what the word really meant. The two poised, elegant women hadn't seemed to notice that their niece came to them dressed like a filthy little boy, or that her manners were shockingly nonexistent, or that, at age twelve, she could barely read or write.

No, these beautiful, strong, independent women— women of infinite gentility—had enfolded her into their sweet embrace. Even now, Lydia could remember their two distinct perfumes. One carnations, the other lilies of the valley. Then, these self-proclaimed spinsters had welcomed her into their home as if they'd been waiting their entire lives for her to appear so that their circle of love would be complete.

"Ladies, with a little more work, we can bring this entire protest to a satisfactory end within a day, so give this everything you've got."

The women cheered.

"Gather into your units, choose your weapons and get to work!"

Chapter Eleven

Myra and Miriam Claussen casually walked toward the barbershop, each of them carrying enormous baskets in one hand and their bulging reticules in the other.

"Do you have the sign?" Myra whispered, *sotto voce*.

"Of course, I have the sign," Miriam muttered under her breath.

They could hear Mr. Bramblyhurst setting up inside his shop. From the opposite end of town, they could pick out the last few notes of the postlude being played in the distance.

"Tack it up, tack it up!"

Miriam quickly hung the placard next to the front door.

Free haircuts and shaves for the first 20 men.
Form line here.

The door rattled as Mr. Bramblyhurst unlocked it, but thankfully, he didn't open it.

A wave of miners began to appear, moving from the Meeting House to the cook shack for the first meal of the day. Myra and Miriam began calling out, "Free shaves and haircuts!"

It only took a few minutes for a line to form. Miriam made her way down the queue counting. When they had twenty men, she lifted her arm to show Myra that they'd reached their limit.

Myra immediately opened the door. "This way, gentlemen. Move toward the rear until everyone is inside. Thank you. Thank you."

"What's going on here?" Mr. Bramblyhurst called out as he stepped in from the back room. "Some of you will have to come back later."

As the last gentlemen stepped inside, she and Miriam slammed the door shut, set their baskets on the ground, then removed a pair of revolvers from their reticules.

"You're all under arrest!" Myra shouted. "Get down on the ground!"

The men whirled to face them, their eyes widening as they took in the sight of the twins brandishing their weapons.

Miriam chanced a glance at her sister. "They aren't under arrest," she muttered under her breath.

"Oh." Myra gathered her thoughts. "You aren't under arrest, but you're now our prisoners, so sit down!"

The men mumbled in confusion, but the sound of a pair of hammers being cocked caused them to lower themselves to the floor.

"Excellent, excellent!"

Myra waited a beat of silence. Two. Then looked at Miriam. "What were we supposed to do next?"

"The baskets."

"Oh, yes."

"Gentlemen, you will not be allowed to leave this barbershop for any reason until we tell you...that...that you can go."

She glanced at her sister in time to see Miriam roll her eyes.

"Get the windows, Miriam!"

Miriam quickly went to pull the blinds on the large picture window. Then, she moved to the door, flipped the sign to CLOSED, and pulled the smaller shade over that one as well.

"The back door, Miriam."

Miriam hurried to do the same to the storage room, effectively closing them all into the shadowy narrow shop.

"Well done, Miriam."

"Thank you, sister."

"Gentlemen, we apologize for the inconvenience, and presently we'll explain ourselves. In the meantime…"

Miriam lugged the baskets to the center of the room and whisked off the checkered cloths to reveal a mountain of food.

"Is anyone hungry?"

The bell to the company store jingled overhead as Emmarissa Elliot and Louise Wilkes stepped inside.

"He's alone," Emmarissa whispered to her friend, referring to Marty Grooper who ran the establishment.

"Then let's get this done before someone else comes in."

Emmarissa hesitated. "Let's try to do this without the guns first. Follow my lead."

"Just be swift about it!"

The two women strode to the counter.

"Mr. Grooper," Emmarissa said, leaning forward as if she didn't want her words to be overheard.

"Yes, Miss…"

"Elliot."

"How can I help you, Miss Elliot?"

She dropped her voice even more. "I wonder if I could ask your advice on a delicate matter?"

This time, it was Mr. Grooper who leaned forward. "Of course."

"And I can rely upon your discretion?"

"On my word, yes."

Emmarissa scrambled for a way to get the man to move to the middle of the store, away from the shield of his counter.

"I seem to be having a problem with my…" she dropped her voice to a whisper "…my garters, Mr. Grooper. And since this is an all-male establishment, I don't suppose that you have any on hand."

The man visibly swallowed. "No. No, we've never had any call for them."

"I know it's an imposition, but…could you take a look at the metal buckles and see if there's something you can recommend? Either a substitution—or perhaps a repair?"

He reached to straighten his slender string tie. "I—I'll do my best."

As Emmarissa had hoped, he walked around the glass cases of knives and boots and safety lamps to join her in the center of the room.

Emmarissa shot a warning glance to her friend, then lifted her skirts, one inch, two, lifting up, up, up to the top of her boot.

Mr. Grooper crouched closer.

Clang!

The man dropped unceremoniously at her feet.

Looking up, Emmarissa found her friend brandishing a cast iron skillet from a nearby display.

"I hope you didn't hit him too hard."

Louise seemed blissfully unconcerned. "'Twas nothing

more than a glancing blow. Let's take him into the back and tie him up."

They had done little more than hook their arms beneath his when the bell jingled.

Emmarissa dropped her side of the storekeeper and tried to shelter the man from view. But it was no use. Ephraim Zapata, the machine shop foreman, gazed at them in confusion.

"Mr. Zapata! We need your help," Louise suddenly exclaimed. "We were speaking to Mr. Grooper and he…well, he simply collapsed on the floor. Could you help us take him to the back room? I'm sure he has a cot there. If we could lay him down and get him some water, maybe we could revive him."

Zapata rushed to sling the wizened man over his shoulder. Trailing along behind him, Emmarissa grinned at the man's unwitting assistance. As soon as Louise and Zapata had passed into the back room, Emmarissa quickly shut the heavy green curtains that separated the store from the back rooms.

Clang!

Grinning, Emmarissa tied one of Mr. Grooper's heavy grocer's aprons around her waist and stowed the reticule with her revolver under the counter. She was straightening when the bell over the door jingled.

"Good morning, Mr. Barsad," she proclaimed, raising her voice enough to be heard by Louise. "I'll be happy to help you with your purchases, but first…do you think you could help me in the back room?"

It was nearing lunchtime, but Gideon still hunched over the papers on his desk. He'd pored over the warning letter sent to him by the Pinkerton offices in Denver that oversaw many of the smaller branches throughout the territories. As Gideon had outlined to his men, so far, officials had nothing more concrete than rumors of a plot to steal the silver ore being shipped from Aspen Valley to Denver. But credible sources spoke of a sizeable group of men being gathered, as well as weapons and horses. If the various reports were to be believed, the attempt would be made somewhere along the journey, after the ore had been loaded onto railway cars. But Gideon should remain alert, especially now that the news had begun to circulate that the railway line into the valley had been damaged.

Gideon rubbed at the ache centering between his brows as he continued to study a log of interviews made by several detectives in the territories. If news of the ruined tracks had become common knowledge, even a child could see that a huge whopping weakness had opened up in the Batchwell Bottoms Mine's security.

More than ever before, Gideon knew he should be focusing on the logistics of reestablishing the telegraph lines, getting the women out of the valley, and hauling the stockpiled ore to the nearest section of undamaged track. Instead, he couldn't seem to think of anything but the Wanted poster still hidden in his desk. One with a rudimentary sketch of a striking woman and her name: Lydia Angelica Tomlinson.

It couldn't be his *Lydia.*

Yet, there was no reason to think that it wasn't.

But bank robbery? Lydia?

Even her name seemed to decry such a charge.

Lydia *Angelica* Tomlinson.

Her middle name suited her. Especially on those days when she allowed her hair to curl around her face in those wispy ringlets.

Gideon surged to his feet and strode to the window overlooking the boardwalk. Once again, the street was eerily quiet and his nape prickled. Growling to himself, he rubbed the back of his neck with his palm.

"Problems, boss?"

He glanced up to find Dobbs clattering down the staircase that led to the upper rooms where the Pinkertons slept.

"You're looking like a dandy. What's the occasion?"

Dobbs wore his Sunday-go-to-meeting suit, tie and bowler hat. Even his mustache had been freshly trimmed. But at Gideon's query, some of his enthusiasm seemed to dim.

"Errands." He added quickly, "It's my afternoon off."

"I'm aware of that. You simply seem spiffed-up for… errands."

Gideon knew full well that the man had probably arranged to meet one of the women, even though every man in Bachelor Bottoms had been forbidden to do so. Save a funeral, there was no other reason that would warrant such grooming.

As leader of the Pinkertons, Gideon supposed that he should chide the man for breaking the rules—especially since the Pinkertons were supposed to be in charge of keeping the male inhabitants at arm's length.

But even as he opened his mouth to lay down the law, Gideon didn't have the heart to do it. The women would be gone soon—within a week, if he could possibly arrange it.

Gideon's gaze returned to the window and the muddy street beyond. "Enjoy yourself, Dobbs. You might not have much time off once we start hauling the silver out of the valley."

He could see Dobbs's grinning reflection in the glass.

"Thank you, sir."

The man dodged to the door, but hesitated before stepping outside. "I don't know if this means anything, but I had a sudden thought about that man they sent from the Ogden office… Eddington?"

Gideon nodded.

Again, Dobbs seemed to choose his words before speaking. "I can't stop thinking about him. He was too old for the territories, you know? And his tunic seemed a little short in the arms. But the thing I keep picturing are his boots…"

Gideon felt the prickling again. "What about his boots?"

"They were brown. Around here, the uniform calls for a blue jacket, black pants and *black* boots." Dobbs touched a finger to the brim of his hat. "Have a good afternoon, sir."

Then he stepped outside, closing the door behind him.

Gideon remained where he was for long moments, his mind chewing over the information Dobbs had imparted even as Gideon watched the man saunter down the boardwalk in the direction of the Dovecote. From the opposite side of the room, the hidden Wanted poster seemed to call him like a siren's song, but he refused to pull it out one more time. He'd already studied every word—and had found the description of her crime too brief to be of any help.

Wanted!
Lydia Angelica Tomlinson, age twenty-three.
Bank Robbery and Cattle Rustling!

Miss Tomlinson is a known accomplice of the Tommy Gang and participated in the robbery of the Crescent City Bank, Chicago, Illinois.
Subject must be apprehended and turned over to the Territorial Marshall to claim the $2000 reward.

He still couldn't wrap his head around the idea of Miss Prim-and-Proper Lydia Tomlinson robbing a bank. And the thought of her riding with the Tommy Gang—one of the most vicious groups of outlaws in the territories—didn't sit right, either. Near as he could remember, the Tommy Gang had been apprehended nearly eleven years ago. That would have made Lydia about…twelve?

Gideon shook his head to rid it of such thoughts. Without a working telegraph, he had no way to gather more information on the subject.

No way except questioning the woman herself.

Yet, he still found himself hesitating in that regard. If this news had come to him a month ago—even a week— he would have locked the woman in one of the temporary cells, *then* started his interrogation. But today…

He kept remembering the vulnerability he'd witnessed in Lydia. He would bet his life on the fact that Eddington had been a stranger to her. And something that he'd said had frightened her to the core. If only Gideon had been close enough to hear the words.

He shook his head to rid it of the "if onlys" and reached for his hat.

Enough of this. It was high time he focused on his job and only his job. He'd get one of his men to cover the office for a few hours. Then Gideon would round up Miss Lydia *Angelica* Tomlinson and have a little chat.

Even as his determination swept through his muscles and willed him out of the door and onto the boardwalk, the sensation was followed by an answering trickle of dread.

Not because he might offend Lydia with the accusation.

But because he might discover that the charges were true.

Lydia waited until midafternoon to seek out Iona in the cook shack.

"How are we doing?" she murmured.

Iona drew her to the rear of the kitchen area where she had hidden their checklist under a pile of folded dish towels.

"We have twenty men sequestered in the barbershop. So far, all of them have agreed to help us with our protest—except Milton Plum, who is in charge of the cattle in the south pasture just beyond the Dovecote. He'll only help us for twenty-four hours. After that time, he insists he has several cows ready to give birth within the next fortnight, and he daren't leave them unattended."

"Very kind of him to oblige us for as long as he can."

"Emmarissa and Louise have nearly reached their capacity at the company store. They are fairly certain that they'll be able to hold at least thirty men in a comfortable fashion, but they are requesting ice."

"Ice?"

Iona giggled. "Apparently, they've been apprehending most of the gentlemen by means of a cast iron skillet."

Lydia winced, then joined in on the laughter.

"As soon as we can spare a few women, I'll send them onto the mountainside to fill some pails with snow."

"Not all of their captives are so willing to join in our protest. Thankfully, the rest of the men overwhelmed them, so they are bound and gagged for the time being."

"Bravo!"

"Mr. Creakle was captured early this morning outside Miners' Hall. He kindly volunteered to help lure more men inside, so we have nearly fifty men who are confined to the Hall and the infirmary." Iona flicked the paper with her fingertips. "All totaled, we have almost one hundred men who are off the streets and—either willingly or unwillingly—have become a part of our protest."

Lydia's breath seemed to leave her in a rush. One hundred men. They'd set that number as their goal, but frankly, none of them had ever believed they would attain it.

Unfortunately, following on the heels of that milestone

was her greatest worry. "We don't have much time. We've got to move straight on to the next phase of our plan."

In order for that to work, Gideon Gault would have to be taken out of the equation. The man still had too much power in the community.

"Have any of the Pinkertons been rounded up during our efforts this morning?"

"It was unavoidable, I'm afraid. We have twelve. Two in the barbershop, four in the company store, and the rest in the Hall. As soon as Mr. Gault realizes they're gone, he could raise the alarm and use some of the men from the mine to overwhelm us." Iona's features clouded. "The only reason we're able to keep this many locked up is because most of them are willing participants."

"I know, I know. But every time I walked past the Pinkerton office, there was someone with him." Lydia tried to think of a way to corner the man, alone. Unfortunately, with each scenario she concocted, she found herself thinking instead of the way that Gideon had walked her home, held her hand, kissed her knuckles…

"When have you arranged to meet Mr. Bottoms at his cottage?"

"Two o'clock."

Lydia glanced at the fob watch pinned to her chest.

"That gives me less than an hour. Has Gideon come to the cook shack to eat at all?"

"No."

"Then maybe he'll—"

"Miss Tomlinson!"

The two women started guiltily when the object of their discussion appeared in the doorway.

Iona whipped the paper behind her back and Lydia stepped to the side to shield the older woman since the color had drained from Iona's cheeks.

"Mr. Gault. How nice to see you. Have you come for something to eat?"

"No. Thank you. I wondered if I could have a word with you."

"Of course."

When she didn't move, he added, "Alone."

"Oh. Yes, of course. Shall we go to Mr. Batchwell's private dining area?" Immediately, her brain scrambled to inventory the contents of the room at the end of the hall that was primarily reserved for the owners.

Gideon frowned, his gaze sweeping over the other women who were already beginning preparations for the next meal.

"No. I'd much rather walk, if you don't mind."

Her heart sank, knowing that there was no way she could overpower Gideon in the open. Nor could she bring the revolver that she'd hidden in a shopping basket.

Turning, she fiddled with the strings of her apron.

"Get someone to follow us," she murmured for Iona's ears alone before handing the protective garment to her friend.

Iona bit her lip, but nodded.

"Will I need a coat?" Lydia asked as she moved back toward Gideon.

"I don't think so. It's warm outside and there's no breeze. We won't be long." He gestured to the hallway behind him that led to the private dining room as well as a side door. "If you don't mind, we could head toward the river and walk along its banks. I haven't checked the flood levels yet today."

Briefly, Lydia wondered if he meant to push her into the river and thereby rid himself of her interfering ways once and for all. But she immediately pushed the preposterous thought away. After all, *she* wasn't the one who had become an unwitting target.

Again, she shot a glance behind her. When she saw no sign of Iona, she prayed that the woman had gone to summon help. A long walk upon the secluded river bank might be the perfect place to capture Gideon Gault once and for all.

Gideon waited until they'd moved away from the buildings, beyond earshot, behind the stands of aspen and matted grass to the riverbank. Here, there was a measure of privacy—but even more importantly, a sense of wide, open spaces and fresh air and nature.

He wrestled against the sensation of doom that hung at the periphery of his senses. With all the dire news he'd received, his mind grappled with the effects of his heightened emotions. It was at times like this, when his heart pounded and the outside pressures began to build, that the past threatened to swamp him. The memories were there, the bottled-up emotions, the sense of frustration and desperation, the impression that there would never be enough clean water to wash away the things he'd witnessed in that Georgia prison.

Gideon swallowed, trying to push away the images, knowing that he couldn't lose control. Not now. Not with her.

But his body and his mind could often prove traitors to his wishes. In times of stress, the things he'd witnessed, the overwhelming misery, were so much harder to push away.

"Gideon?"

Lydia regarded him curiously and he took deep breaths through his nose, focusing on her face. That sweet face with its halo of curls.

"Do you have a middle name?" he blurted.

"Yes. Angelica."

The Wanted poster was true in that respect.

Gideon bent to scoop up a rock, then threw it toward

the river. A part of him, ever the professional, noted that the river had risen another six inches. At this rate, it could overflow its banks within a day or two.

"Gideon?"

He turned to Lydia, a part of him resisting the words he needed to utter, the other, the ever-dedicated Pinkerton, insisting that the time had come.

Knowing that he couldn't delay any longer, he unbuttoned his tunic—the Pinkerton blues—and removed the poster, still folded in quarters.

"I received this yesterday. It was brought here by the messenger from Ogden, along with the correspondence you received from your aunts."

She regarded him curiously before reaching to take the heavy paper. Slowly, ever so slowly, she unfolded it—and in those brief moments, the ghosts of Andersonville pressed in on him again. Because Gideon knew that, whatever happened next, things could never be the same between them. Either she would despise him for believing her capable of such a crime.

Or he would discover that the claims were true.

As if sensing his turmoil, she looked up and Gideon did his best to remember that very instant when she gazed at him with such open confusion, and trust, and…and beauty. More than anything, he wanted to sear that image into his brain so that he could pull it out and look at it, again and again, like a tattered cabinet photograph, whenever the darkness threatened to consume him.

He watched the way her eyes scanned the illustration—little more than a few ink strokes to indicate long hair, two eyes, a nose, a mouth. It could have been a sketch drawn by a child, it had been rendered so vaguely. Then he watched her gaze drop to the heading, then scan the rest of the text.

He waited, sure that she would deny it—that she would rail at him for believing such a slanderous bit of fiction.

Instead, the color bled from her features and her hands began to tremble, causing the poster to crackle like autumn leaves being driven by the wind. Then, she looked up at him. For the first time, he found no spark of passion in her eyes. Rather, they filled with an infinite sadness and a hopelessness that he had seen in his own gaze all too often.

Then she turned and began striding back toward the cook shack.

"Lydia!"

She didn't pause, so he was forced to quicken his pace until he could snag her elbow.

"Aren't you going to say something in your defense?"

"Why? It's apparent that you've already made up your mind, so what could I possibly say to alter your opinion?"

"I brought you here so that you could explain."

"Explain what? It's my name on that poster. My face."

He could feel her trembling violently against him. But rather than increasing her guilt, it merely seemed to underscore her innocence.

"That face could belong to half the women in the Dovecote."

She wrenched free from his grasp, but instead of dodging toward the safety of the cook shack, she wrapped her arms around her waist.

"But none of their names are attached to the charges. Only mine."

Gideon scrambled for a logical answer—other than the most obvious one. For days now, his instincts had been poking at him, and images darted through his head like a swarm of angry bees.

The too-quiet streets.

A measles epidemic.

A Pinkerton who wasn't a Pinkerton.

This time, when he took Lydia by the elbows, she didn't back away. He was careful to hold her gently, so she would know that, if she wanted her freedom, she need only step back.

"Why would someone do this to you?" Gideon asked softly.

She blinked, obviously taken aback that he'd decided to champion her innocence. But as he looked down into those blue, blue eyes, eyes that truly were the mirror to her soul, he found no guile. If anything, she seemed to experience the same turmoil that raged through his own soul.

Then she looked away before he could see too much.

"Lydia? Do you know who would accuse you this way?"

Her lips pressed together and she remained mulishly silent.

"You need to tell me so I can help you."

She offered a short burst of mirthless laughter. "Why would you do such a thing? You're a Pinkerton."

"I'm not territorial law, Lydia."

She seemed to hesitate, then shook her head. "Don't try to help me, Gideon. It's a useless endeavor."

"Why?"

He saw her lower lip tremble slightly before she bit it. Tears gathered at her lower lashes, but she blinked them away.

"Because the charges are true."

Chapter Twelve

Lydia didn't bother to turn around as the cell door clanged shut behind her. She had no intention of explaining herself to Gideon Gault—or to anyone else. Nothing she offered could rectify the situation. The past had caught up to her as she'd feared that it would someday. Quite clearly, promises had been broken and she would be the one to pay.

"Lydia…"

She could feel Gideon looking at her from the other side of the bars. Somewhere, beyond him, she heard the shifting of the jail's only other occupant, a man apprehended for the murder of Jenny Reichmann, the mother of Willow's and Charles's adopted children.

Gideon seemed to become aware of the man as well, because he cleared his throat.

"I'll come back later and we'll talk."

Lydia remained with her back to him, knowing that she couldn't look at him—couldn't see the confusion and… *betrayal* in his eyes—without breaking down.

Don't think about that now.

But even when she squeezed her eyes shut, she relived that moment when she'd admitted that she was guilty of bank robbery and cattle rustling. Gideon had eyed her with stark disbelief. He'd even had the audacity to laugh.

Until he'd realized that she wasn't laughing with him.

She heard the sharp staccato sounds of his boots as he ascended the stone steps leading out of the stone cellar beneath the Mining Office. Only after he'd closed the heavy wooden door with a dull *thump* did she sink onto the cot.

"What you in here for, missy?"

She ignored the query thrown at her from somewhere beyond her sight. Shivering, she tugged at the blanket folded at the end of the unmade mattress and wrapped it around her shoulders.

Ruined.

Everything that she'd fought so hard to obtain lay in tatters at her feet. The life that she'd built with her aunts, the independence she'd won, the causes she'd championed. Even her attempts to bring a better life to Bachelor Bottoms would probably be negated. All because of her blood.

Tainted blood.

A chill shuddered through her entire body, causing her to clutch the blanket even tighter. She knew full well how gossip traveled in Aspen Valley. The news had probably spread through town before Gideon had finished twisting the key in the lock.

Lydia Tomlinson had been arrested.

Nighty-night under the starlight bright...

Her father had sworn that he would find a way to punish her for her betrayal. Clearly, his words had been prophetic.

She stiffened when a soft noise came from above, warning her that Gideon had returned.

So soon? What could he possibly want from her now? She had no intention of telling him anything more. She couldn't bear to see the disappointment deepen in his eyes.

"Lydia!"

The whisper was soft, urgent, but clearly female.

Lydia jumped to her feet, the blanket falling unheeded to the floor.

"Stefania? Over here!"

Two shapes separated from the dimness of the stairwell as Stefania and Millie rushed toward her.

"What on earth happened? Did he find out about the men we've captured?"

"No." Lydia blinked, certain that the women were a figment of her imagination. "How did you get in here?"

Millie grinned. "I took Dobbs's keys from him when he agreed to join the men in the infirmary."

So, it was Dobbs who had been sending Millie love letters and snowdrops for the past few weeks.

"Hurry! We've got to get you out of here. We don't have a minute to lose. Willow is heading toward Batchwell's house and it's time for Iona to meet with Mr. Bottoms."

Unaccountably, Lydia felt a burst of hope. She had no illusions. All too soon, she would be back behind bars, and her speaking engagements in California would be a thing of the past. But she could finish what they'd all started here in Bachelor Bottoms. She could help make this a community of families.

As soon as Stefania turned the key, she burst out of the door.

"Hey! What about me?"

At the far end, the bars rattled, but she and the girls ignored the noise. Creeping up to the outer door, Lydia opened it a slit, peering in either direction to make sure their escape would remain unnoticed.

The alley looked quiet. The street beyond completely empty.

"We've already captured most of the men who were off

shift," Millie whispered. "So, unless you can see Gideon Gault…"

No. There was no sign of Gideon, but Lydia wasn't taking any chances.

"Stefania, you and I will go around the back way, along the lane leading to the miners' row houses. Millie, you go to the cook shack and get everyone else. Then we'll meet on the lane that leads up to the owners' homes."

The other women nodded.

"Ready? Go!"

Gideon strode into the livery.

"Smalls? Are you here?"

His only answer came from the shifting of animals in their stalls and the bleating of the goats kept at the far end.

"Smalls?"

Sighing, Gideon strode to the spot where his own gelding was kept, knowing that he had to get out of here, had to ride, had to feel the wind against his face or…

Or what?

It wasn't the images of Andersonville that crowded in close. It was Lydia, her head down, looking so small and fragile within the stone walls of the jail cell.

How could she be guilty of the crimes she'd admitted to doing? Yes, he'd known that Lydia could be militant and skirt the rules of Bachelor Bottoms. But there was an innate dignity about her, a passion for championing the underdog. He couldn't imagine her storming into a bank and demanding that they hand over their cash.

He snorted, throwing his saddle over the roan's back.

If that image was preposterous, it was even more nonsensical to think of her sneaking into a pasture in the dead of night to herd cattle away from their owner.

So, what had made her say she was guilty of such crimes?

As he finished tightening the girth and reached for the bridle hanging on a nearby peg, he tried to think of something—*anything*—that she'd said that could give her a motive for her behavior.

Aunts.

She'd said that she'd lived with a pair of maiden aunts.

Where?

Boston.

For how long?

Think, think!

Gideon led his animal out of the livery and swung onto its back. Then, nudging it with his heels, he urged it into a walk, a trot, a gallop, until he was riding out of town, the wind flowing around his face, the animal below him gloriously stretching out to its full speed. In a matter of minutes, Gideon had left Aspen Valley behind. Following the wagon tracks, he headed up, up to the spot where the ruined railway cars now sat completely exposed like children's blocks thrown haphazardly down the hill.

Mindful of the rocks and broken tree limbs from the debris field, Gideon slowed the animal beneath him, picking his way through until he reached the mouth of the canyon. Breathing hard, Gideon looked down, down, into the winding ravine.

Although snow still lingered in the upper elevations, around the riverbanks, he could see the snaking path of the road. A few stubborn patches of slush and ice remained in the shady spots, but the primary problem now would be mud. Thick, cloying mud that would cake onto the rims of the wagon wheels—especially if they were loaded down with women and baggage. But if they waited much longer...

He noted the snake of the river, the swollen banks, the glint of whitecaps in the rapids. If the warm weather continued unabated, there would be flooding. The road could be swamped or washed out completely.

If he were to get the women out at all, it would have to be in the next few days.

For the first time, Gideon didn't feel a jolt of relief at the thought. Instead, his anxiousness seemed to increase.

Why was he so torn? It wasn't as if he and Lydia…as if she…

He shouldn't even be thinking that way. She'd made it clear that he was nothing to her but a spirited opponent. Perhaps even a friend. While he…

What did he feel for Lydia?

Gideon tried to summon all of the old arguments—that he wasn't a marrying kind of man, that he could never settle down to such a life…

That no woman should be burdened with the images that haunted him.

But the thoughts didn't pull their weight the way they used to do. Instead, the idea of living the rest of his life alone pressed as heavily on his shoulders as his past.

Why hadn't she trusted him enough to tell him the truth?

Even if she'd committed those crimes, she could have confided in him. He would have done his best to help her. But without a full accounting, his hands were tied.

Frustration sizzled, building up, threatening to burst through his chest, but just as quickly, it fizzled away when he realized that he'd done nothing to inspire Lydia's confidences. He'd been unwilling to listen to her arguments about Bachelor Bottoms—and he'd done his best to dissuade her from pursuing her goals. He could rail at her for not telling him more, but had he told her anything about himself save a few miserly details?

The gelding shifted restlessly beneath him, reminding Gideon that his duties lay behind him in town. He'd been hired to do a job, and the moment had come for him to see things through. As per the owners' instructions, he needed to get the women out of the valley and set them back on the journeys they'd originally planned. Then, he had a stockpile of ore to guard and transport to the nearest railhead so that it could be shipped to Denver.

After that…

Well, maybe it was time to move on. Maybe he'd been at this job, this location too long. Maybe the mountains were closing in on him, making him skittish and likely to do things that were completely out of character. Maybe once he had some space and some time alone, he'd feel like his old self again.

But the thought seemed hollow. His gut told him that nothing would ever be that simple again.

"Is everyone ready?" Lydia whispered from where she and nearly a dozen women crouched behind a clump of sumac.

As she surveyed the group, the women nodded. Many of them held revolvers or rifles, while a few felt more comfortable brandishing rolling pins or skillets.

"Remember, we want to keep this whole affair as civilized as possible. Our objective is to have the two owners under our control so we can extend a list of demands and explain our argument. Hopefully, they'll listen to reason."

"And if they don't?" Louise asked fearfully.

"Then we use the solidarity of the miners we've engaged in our protest to curtail production in the mine itself. Hopefully, once it becomes apparent that the profitability of their enterprise is in danger, they can be persuaded to negotiate." Lydia offered them an encouraging smile. "Remember, we're fighting for so much more than ourselves. We're fighting for our community. Bachelor Bottoms has done well by itself. But this sterile environment cannot contain itself. Even before we arrived, the men were growing restless with their lot. True, some of the workers are bachelors who are here for the money and the adventure. But so many more of them are husbands with families, or men with sweethearts waiting for their return. Such isolation can only be maintained for a limited time before the heart revolts against such strictures. We've already seen how this valley has blossomed with the addition of a few feminine hands. Imagine what this place could be if there were homes and schools. If the sound of children's laughter filled the air."

The women around her murmured in agreement. Even Louise's shoulders drew to a determined line.

"If we can do this…if we can capture Batchwell and Bottoms—*today*—our goals will be in sight."

"Bravo!"

"Are we all ready?"

The small space resounded in a chorus of whispers.

"Yes!"

"We are!"

Lydia pointed to Willow.

"Willow, you go first. Get Boris to go into town on some sort of errand. As soon as we see him leave, we'll send Iona in to meet with Phineas Bottoms."

Willow nodded and turned the wagon carrying the twins. It rumbled softly over the uneven ground, marking their progress toward the mansion.

"Iona?"

Iona looked up. She was obviously trembling.

"Yes. Yes, I'm ready."

Lydia took the older woman's hands in her own, noting the chill to her fingertips.

"Everything will be fine."

"I know. But, I… I don't want Phineas to think ill of me."

Lydia suddenly realized that, for Iona, their mission had become entirely personal. With each encounter she'd had with Phineas, a glow had begun to settle over her.

"If he's the man we think he is, he'll be thinking of you, Iona."

The woman offered a bashful, girlish smile.

"Is it that obvious?"

Lydia squeezed her hands again.

"You deserve every happiness, Iona."

Her friend laughed nervously. "Even at my age?"

"There's no age limit on happiness, Iona. Nor, apparently, on romance."

"There he is! There's Boris!"

The women hunkered even lower behind the copse of trees, waiting until the crunch of footsteps approached, then continued past them down the hill. Only after the sound had completely faded did Lydia whisper, "All right, everyone. Step one has been completed. Iona, you're next."

Willow made her way up the back staircase, then navigated the hall to Mr. Batchwell's bedroom.

She knew she was taking a chance in bringing the twins with her. Despite the women's plans for a non-violent protest, anything could happen.

But Willow doubted that taking the owners hostage would provide the outcome they all desired. She'd received the brunt of Batchwell's ire in the past—and she had no illusions that anything other than her cooking had allowed her to encroach on the man's inner sanctum.

To that end, she'd decided to wage her own silent battle

against the crochety old gentleman. And for that, she intended to employ her sweetest weapons.

"Good morning, Mr. Batchwell."

The man looked up from the book he'd been reading and scowled.

"Don't you have someone who can watch those things?" he groused.

"Actually, no. There's quite a lot going on in town lately. The pass is nearly clear and most of the women are busy with last-minute preparations. I thought I would do some baking in those huge ranges you have downstairs. Since I'll have my hands full, I was hoping that you could keep an eye on the children. Adam is still asleep. The poor thing had a fitful night, I'm afraid. So, he'll give you no trouble at all. Eva, it seems, is ready to play."

She bent toward Mr. Batchwell with Eva cradled in the arm closest to him. As Willow had hoped, her daughter caught sight of Batchwell's bushy sideburns and grinned, her arms waving.

Almost of their own volition, Batchwell's hands reached for the baby and pulled her to his chest. Immediately, Eva began to coo and hum.

Not wanting to do anything to tarnish the moment, Willow turned to the bed where she grasped a pillow and blanket. Arranging them on the floor, she set Adam in the nest she'd formed.

Adam's eyelids flickered, then proved too heavy for him to open, and he quickly settled back into sleep.

Batchwell tore his eyes away from Eva to look down at her twin.

"He's a tough little bruiser, isn't he?"

"Yes, he is," Willow said proudly. "But that one's just as stubborn."

At the sound of her mother's voice, Eva glanced up,

but she soon returned to exploring the tip of Batchwell's bulbous nose.

"Ach, she's a bonny lass, she is," Batchwell said, so softly that Willow nearly didn't hear him at all.

Willow took that moment to walk toward the doorway. Once on the other side of the threshold, she paused. "Is there anything in particular that you'd like me to bake today, Mr. Batchwell?"

The man didn't answer. Clearly, all his attention centered on the baby in his arms.

"Ring the bell if you need me," Willow murmured. Then, smiling, she hurried downstairs again.

Iona didn't need to announce her arrival at the cottage. She was several yards away when Phineas opened the door and welcomed her inside.

"Mrs. Skye."

Iona couldn't account for the way that the mere sound of her name on his tongue caused a frisson of delight to skitter down her spine.

"I think we know each other well enough that you should call me Iona."

"Very well… *Iona*. And you must call me Phineas."

Iona stepped inside his home, finding it exactly as she'd imagined—compact, quaint, warm.

"Phineas, I need you to listen to me," she said, turning to him. Brazenly, she reached to take his hand. "Something is about to happen—I don't have time to explain. Just trust me. You *do* trust me, don't you? Even though we've only known each other a short time?"

He gripped her tightly, covering their twined fingers with his free hand. "Iona?"

"Please, tell me you trust me. I'll explain everything

later, but I want—no, *need*—to know that you won't think badly of me. I've grown to care for you so much."

His blue eyes brightened at the words.

"I couldn't bear it if you thought I'd tried to deceive you."

"Iona, I—"

The door suddenly burst open and the women stormed in. Instinctively, Iona stepped in front of Phineas, shielding him from the group, still gripping him tightly. He must have seen the weapons, heard the women's cries, because he pulled her tightly against him, an arm wrapping around her waist. And even in that moment of confusion, the warmth and strength of his embrace caused tears to prick at the back of her eyes.

It had been so long since she'd felt this way.

Young.

Feminine.

And oh, so in love.

Bang!

The women screamed and dropped to the floor when one of the revolvers suddenly discharged. A chunk of ceiling rained plaster on them all as Phineas threw Iona to the floor, then protectively shielded her beneath his hunched shoulders.

Iona squinched her eyes shut, waiting for another volley. But there was only an uneasy silence, then Louise offered breathlessly, "So sorry. I must have accidentally left one of the bullets in the chamber."

Above her, Iona could feel Phineas trembling above her.

Please, Lord. Don't let him be too angry with me.

But when Iona dared to look up, she saw Phineas shaking with silent laughter. He rose to his feet and offered his hand to Iona, pulling her up next to him.

"I take it that I'm the next captive in this wild revolt?"

The women eyed him nervously.

"Don't worry, I won't give the game away." He pointed to the picture window that overlooked the town. Next to his tufted chair was a telescope mounted to a brass tripod. Phineas offered a delighted laugh. "Caught you throwing a blanket over a fellow a few days ago. That tipped me off." He pointed a finger in their direction. "You gals are slick, I'll give you that. Especially this morning. Now, that was a sight to behold. How many men have you taken so far?"

Lydia opened her mouth, then closed it again, clearly unwilling to divulge the information. But Iona—loving this man even more than she had moments ago—decided that if she'd asked for his trust, he deserved some in return.

"Over a hundred."

Phineas's eyes widened; his mouth opened. Then he let out a hearty guffaw. Only after he'd wiped away the tears brought on by his merriment did he manage to hold up his hands in surrender. "Well, tie me up before the Pinkertons come running. They'll have heard the shot in town. But, do it in that chair over yonder so I can keep my eyes on the fun."

Gideon had just reached the outskirts of town when he heard gunfire.

Reining his horse to a stop, he tried to determine the direction of the report. But in such a narrow valley, the sound echoed off the hills, making a determination difficult.

Standing in the stirrups, he glanced behind him, thoughts of the suspicious messenger fresh in his head. But there was nothing. Even more unusual, there was no one ahead of him, either. The street lay empty in the afternoon sunshine. If it weren't for Bertrum Smithers's old blue heeler trotting toward the cook shack, Gideon would have thought the community had been abandoned. It was

only when one of his men came running from the direction of the mine that he felt a momentary relief.

Gideon urged his mount in that direction, meeting the
man halfway.

"Did you hear that?"

Winslow panted slightly as he drew to a halt. "Gunfire?"

"Yeah."

He pointed up to the hill toward the owners' houses.
"I'm not sure, but I think it came from Bottoms's place."

"Gather what men you can and meet me up there."

Gideon turned his mount toward the row houses.

"But most of them are in the mine!"

"I don't care. Get them!"

Chapter Thirteen

"Gideon Gault is on his way up the hill, and he's on horseback," Phineas called out.

Lydia and the other women had been conferring about how best to apprehend Mr. Batchwell, but the announcement brought them up short.

"You three stay here," Lydia said to Iona, Stefania and Millie. "The rest of you come with me. We have to get into the mansion before Gideon figures out what we've done."

They burst out of the door, brandishing their weapons, at the same time that Gideon appeared at the top of the hill. He seemed to size up the situation like a practiced general, because he didn't stop. Instead, he rode full speed to Batchwell's home, vaulting the horse over the back fence. Before Lydia and the other women could even make it to the gate, he ran into the side door—the one that they'd arranged to have left unlocked for their own attack—and slammed the door. As she raced to close the last few yards, Lydia heard the bolt strike home.

She should have sent someone to Batchwell's home the moment the revolver had gone off.

"What do we do now?" Hannah asked, pressing a hand to her side as she fought for breath.

Lydia thought for a moment, then shook her head. "He'll have the remaining Pinkertons here in a matter of minutes—and they'll be carrying weapons that are fully loaded."

The women turned, en masse, to stare accusingly at Louise.

"I said I was sorry. I was sure that I'd emptied all of the bullets out. But I was in a rush and I…must have…missed one…" Her words petered out as the weight of her friends' gazes grew even heavier.

Lydia stomped her foot in frustration, strode a few feet away, then paused, trying to think things through as quickly as she could. Finally, she turned back to her allies.

"All of you get back to Phineas's house. We need a show of strength so they don't decide to attack the cottage and rescue the man."

Hannah snorted. It wouldn't take much rescuing since Iona had tied him so loosely to the chair that even a toddler could have escaped the bindings without much bother.

"Go on, now. I'm going to hide over there in those trees and take note of who comes to Batchwell's rescue. Then, when I have a better idea of what we're up against, I'll be back with more help."

"Maybe you should have our reinforcements load their weapons," Hannah suggested.

"No! No, we're not going to do that. So far, we may have stretched the rules of propriety, but we haven't broken any laws. All the men have agreed to help us, including Mr. Bottoms. I won't have any of you go to…to prison for anything we've done." She stumbled over the words, knowing that she would not escape the same fate. "Go!"

She waited until the others had returned to Mr. Bottoms's house, then she quickly moved to the same copse of trees where they'd hidden before all this had begun. Through it all, her heart pounded against her ribs.

What must Gideon Gault think of her now?

Gideon bolted into the kitchen, coming to an abrupt halt when he found Willow measuring flour from a bin. At the sight of him, she squeaked and dropped the scoop, causing a puff of flour to explode into the air.

"Gideon!"

"Where's everyone else?" Gideon demanded, removing his sidearm.

Willow shrank against the counter. "M-Mr. Batchwell is upstairs with Adam and Eva, a-and Boris has gone to t-town to get something to eat."

"And the women?"

"Women?"

"Where are all the women who came with you?"

Gideon's gaze was already scanning the room, the hall, the staircase. In this house, there were hundreds of little hidey-holes where Lydia's cohorts could be lying in wait.

"No one else is here. There's only Mr. Batchwell, the twins, and…and me."

He searched her features. But if there was one thing he'd learned about Willow Wanlass, it was that she had no talent for lying. She telegraphed every thought and emotion she experienced in her wide blue eyes and expressive features.

And right now, she was frightened.

"Put the gun away, Gideon." Her chin tilted in the air in false bravado. "Please. My children are here." When he hesitated, she added, "I give you my word, no one else is here."

It wasn't so much her vow that convinced him. It was that mother bear stance. She would protect her little ones, even if she thought she needed to protect them from *him*.

Images swam through his brain—dinners with the Wanlass family, Willow doting on Gideon as if he were family, the twins.

He lowered the revolver to his side.

"Why are you here, Willow?"

"I come every afternoon to cook for Mr. Batchwell."

"Since when?"

"A few days now. Since Charles discovered that Boris was nearly beside himself from all of Batchwell's demands."

That statement had a definite ring of truth.

"Do you know what the women are up to?"

A flush tinged her cheeks, but she remained mulishly silent.

"It's Lydia who's the ringleader, isn't it?"

Again, she refused to answer, but her expression told him what he needed to know.

How had Lydia managed to escape the jail cell? She couldn't have been inside for more than ten minutes.

"Tell me what they plan to do next, Willow."

She shook her head. "I—I can't."

"'Can't' or 'won't'?"

"*Can't*! I don't live in the Dovecote anymore, remember? I'm not privy to their plans. I was merely asked to send Boris to town and leave the side door open."

The words were said so grudgingly, that Gideon felt bound to believe them. There was an air of rushed confession to the statement—as if the thought of any sort of deceit had proved too onerous to bear.

"Get upstairs, Willow."

"But—"

"Go upstairs where it's safer. They've already fired on someone once, and they may decide to do it again. I've got reinforcements coming, but until then, I have to do whatever I deem necessary to keep Mr. Batchwell safe. So, go upstairs and see to your children."

She seemed rooted to the floor for several long seconds, but then she wiped her hands on a dish towel gathered up her skirts and headed toward the staircase.

Gideon, on the other hand, moved to the door, gently drawing aside the curtain with the tip of his finger.

"I know you're out there, Lydia," he murmured to himself. "Show me what you intend to do next."

As if she'd somehow heard him, Lydia stepped into sight. She moved to the gate leading into the yard, carefully keeping the intricate wrought iron between them. When she stood there for several moments, not moving, Gideon realized that the next move would have to be his.

Cautiously, he unlatched the door, opened it, then stood within the threshold. But mindful of the fact that she might not be as alone as she appeared, he went no farther.

"What in heaven's name is going on here, Lydia?"

She actually seemed pained.

"You know full well what we're trying to do, Gideon. I was quite up front with our intentions."

"You said you wanted to change the rules, not stage a coup."

She shrugged. "Desperate times often call for desperate measures."

"You can't honestly think that kidnapping the owners would put them in the proper frame of mind to alter their views."

"Perhaps not. But eventually, they would have to negotiate."

Gideon shook his head. "That would never happen. These are powerful men with plenty of money at their disposal. It's only a matter of time before you'll be overpowered."

"Granted. But time is something that is already in short supply. You're already making plans to force us out of the valley. At least this way, we've stood up for ourselves—and for the men who are tired of living alone."

"They agreed to the rules before they came here."

"True. But agreeing to some imaginable existence isn't the same as living it." She tipped her head. "Did you realize how alone you'd be, Gideon?"

"I have no problems being alone."

"Really? Perhaps if you had someone you cared about, you wouldn't spend so much time riding out of town as if you're being chased."

Perhaps. Or maybe, by being alone, he kept his memories from tainting anyone else.

But even though he'd repeated that thought to himself a thousand times before, the words seemed false this time. If he were to find a woman who loved him, *really* loved him, he might find strength in sharing his struggles.

"You're a bachelor, Gideon. Imagine if you had a wife. Children. How much harder must it be for those men? They spend their lives waiting for the notes from home. Those infrequent reminders of the lives that are carrying on in their absence. Think of Quincy Winslow. The last letter he received before the avalanche was a message warning him that his wife had given birth to twins. It's bad enough, knowing that your own flesh and blood has come into the world a lifetime away, but to then be informed that the babies and their mother were fighting for their lives? For three months, he's had that uncertainty hanging over his head. I can't imagine the torment he's suffered, night and day, wondering what has happened since then. Do you know that he visits Willow and the babies several times a week? Merely to hold another set of twins, to draw strength from their tiny bodies, so that he can convince himself that maybe, just maybe, his own sons have survived?"

Gideon knew full well what Lydia was talking about. He'd been at the Wanlass home on more than one occasion when Winslow had come to visit. And Willow, bless her soul, had understood how much the man had needed those stolen moments with her children.

"There are other ways to change the rules, Lydia."

"Are you sure? Because when I discussed the possibility with you only days ago, you adamantly insisted that Batchwell would never agree to discuss the matter with us."

Gideon desperately tried another tack. "Violence isn't the answer. You can't go around shooting people—and where did you get the gun, anyway?"

She sniffed in indignation. "Do you honestly think that women who were brave enough to travel the breadth of the country to new lives wouldn't find the means to protect themselves?"

Lydia had a point—and Gideon, short-sighted male that he was, hadn't even thought that the myriad trunks he'd helped to carry from the shattered railway cars could have held a stash of weaponry.

"Is anybody hurt?"

The look Lydia shot him could have withered grass at thirty paces. "Absolutely not. The incident was an unfortunate accident by a more…inexperienced member of our group. One that I can assure you won't happen again."

Gideon couldn't account for the relief he felt.

"Stop this now, Lydia. Before things go too far. Before—"

"Before someone ends up in jail?"

The air shivered with the memory that she'd been behind bars less than an hour earlier.

"How did you get out of your cell, Lydia?"

She shrugged. "Someone from the Dovecote let me out. One of your men was rather careless with his keys."

Dobbs. It had to be.

"You know he'll be reprimanded for the lapse. He might even lose his job."

"If the women aren't allowed to stay in Aspen Valley, I don't think he'll be planning to resume his duties. It seems that he's already asked a certain girl to marry him."

The romance had apparently blossomed right beneath Gideon's nose and he'd been too blind to see it. Then again, if he were honest with himself, Gideon would have to admit that he'd been so intent on avoiding interacting with the women—and Lydia in particular—that he'd delegated most of the responsibilities for guarding the brides to his employees.

"You could end this yourself, Gideon, by allowing us to see Mr. Batchwell."

He shook his head. "You know that's not going to happen."

"Then we might have to push you out of your stronghold, Gideon."

"You wouldn't force your way in. I'd have to fire upon your little band of protesters. You wouldn't risk it. Not while Willow's here with the babies."

He knew that he'd struck a point in his favor when her chin dipped, ever so slightly.

"Then, we are at an impasse," she said flatly. "Nevertheless, if you would be so kind, I'd like to ask you for one favor."

"What's that?"

"Relay a message to Mr. Batchwell."

"And what would that message be?"

"'Do the right thing and allow these families to be together.'"

"Or what?"

"Nothing. That's the entire message."

Gideon waited a heartbeat. Two. For the life of him, this whole situation felt *wrong*. A part of him yearned to be on the other side of that fence, fighting *with* Lydia rather than against her.

But he shook his head instead. "He'll never give in, Lydia. Once he hears what's been going on in his camp, he may consider doing more than hauling you and the other ladies out of the valley. He could possibly take legal action. You forget that Batchwell hasn't always been a wealthy man living in a luxurious mansion. He came from humble stock, grubbing in the Scottish mines from the time he was six years old. He fought his way out of the tunnels to become a man of power. This mine is his wife, his baby, his everything. He will see your interference as a threat. And he would regard any concession he might make, any change to the rules, as a sign of weakness. That's something he will not allow to happen."

In the distance, he heard shouting, the sound of hooves on the gravel.

"Get out of here, Lydia," he said. "Before the men get here."

Her eyes widened in surprise.

"Go!"

Still she hesitated. But as the noises grew louder, she finally backed away.

"This isn't personal, Gideon. I'm merely doing what I think is right."

Then she turned, running toward the cottage.

Gideon's eye followed her every step of the way, saw her dodge into the unfinished garden, stumble over the matted grass, then pound on the door. In an instant, the panels opened and she disappeared as the first riders thundered up the hill and galloped toward Batchwell's mansion.

This isn't personal, Gideon.

He closed his eyes for a moment, trying to banish the sight of her, her hands fisted, her chin held high, her eyes flashing with determination.

Gideon knew that she might believe the statement. But from his perspective, she'd been oh, so wrong. In that instant, with the words still ringing in his head, the current situation had become incredibly personal to Gideon.

Because he feared he was falling in love with his ardent little suffragist.

And somehow, he had to find a way to help resolve this mess before the consequences became any direr.

To Gideon's surprise, it wasn't a group of Pinkertons who rode to his rescue. Instead, Charles Wanlass and a half-dozen men from his blasting crew strode through the door and into the kitchen.

"Willow, is she—"

"Fine. She's fine." Gideon jerked his thumb toward the ceiling. "She and Batchwell are upstairs with the twins. Apparently, a group of women from the Dovecote stormed Bottoms's cottage, taking him hostage. One of them accidentally discharged her weapon."

"Anyone hurt?" Wanlass asked, some of the wildness easing from his eyes when he realized his family was safe.

"Not according to Lydia."

"Lydia?" Charles laughed. "What does she have to do with any of this?"

Gideon rubbed at the tight cords of muscle behind his neck. "She and the brides have staged a protest. They want Batchwell and Bottoms to change the rules and allow women into the valley so that the men can live with their families."

A slow smile crept over Charles's features and Gideon pointed an indignant finger in his direction. "Not one word! I already know which side you'd take in the argument. I'm surprised you and that wife of yours aren't in cahoots with the whole lot of them!"

Charles held up two hands in surrender, laughing softly. "Fine. I won't offer my two cents."

Once again, Gideon was struck by the difference in his friend. Until Willow had come along, Charles had seemed to carry the weight of the world on his shoulders. Even his devotion to his ministering duties had seemed a kind of private penance. But somehow, that tiny slip of a girl upstairs had healed something within him. In the space of a few weeks, Charles's entire demeanor had shifted to a reflection of his inner joy and his faith in a benevolent God.

Gideon felt like a traitor when he poked the air with his finger again. "Can I trust you and your men to watch over Batchwell for an hour or so? I need to go round up my men."

Charles turned to regard his fellow members of the blasting crew. "Any of you have a problem with that?"

The men shook their heads and mumbled amongst themselves.

"Looks like you've got an impromptu set of guards. We were pretty much done in the mine, and it's not that long until the shifts change. Take as much time as you want."

"Thanks." Gideon hesitated, then extended his sidearm toward Charles. "Here, you'll be needing this."

Charles shook his head. "I think we can manage for now with the doors and windows locked. If we need something more, Batchwell's got a whole collection of guns in his study."

Gideon nodded, holstering his weapon. "It might be past dark before I come back."

"No problem." Charles scanned the gleaming tile and marble floors. "It appears that we'll all be more than comfortable for the time being. Can't say that I've ever spent much time in a house this grand before."

Gideon stepped forward to extend his hand. "Thanks, Charles."

His friend shook it, then slapped him on the shoulder. "Be on with you then."

Gideon hesitated one last time—not sure what he'd felt driven to say.

Keep an eye out for Lydia, too.

No. That wouldn't be right. Charles was already in a tight spot, stuck between his loyalty to his job and employer on one hand, and his wife and family on the other. So rather than saying anything, Gideon strode outside instead, heading toward his horse. He'd find his men first. Then, he'd lay a trap for Lydia. As soon as the women lost their leader, they would capitulate.

But even as the thought appeared, Gideon was no longer sure he could bring matters to such an easy solution.

Willow waited until she heard the sound of a horse hurrying toward town before creeping into the kitchen.

"Is he gone?" she whispered.

"Aye, he's gone."

She grinned and rushed into Charles's waiting arms.

"You didn't let on that you've been helping the women from the onset, did you?"

Charles lifted her chin with a crooked finger. "D'ye think I'd be spillin' the beans when the man unwittingly handed over Batchwell's mansion to the enemy?"

Willow's nose wrinkled. "Not the enemy. Merely…"

Charles bent to press a kiss to her lips. "A possible salvation, then?"

At that, she laughed. "I think we're somewhere in the middle of those two extremes."

"Do you want me to go tell Lydia that she can come present her demands?"

Willow shook her head. "Not yet. Batchwell's in no mood to listen right now. He heard the shot and I had to explain it away by telling him I'd dropped a baking pan. Even so, he's…fretful and grumpy. Not the best of moods for a reasonable discussion."

"And you want Lydia kept in the dark because…"

Willow made a face. "Because there's something going on between her and Gideon."

Charles's brows rose. "Now I know you're pulling my leg. Gideon's a confirmed bachelor, through and through."

Her lips tilted. "So were you, not so long ago. Give things a few hours. I think, if pressed, she'll try to approach him again. It couldn't hurt to see what comes of it."

Charles laughed softly, releasing her.

"What do you want us to do in the meantime?"

"Go visit with Mr. Batchwell. He won't admit it, but he's starved for company. Give him something to think about besides himself. While you're doing that, I'll get my baking done and dinner made. Any future discussions are bound to go better if he hears them on a full stomach."

Charles nodded, then gestured to his crew. "Come along, boys. Let's go tell the old man about the progress in the new tunnel. That should sweeten his mood even more."

Lydia huddled around the trestle table in the cook shack with the few women who'd been kept there to prepare enough food for their captives and the men who would soon be coming off shift.

"Despite the fact that we failed to apprehend Batchwell, we're in a good position. We have over a hundred men who will fail to show up for work. Perhaps, as soon as the rest of the miners head out of the tunnels, we can convince a few more to join their number. Until then, we have a bigger problem on our hands." Wrapping her hands around her mug of tea, Lydia took a bracing swallow of the strong brew. Then she looked up, finding all eyes turned in her direction. "Gideon Gault. Now, more than ever, he will be determined to stop us."

"So, what are we going to do?"

Lydia glanced at her fob watch, then set her mug on the table.

"We have one hour before the whistle blows at the mine. We need to capture the man before he can spread the alarm any farther than he already has."

"How do you plan to do that?"

Lydia stood. She smoothed her hair with her palms, then tugged at the hem of her shirtwaist.

"Feminine wiles." Lydia took a fortifying gulp of air. "Louise, get that skillet of yours. Emmarissa, find a blanket. It's time we captured ourselves a Pinkerton."

It took less than an hour for Gideon to realize how determined—and systematic—the women had been when they'd begun their protest. While searching for his men, he had discovered that half the buildings in town were locked and shuttered—and he had enough sense to know that it wasn't due to a quarantine. He also knew that most of the men must be willing participants. Otherwise, they could have overpowered their female guards through sheer numbers alone.

On the one hand, he was impressed. The women had managed to stage a full-scale revolt, right beneath the noses of the owners and the security forces who were tasked with guarding the mine. But that thought also rankled. In that moment, Gideon realized how sidetracked he'd become by Lydia Tomlinson and the Wanted poster. He'd intuitively known that something was wrong in Aspen Valley. But he'd allowed himself to become distracted for far too long before waking up to the situation at hand.

And now there would consequences before things could be put back to rights.

He strode into the mine, knowing that he had less than an hour to get a tighter handle on the situation before it exploded in his face. As soon as he was deep enough into the tunnels that he could locate his crew, he drew their attention with a sharp whistle. After a moment's hesitation, the men trotted over to him.

Gideon shot each man with a hard stare. Although most of them held his gaze, a few shifted nervously.

"How many of you are privy to the women's shenanigans?"

He waited, allowing the silence to grow uncomfortable.

Three men finally lifted their hands.

"Hand over your sidearms. You are temporarily suspended from duty."

The other Pinkertons seemed shocked by the order until Gideon explained. "It seems our mail-order brides have staged a rebellion. For the past couple of days, they've kidnapped half the town and locked them up under the guise of a measles quarantine."

The men who'd handed over their revolvers shrank a little. The others displayed a montage of emotions: disbelief, outrage, amusement.

"This couldn't come at a worse time. If you'll remember from your briefing this morning, our home office has reason to believe that there's a credible threat against the stores of silver in the valley. We are vulnerable to an attack—and at the moment, we're left undermanned and outmaneuvered by the same bunch of women we were supposed to be guarding!"

By now, Gideon had their whole attention.

He pointed to a pair of men. "You two come with me. I want the rest of you positioned at the mine entrance. No one goes in or out until I give the order." He then turned to the men he'd suspended. "As for you all, the next few hours could determine whether or not you have a job when you leave this tunnel. You continue overseeing things here, near the face."

Gesturing to the men he'd assigned to follow him, Gideon strode back toward the surface. As they marched toward the dim patch of light at the end of the tunnel, Gideon called out to several other miners he could trust until he had an improvised force of two dozen men.

He led his group to a spot, just within the shadows of the mine, then stopped, crouching down. Using his finger, he drew a map of the town in the dirt.

"We're going to set up a trap. I'm pretty sure if we can get our hands on Lydia Tomlinson, we can convince her to stop this nonsense once and for all. She's the ringleader of this little circus."

He pointed to Bill Marsh. "Bill, you're going to take these men to the Pinkerton offices and get them some weapons. You'll head out this way, behind the buildings, along the river, then come into the building through the rear door."

He pointed to his men. "Garland, Otis, I want you to head to the pass. With everything that's going on in town, I don't want to leave us any more vulnerable than we already are. If you see, hear, smell or even *think* there's something out of place, you come high-tailing it back to warn us."

"You six need to station yourselves on the rooftops." He pointed to the miners in question, then to the sketch of each building. "I want you here at the mining office, the livery, storehouse, cook shack, laundry and warehouse. Lie down as low as you can on the rooftops. I don't want anyone to know you're there. The rest of you, scatter yourselves in whatever buildings haven't been taken by the women. If one of the mail-order brides so much as shows a stitch of lace, I want her apprehended and locked up in the Pinkerton building. You can use our personal quarters upstairs."

"Why not put them in the jail?" Otis asked.

"Because they've got a key to the cells and they've already broken one of their members out today."

Marsh laughed, but he had the sense to quickly disguise it with a cough.

"This seems like a whole lot of trouble for a passel o' women. Why don't we let 'em have what they want?"

"Because we're out to save the jobs of every man in this community. These women think they can force Batchwell to change his mind and allow females to live in the valley."

Gideon heard a few indistinct murmurs and knew that many of the men present probably agreed with them.

"But I want you to think long and hard. Which do you think Batchwell is going to be more likely to do? Give in to the women? Or fire the lot of us and hire a new workforce willing to follow his rules?"

That sobered the group and dispelled the murmuring, just as Gideon knew it would. They'd all been around Batchwell's temper enough to know that the man would do anything to save face in an argument. He wasn't about to let a bunch of women take control of the mine he'd built from a tiny hole in the ground.

"So, what's your plan, Gideon?"

"Right now, Batchwell is holed up in his house. Maybe,

he realizes that the shot came from Bottoms's house, maybe not. Frankly, I'd love to overtake the buildings and apprehend the women guarding them. But I can't take the chance that one of the women might accidentally shoot someone. So, we're going to launch a counterattack. One by one, I want you to isolate those girls posted outside the quarantine zones. As quickly and as quietly as you can, you're going to sneak up behind them, apprehend them, and lock them up. Once we think we have most of the ladies' lookouts, we'll start 'liberating' their hostages and talking some sense into them. If we can do it before the shift changes, the men can head to work as they normally would and Batchwell will be none the wiser. Then we can concentrate on freeing Bottoms. By nightfall, this could all be over. Come morning, we'll make the final arrangements to take the girls out of the valley. They'll be in Ogden before Batchwell catches wind of the total scope of this fiasco. Hopefully, that will mollify him enough that he won't start firing the whole lot of us."

Marsh pointed down to the map. "Where will you be in all of this?"

"I'm going to do my best to get myself captured."

Marsh's mouth gaped, but he quickly snapped it closed again.

It was Otis who asked, "Why on earth would you do that, sir?"

Gideon allowed himself a faint smile. "Because it's the quickest way for me to get to Lydia Tomlinson."

Chapter Fourteen

Gideon waited until he was sure that he'd given his men enough time to gather their weapons and assume their positions. Then he strode from the tunnel, head down. Once he reached the boardwalk, he slowed his pace. Removing his pocket watch, he pretended to fiddle with the stem.

All the while, his body remained tensed. Alert. It took every ounce of energy he possessed to remain casual and slightly distracted.

It wasn't until he neared the cook shack that his nape began to prickle in warning. With so many years spent as a soldier—and eleven months spent as a prisoner of war—he'd learned to guard his back. A stray crust of bread in Andersonville could be enough for a gang of men to jump a person and beat him senseless.

But rather than avoiding the danger, Gideon turned toward it, knowing that the cook shack would be a logical place for the women to make their move.

Slipping the watch back into his pocket, he opened the door and made his way toward the table where a stack of mugs was kept next to a tureen of hot coffee—yet another convenience that the women had brought to Batchwell Bottoms. He could only pray that whoever lay in wait didn't realize that he'd never been a coffee drinker.

Sure enough, he'd only gone halfway when the door opened behind him. Gideon was sure that he heard the swish of skirts. Then a blanket dropped over his head.

Clang!

He only had a moment's wherewithal to note a shuddering pain that shot from skull to boot tips. Then his world went black.

Lydia rushed out from the cooking area where she'd been conferring with the other women.

"Why'd you hit him so hard?" Myra demanded.

"He has a gun, Myra. Unlike ours, his is loaded."

Lydia shushed their bickering and sank to the floor. A lump was already forming on the back of Gideon's head.

Gingerly, she reached to touch the spot and the man moaned.

A part of her shrank in desperation. She'd known that some of the women had taken to a skillet as their weapon of choice, but it wasn't until now, with Gideon sprawled at her feet, that she'd seen the effects. The thought of Gideon bruised, dazed, unconscious, was causing inexplicable tears to prick at her eyes.

"Gideon?"

He groaned, but he didn't open his lashes.

"What should we do with him?" Miriam asked in such a practical tone that she could have been inquiring where to tote a basket of laundry.

Honestly, Lydia hadn't thought that far. She'd merely wanted Gideon to be out of the way so that they could finish their protest. She hadn't considered anything beyond getting him off the street.

"We can't leave him here," Myra said fearfully. "Anyone could come in."

Miriam nudged him with the toe of her shoe. "We could take him to the jail. It's probably the safest place since we have Dobbs's keys, and according to him, Gideon is the only other person with a set."

She knelt and rummaged through his vest pockets—and Lydia had to bite her inner lip to keep from snapping at the woman to be gentler.

Crowing in delight, Miriam stood with the keys suspended between her fingers. "Here we are!" she announced as she dropped them into her pocket.

"Come along, Myra. You take the arms, I'll take the legs. Stand back, Lydia."

But Lydia couldn't move. It seemed wrong, to cart the man around like a rolled-up carpet.

"No!"

The women regarded her questioningly, so she schooled her tone.

"We can't haul him across the road to the jail cells."

The two women still clutched him beneath the arms and around the legs.

Miriam frowned. "Why not?"

"He's too heavy, for one thing. It's over thirty yards to the Mine Office, and then we'd have to take him down a flight of stairs."

That seemed to give the women pause.

"Besides, we can't chance Batchwell or Bottoms seeing us carrying their head Pinkerton through the streets. Bottoms may have been cooperative so far, but Batchwell would have a fit of apoplexy."

"She's right, Miriam."

"Then what should we do?"

Lydia's brain scrambled for a logical solution—one

where Gideon could be kept out of sight, but not be subject to more abuse.

"Take him into the private dining room. I'll see what I can find in the kitchen to tie him up."

She rushed into the preparation area, trying to close her ears to the thuds and scrapes as the Claussen twins each took an arm and began to drag Gideon across the length of the miners' eating space, down the hall, then into the owners' private dining room,

For a moment, she gripped the counter, knowing in her heart of hearts that she'd just severed her relationship with Gideon. He would never forgive her for this—how could he? She'd flouted his authority and taken him prisoner. No man would ever forget such an assault to his pride.

Her hands trembled violently as she reached for a pile of dish towels. Over and over again, she tried to tell herself that it didn't matter. No affair of the heart was worth sacrificing the greater good. She had the opportunity to help dozens of families to remain together.

But for the first time since becoming an ardent suffragist, she found herself thinking: *At what price?*

For years, she'd insisted to herself that she was happy alone, that she didn't need anything but her causes to make her life rich and fulfilled.

But since coming to Bachelor Bottoms, chinks had begun to appear in the defenses she'd built around her heart. First, she'd seen the way that Sumner and Jonah Ramsey had fallen in love. Jonah had been so accepting of Sumner's career—indeed, he'd supported it wholeheartedly. Lydia had never thought that such a thing could ever be possible. A man's man supporting his wife's interests outside the home.

The second chink had occurred with Willow and Charles. From the moment Lydia had met her friend, Willow had been incredibly shy, almost fearful. But the moment she'd set eyes on the abandoned twins, there had been no obstacle she wouldn't surmount for their well-being—even marrying a total stranger. And Charles... well, Charles had taught Lydia that a man could be kind and loving and devoted to his wife and children—qualities she'd only seen in her aunts—and still be fierce and protective. Her own father had certainly never displayed such tendencies. Clinton Tomlinson had bemoaned Lydia's existence for as long as she could remember. If she hadn't been so handy—as his servant and an unwitting accomplice to his crimes—he probably would have left her in the desert to starve.

And then there was Gideon...

She'd tried so hard to remain cool and objective in his presence. But somehow, he'd found a way around the fortress binding her heart. For a brief time, he'd made her feel...

Special.

Worthy.

Whole.

Lydia shook herself free from such thoughts. What she was experiencing was a momentary lapse, that was all. No doubt, her chaotic emotions were due to the trauma of the avalanche, three months spent sequestered in a mining camp, and Gideon's ability to hold his own in a spirited debate.

But even as she tried to pound that thought home, there was a part of her whispering that it wasn't true. She'd begun to care for the man. Worry about him. Did he eat enough? Did he sleep enough? What caused that crease of worry to appear between his brow? And what wartime memories sent him striding toward the livery and galloping pell-mell out of the mining camp—as if the valley walls were about to close in and crash down upon him?

The fact that a complicated man like that had taken her
hand and walked her home, kissed her hand…

"Lydia?"

Miriam's impatient voice called from the other room.

"I'm coming!"

Even then, she didn't immediately move. A little voice
whispered that she could end this, right now, before anyone else could be hurt.

"Lydia!"

Hugging the towels to her chest, Lydia rushed into the
other room—only to find that Gideon was beginning to
rouse and Myra and Miriam were attempting to hold him
down.

"Tie him up! Hurry!"

"Lydia!"

Dropping to her knees, she began to lash his feet together with a few knotted dish towels.

"Put his arms behind his back, Myra!"

The twins grappled to bring his wrists together and
Lydia immobilized them as well. Then, mindful of the
miners who might stop in the cook shack for a snack, they
used one last dish towel to gag him.

Finally, breathing hard, the women stood, just as Gideon's
eyes began to flicker.

Miriam's coronet of braids had come free and she began
pinning them back into place. Her twin sank into one of
the nearby chairs, panting.

"I swear, if there weren't so much at stake—if I didn't
love Rulon Dell so much my heart could explode—I'd walk
out of the valley myself," she gasped.

Miriam reached to squeeze her sister's hand, then
turned to Lydia.

"What now?"

"Go into the other room. Keep an eye on things in the

cook shack and keep everyone away from this room."
Lydia took a deep, fortifying breath, but it didn't ease the
gallop of her heart. "As soon as he wakes up, I'm going to
try to talk to him. One last time."

The twins seemed skeptical, but they finally nodded
and left the room, closing the door behind them.

Lydia stood for several long moments, then sat in a
chair, and then, unable to help herself, she sat on the floor
next to Gideon, pulling his head onto her lap. Her fingers
shook as she reached out to push back the hair tumbling
over his brow. So soft. Silky. Fine. She gingerly stroked
the rising goose egg, knowing he would have an awful
headache.

"I'm sorry," she whispered, so softly, that he probably
wouldn't have heard her, even if he'd been awake. "I'm
so, so sorry."

Gideon fought against the blackness that smothered
him with the weight of his memories. Panicking, he fought
against them. But powerless against the onslaught of images that flashed through his mind like a cannon volley.

The terror of battle.

Blood.

Pain.

Then a desolation so complete that his spirit shrank
against it.

They'd brought him back to Andersonville.

Immediately, he was awash with the foul stench of
suffering and filth. An oppressive heat blanketed him,
drawing him deeper and deeper into that world—until he
wondered for a moment if everything he'd experienced in
the last few years had been a fever dream.

His sisters.

The mountains.

Aspen Valley.

Had he imagined it all? Had his brain concocted the scenes so completely that he'd actually believed the war had ended and the next stage of his life had begun?

But then, somewhere in his suffering, he felt a cool hand touch his brow and a softness beneath his head. Clinging to that solace, he forced himself to breathe…in…out. If he listened carefully, he thought that someone called to him. Could it be one of his sisters?

Dear Lord in Heaven. Help me. Please help me.

If he were still in Andersonville, if this had all been a figment of his imagination, he didn't know that he could fight anymore. Not after he'd felt the first stirrings of hope.

Hope.

The thought brought to mind the face of a woman. Not one of his sisters. No, this woman was willowy and elegant, completely out of his sphere.

Had he imagined her too? Had he imagined the way that she'd filled him with curiosity, then frustration, then a grudging admiration.

And more, so much more.

He couldn't remember the last time that he'd felt a stirring in his heart. Oh, he'd had his share of mad crushes when he'd been a young man, but this was different.

Still maddening.

But sweet. Like the soft rays of the sun in the morning.

Or the first breath of spring.

Somehow, without his being aware of it, she'd awakened the long-dormant recesses of his emotions, and he'd come to life. And just like the mountains around him, there were still a few stubborn patches of snow that remained, but underneath them, his spirit grew green.

His eyes flickered, and he panted softly when he realized that he wasn't in the cobbled-together lean-to of canvas and branches that he and his fellow cavalry officer had fashioned to protect themselves from the blazing Georgia sun.

He was inside. In a place he knew. And hovering above him was that beautiful face.

Gideon watched in consternation as her eyes brimmed with tears. A single drop fell from the dam of her lashes to land on his cheek.

What on earth had happened to make her cry?

Lydia never cried.

Immediately, his brain seized on the name.

Lydia.

"Shh. You mustn't talk or make a sound or the others will come to investigate."

Others.

Gideon frowned. His thoughts remained muddled. Then he hissed when a bolt of pain shot from his head to sizzle down the length of his spine.

"Shh."

He felt her fingers, cool and lithe against the nape of his neck. Then a wad of cloth lifted from his mouth and he could finally breathe again.

"Wha—"

He tried to lift a hand to the ache on his skull, but found that his wrists had been bound behind him. And his feet...

Immediately, he struggled, trying to free himself, to sit up. Again, a wave of memories threatened to swamp him.

He had to get free.

He had to protect himself!

"Shh. Shh! They mustn't know you're awake or they'll come and escort you to the jail. I've put them off for now, but the twins will be back the minute they hear that you're awake!"

Gideon forced himself to lie still, even though every muscle in his body thrummed with panic.

"What have you done?" he whispered, his throat hoarse.

Again, her eyes filled with tears. "I'm so sorry. I never meant for any of this to happen. It was supposed to be a peaceful protest—and it was working! We had enough men willing to sit out their shifts so Batchwell would realize it was in his best interest to negotiate a new set of rules."

Gideon tried to shake his head, but the action caused his brain to slosh against the enclosure of his skull, so he forced himself to become motionless again.

"We've been through this before. He'll never agree. He'd fire every man in the valley and start over again if he thought it would be the only way to save his precious mine."

Lydia adamantly shook her head. "No, don't you see? If he fired everyone, it would take months to hire new workers. Maybe even a year. He'd never allow the mine to lay dormant like that. Especially now that the new tunnel has hit a seam of silver bigger than anything they've ever found before."

Even through the sickening throb of his head, Gideon realized that Lydia might have a point.

"And we're not asking for a complete overhaul of the rules. We only want one minor change. That married families be allowed to coexist here. Batchwell can keep his bachelors segregated. If they want to do their courting, they can do it in Ogden on their days off, as they've always done."

Gideon knew he must have a serious injury, because Lydia was starting to make sense.

"Can you help me sit up?" he rasped. "The way my head is thumping, I'm afraid I'm going to be sick."

She immediately jumped to her feet and hooked one

arm beneath his. Slowly, awkwardly, he was able to force himself into the seated position. Then, with some scooting and scuffling, he managed to rest his back against the wall.

"Go on," he said, even though he knew that allowing Lydia to talk was probably the last thing on earth that he should let happen. She could talk a man into…

Changing his mind.

She sank on the floor beside him, and the faint scent of lemons and gardenias washed over him.

Gideon nearly smiled. Who knew that he could be so entranced by a woman's perfume?

"I'll admit that when I first sat down with the women and helped to devise this plan, I was short-sighted."

Gideon snorted.

Even Lydia had the grace to make a face.

"You were right. I thought that gathering up half the men in the valley would be enough. I was so focused on what I felt was an injustice that needed to be rectified— families being able to live together—that I forgot to figure in the human element."

"Which is?"

"I failed to appreciate the…*personal* investment that Mr. Batchwell has made in the mine. I regarded his involvement as little more than a businessman trying to protect his interests. I suppose I could claim that I didn't know enough about his background to understand the depth of his commitment to this enterprise. But that wouldn't be entirely true. I regarded this whole endeavor from a very selfish point of view. I wanted to leave my own mark on this community, undertake one great, monumental cause before I left the valley."

Head down, she seemed to study her interlocked fingers.

"Now that you've told me a little more about Mr. Batchwell, I can understand his motives. I know what it's like to have nothing—no food, no warm place to sleep."

She looked up then, meeting Gideon's gaze with a bleakness that took his breath away.

"No one to love you."

Gideon's heart seemed to lurch sideways, then lodge in his throat.

"How…"

One of her shoulders lifted in a melancholy shrug.

"My father is Clint Tomlinson, of the infamous Tommy Gang."

In an instant, the rock in his throat fell like a lead anvil into his stomach.

No, no, no.

Everyone in the territories knew about the Tommy Gang. Nearly a year before the war had begun, during Bloody Kansas, he and his infamous band of Border Ruffians had swept into the disputed states, terrorizing those suspected of abolitionist sympathies. They'd raided the homes of Free Staters, then robbed, looted and pillaged their way west. When the war broke out, the group seemed to vanish for a time. Rumor had it that Clinton Tomlinson and his men had enlisted in the Reb Army. But they hadn't lasted long under the discipline of a regular unit. They'd soon deserted their posts and headed for the territories.

"I thought the Tommy Gang was in prison."

Lydia's mouth twisted. "They were. I helped put them there. For my testimony, I was told that all charges against me would be dropped. You see, my father used me as a lookout or insisted that I create a diversion. Sometimes, I simply held the reins of their mounts when they stormed a bank. At other times, I would be asked to approach someone as if I were lost, or open gates and scatter livestock. Through it all, my father terrified me with stories of what would happen to me if the gang were ever caught. When I finally found the courage to turn them in, I did it knowing that I would probably spend the rest of my life behind bars."

Gideon swallowed, trying to wrap his brain around the story he was being told. "The Tommy Gang went to jail in what…sixty-one? Sixty-two? You couldn't have been more than—"

"Twelve. I was twelve." She shot him a smile that could have lit up the skies. "That's when I went to live with my aunts. They were so good to me. They still are. They're the ones who warned me that my father and his gang had escaped. The news was in those letters you gave to me."

Gideon's pulse started to knock out a heavy, insistent beat that drummed against the knot on his head.

The Wanted poster.
The Pinkerton who wasn't a Pinkerton.
An unknown threat to the storehouse of silver.

"Lydia, you've got to turn me loose."

She seemed to consider his request, then shook her head. "I can't. You see, in my selfishness, it wasn't only Mr. Batchwell that I failed to consider. I also didn't factor in the depth of emotions I would unlock within the women themselves. They've fallen in love, Gideon. I admit that I never really knew how…*all-consuming* love could be until…until lately. I never took into account the pain involved in being told that you couldn't be near your sweetheart. It's cruel, Gideon. Batchwell has to understand that fact, if nothing else. I think if he were to look at the problem, not from a business aspect, but from a human aspect, he could be made to understand things just a little better."

"Lydia, he'll—"

"No, wait. Hear me out. I understand how important it is for him to save face, to feel like he's totally in charge of the situation. As you stated before, he needs a way to alter the rules without appearing weak. And I think I've come up with a solution."

She rose to her feet, kneading her hands together.

"There's a loophole to the rule. One that's already being used."

Gideon's brows creased in confusion.

"I don't understand."

"Sumner and Jonah Ramsey. After they married, they moved to Jonah's homestead, which is off company property. According to Sumner, Batchwell couldn't fire Jonah because, technically, he's obeying the rules as they are outlined."

"And how will that help the rest of the men?"

She knelt so that they were eye to eye, and he could see the renewed passion reflected in her gaze.

"Charles and Willow have been talking about going to the land office as soon as the pass opens. They intend to see if they can get the parcel next to Jonah's property. From what he remembers, there are still several allotments that haven't been claimed."

"So?"

"With this new seam of silver, Batchwell's going to need more men, correct?"

Gideon nodded. From some of the discussions he'd heard, the owners were thinking of adding another hundred miners to the workforce.

"Those men will need housing."

"Sure."

"So, what if, instead of adding more row houses in town, Batchwell and Bottoms bought a piece of property bordering the land they already have. There would be plenty of room there for them to build family dwellings. I bet the men would willingly build the structures themselves in their off hours!"

Lydia's enthusiasm was infectious. Gideon felt his own brain snag on the idea, poke it, prod it. For the life of him, he couldn't think of a reason why it couldn't work, why it wouldn't work...

If they could just get Batchwell to agree.

"Don't you see? Technically, the women wouldn't be a distraction. They'd be away from the heart of the mining town and the single men, immersed in their own family-oriented community. Yet, they'd still be near enough that they could attend services at the Meeting House, work in the cook shack, and tend to the wounded when needed. It's the perfect compromise."

"You're forgetting. Batchwell isn't your only problem. Bottoms would have to agree as well."

Lydia's eyes twinkled with some secret knowledge. "Somehow, I think he'll look favorably on the plan."

"I don't know if you'll ever get Batchwell to calm down enough to even consider the proposal. As soon as he hears that you've held the valley hostage, he's likely to explode like a case of dynamite."

"Leave that to me." Lydia jumped to her feet.

"Wait! You need to untie me, Lydia!"

She paused, her hand on the doorknob. He could see her determination wavering. She even swayed in his direction. But then she shook her head.

Returning to his side, she lifted the gag from where it had fallen nearby.

"I'm sorry, Gideon. It's for your own protection."

He fought against her, trying to rear away from the rolled-up dish towel. But with his hands tied behind him and his head still pounding, his efforts merely made him sick. He was forced to become still to make the waves of nausea go away.

Lydia cupped his face with his hands. In that moment,

despite everything that had happened, he'd never seen anyone so beautiful. Her gaze had softened, her face filling
with such a wealth of tenderness and wonder that he had
a hard time believing it had been directed solely at him.
If he hadn't known any better, he would have thought he
saw a portion of his own fragile feelings for her reflected
in their depths.

"Don't you see, Gideon? I'm leaving you this way for
your own good. If this doesn't work, if I can't make Batchwell see reason, you can honestly say that you had no part
in any of it."

To his amazement, she leaned close, pressing a kiss to
the corner of his mouth.

"I know you'll probably never forgive me for this,
Gideon. And I'm sorry. I really am. But I can't leave this
valley knowing I didn't try my best. So many lives are at
stake. Against all that, my own happiness isn't worth a
hill of beans."

He opened his mouth for one final argument, but she
took that opportunity to shove the towel in his mouth, then
tie it behind his head. He tried to speak, tried to call her
back. But she rose to her feet and left the room, quietly
shutting the door behind her.

Chapter Fifteen

I can't leave this valley knowing I didn't try my best.

Panic rose in Gideon's chest as Lydia's words echoed through his head. But his apprehension had little to do with the way he'd been hog-tied with a set of dish towels.

So many lives are at stake. Against all that, my own happiness isn't worth a hill of beans.

He suddenly understood. After everything that Lydia had told him—and knowing enough of the Tommy Gang to piece together the rest—he finally realized why Lydia had been so adamant against marrying and having a family of her own.

He didn't doubt that she felt the need to champion women's suffrage and equality. As a child, she must have felt helpless. Clinton Tomlinson had a reputation for being ruthless. He'd shot one of his own men in the back for bumping into Clinton's horse. How much more ruthless would he be with his own blood? Gideon could only imagine that, from the time she'd proved useful to Clinton, he'd demanded absolute obedience from his daughter. The man had taken her on his raids, forced her to participate in them, then had threatened her with horrible images of what would happen to her if any of them were ever caught. The thought of her being so young and exposed to so much savagery filled Gideon with such a boiling wave of anger and protectiveness that he could scarcely breathe.

Yet, through it all, she'd found the courage to turn her father in, thinking all the while that she would go to prison for her efforts. And now, after fighting so hard for her future, she'd placed herself in a position where Batchwell could see her put behind bars as well.

No.

Gideon fought against the dish cloths that restrained him, knowing that he had to stop Lydia before she approached Batchwell. There might still be a way to present the compromise. If they could bring an end to the protest and get the men back to work before the evening shift change, maybe, just maybe, they could avoid the brunt of Batchwell's anger.

The door cracked open, silently, stealthily. Gideon grew quiet, praying that Lydia had come to her senses and come back to untie him.

But it wasn't a woman who stepped inside.

It was Jonah Ramsey.

For a moment, Jonah stood frozen, taking in the sight of Gideon bound and gagged on the dining room floor. Sumner hadn't been lying about the measles. Gideon could see the faint evidence of the telltale rash on his neck and hands.

The man stepped inside and closed the door. He leaned against the wall and folded his arms, managing to look stern and amused at the same time. Then the room vibrated with the sound of low laughter.

"I'm gone a couple of weeks and the whole place falls apart," he said once he'd managed to tamp down his mirth.

Gideon struggled against his bindings. He tried to order his friend to untie him, but the only thing that emerged were garbled noises—which only seemed to make Jonah laugh harder.

Finally, he pushed himself upright. Even then, he took his blessed time crossing the room.

"I tell you, I nearly took my life in my hands by coming here today. Sumner has been fussing over me like a mother hen. The way she was acting, you'd think that I was at death's door most of the time. For the past week, I've been about ready to go stark, raving mad. This morning, I finally caught on that she wasn't desperate about my health. She was desperate to keep me out of town. Once I figured that much out, I knew the women were up to something. The warm weather was bound to make them desperate."

Jonah reached for the gag. "They've got this tied in a half-dozen knots," he muttered to himself as he worked. But finally, the gag fell away.

"How'd you know I was here?" Gideon gasped, gulping for air.

"My first stop was the mine. One of your men filled me in. Where on earth is Charles? I left him in charge of the tunnels."

"He's guarding Batchwell. The women have kidnapped half the miners and they're holding Bottoms as a hostage in his own cottage."

Jonah chuckled again.

When was he going to stop laughing and turn him loose?

As if Gideon's thoughts had been spoken out loud, the cloths binding his wrists gave way and Jonah made quick work of the ones at his feet.

He stood, then reached out to haul Gideon upright.

Gideon swayed for a moment, his hands and feet tingling as the circulation returned to them.

"What's the plan?" Jonah asked.

"I need to get to Batchwell's place before the women do. In the meantime, gather more miners from the tunnels. Outfit them with revolvers and rifles from the storehouse and storm the buildings where they're keeping the men."

"You plan to shoot the girls?"

Gideon shot Jonah a pithy look. "No. But I'm betting that, with a show of force, we can get them to give up this nonsense and get the men back to work. The sooner that happens, the better off everyone will be."

Jonah nodded. "Fair enough. Then what?"

"Then meet me at Batchwell's. I'll wait until you get there before I talk to the man. Maybe with you and Charles there, we can keep him calm."

Jonah started laughing again. "So, we're resorting to wishful thinking, are we?"

"Just do it, Jonah."

Jonah shot him a mock salute, then headed for the door. Gideon didn't even wait for his friend to leave. He was already climbing out the window to the side alley beyond.

Lydia kept her head down as she hurried across the street, down the narrow lane leading to the Meeting House, then to the road that wound from the tail end of the miners' row houses, up, up to the owner's homes. She'd walked little more than a third of the way, carefully averting her face from view, her eyes smarting with tears, when she became aware of a pair of riders galloping furiously onto the main thoroughfare from the opposite end of town.

She paused, high enough on the hill now that she could see them head pell-mell toward the mining office. There, one of the men brought his mount to a skidding halt while the other one continued his furious pace toward the mine.

Lydia wasn't even conscious of changing course, her step quickening as she returned toward the heart of Bach-

elor Bottoms. As the first deep tolls of the warning bell
rang through the valley, she broke into a run, arriving at
the Mining Office as a few men began to poke their heads
above the false fronts of the buildings.

"There's a large group of men heading into the valley!"
the rider shouted to anyone within earshot. "It looks like an
advancing army! They're loaded to the eyeteeth. They've
even got a cannon!"

Lydia came to a shuddering halt.

She rested a hand against the building to steady herself
as Jonah Ramsey jogged into view. Lydia didn't have time
to wonder when he'd managed to arrive in town. Like the
leader he was, he immediately commanded the attention
of anyone within earshot.

"It's got to be the attack that the home office tried to
warn us about. You! Get over to the mine. I want every
man you can find. Send them to the storehouse and start
handing out the weapons and the ammunition. I doubt
we've got more than twenty or thirty minutes until they
break through the canyon."

Lydia's feet seemed to move of their own volition, back-
ing away from the crowd gathering around the alarm bell.
Whirling, she picked up her skirts and ran to the Miners'
Hall.

She was several yards away when the door opened and
Hannah nervously poked her head out.

"I take it that they've figured out what we've been
doing?"

"No. Let the men go."

"What?"

Greta joined her friend in the doorway.

"Was ist los?"

"The Tommy Gang. They're riding toward town. They

mean to steal the silver and who knows what else. We've got to warn people! We have to fight back!"

"Lydia!"

She whirled, unable to believe the evidence of her own eyes. Just when she needed him most, Gideon came running toward her.

Lydia ran into his arms. "Please! You don't know him like I do. He'll do anything in his power to get what he wants. You've got to warn everyone. I can ride toward the pass and head him off. As soon as he sees me—" she sobbed, panic twining in her chest like a living thing "—I can stall him for a few minutes while you get the women to safety. T-take them into the mine, or have them run out of town. P-please."

To her amazement, Gideon didn't chastise her. He didn't blame her for the danger heading toward them. Instead, he pulled her into his arms and issued orders over her head.

"Greta, Hannah, send the men to the storehouse. We need as many people armed and ready as we can manage."

Lydia reared back, gripping his arms. "No. No! That won't do any good!"

When Gideon's gaze met hers, she was shocked to see that it held no recrimination. Instead, his coffee-brown eyes swirled with a curious mixture of warmth, urgency and a fierce protectiveness.

"We can hold them off, Lydia. A good number of these men are veterans. They can handle a wea—"

"There's no bullets!"

Gideon stopped in midsentence, his eyes narrowing in confusion.

"What?"

"You won't find any bullets in the storehouse! We emptied all of the boxes and crates and took the ammunition back to the Dovecote. It's hidden in several dozen trunks all over the dormitory!"

Gideon made a sound that was half laugh, half strangled moan. Then his eyes swept the town.

"Get the weapons anyway. I want men stationed in every doorway, at every alleyway, on every rooftop. But keep out of sight." He grasped Lydia's arms. "How many women are here in town?"

She scrambled to think.

"A-about thirty, I'd say."

His grip tightened ever so slightly and he said, "Do you think you could get the ladies to the Dovecote without being seen?"

She thought of the tall stands of pine and aspen that surrounded the Dovecote. "I think so, yes."

"Go the long way there, down by the riverbank, so that you won't be seen from the roads. They'll have a spotter watching the town soon, if they haven't already. Bring as much ammunition back as you can carry and take it to the cook shack. I'll have men waiting there to redistribute it to everyone with a weapon. Can you do that?"

"Yes. Yes, we can do that!" She pointed to Greta. "Get the women from the infirmary. Hannah and I will round up those in the store and the barbershop and the cook shack."

"Jawohl!"

Lydia broke free from Gideon and dashed across the street.

"Lydia!"

She glanced over her shoulder at Gideon's call.

"Be careful, you hear me? I don't want to hear that anyone's been hurt, least of all you!"

He regarded her so intently, so fiercely, that a warmth ignited in her chest. The thinly veiled message was clear, and yet, incredible.

Gideon Gault cared about her safety.

He cared about *her*.

Despite all the trouble she'd given him.

"The same goes for you," she said back, hoping that he understood. Please, Lord, let an inkling of what she felt for this man be transmitted in their seemingly innocent exchange.

"After this, you and I are going to talk," Gideon added, his tone filled with warning.

The words should have filled her with dread, but she felt a tingling anticipation instead. "Yes. We'll talk."

"Lydia!"

She turned to find Hannah watching her impatiently.

Knowing that they didn't have time to waste, Lydia tucked away the thought of her short exchange with Gideon.

Later.

Later, she would pull out the memory from every angle, examine it minutely, polish each tantalizing detail.

But right now, she needed to help protect this town.

Her town.

In that instant, as she raced to the company store, she suddenly understood what the other women had been fighting so hard to retain.

This was their home.

Their *home*.

And no one was going to take it from them, least of all Lydia's father.

That moment, when Gideon was forced to turn his back on Lydia and start organizing the men, was one of the hardest that he had ever experienced in his lifetime. It took every ounce of his control not to rush toward her, sweep her off her feet, and carry her away to some hidey-hole where she would be safe until this confrontation was over.

But he didn't have the time to surrender to his own emotions. Not when so many lives and the future of the mine itself was at stake. They needed that ammunition to protect themselves and the livelihood of the community. If people were hurt—killed—and the cache of silver stolen, it would take years for the mining company to recoup its losses. Which meant that hundreds of men could be laid off, and their families could go hungry.

No.

That wasn't going to happen. Not on his watch. He may have given the women too much lead in the last few weeks, but he knew how to do his job. He'd been an officer in battle, and the old instincts were stirring quick and strong. As the men poured from the buildings, he began assigning them to groups, each with an area of town to defend, a commander, and a runner. The runners were immediately sent to the cook shack. As soon as the ammunition arrived, they would start ferrying it to their groups. The rest of them would gather their weapons from the storehouse and get into position.

"How are things going?" Jonah asked, breathing hard from his run to the mine. Behind him, men funneled out of the yawning entrance, carrying pickaxes and shovels and mallets—anything at all from their tools that could be used as weapons.

"Take half of your group to the warehouse," Gideon ordered. "Tell them to be inside the shed and ready to defend that silver with anything they've got. As soon as I have more men with weapons and ammunition, I'll post them outside the building and on the roof."

Jonah nodded. "What about the rest?"

"Outfit them with rifles and send them back to the mine.

I want a good half-dozen men at the mouth of each tunnel. I don't want Clinton Tomlinson thinking he can force our hand by destroying the passageways or the equipment."

"You've got it. But what about that infernal cannon they've got? We're powerless to that kind of weaponry."

Gideon whirled to point at Marsh. "Keep ringing that bell until you see Charles Wanlass heading down the hill."

"Yes, sir!"

Jonah's brows rose. "I take it you've got a plan."

"Oh, yeah. I've got a plan. I just have to hope that Lydia, Willow and your wife don't skin me alive when they get wind of it."

Willow froze, a pan of biscuits hovering halfway to the oven when she heard the distant tolling.

"Isn't that…"

Charles grew still as well. "Yeah. It's the alarm bell."

Since Batchwell and the babies had been dozing, Charles and his men had returned to the kitchen. Willow supposed that the warm, sunny room with its scents of spices and roasting meat had been preferable to these rough-and-tumble miners rather than the overly-decorated, shadowy confines of Batchwell's bedroom. The men had gathered around one end of the farm table with cups of tea, coffee and Charles's favorite oatmeal raisin cookies—the treat made all the more delicious since she'd announced that the storehouse's stock of tea, cinnamon and oatmeal were nearly gone.

Charles pointed to one of his men—Edward Shupe, if Willow remembered correctly.

"You stay here with Willow and Batchwell. Get a rifle from Batchwell's gun collection, just in case. The boys and I will go to town and see what's wrong."

Willow hurriedly set the pan on top of the range and bumped the door shut with her hip.

"Do you think something has happened in the tunnels?" she asked worriedly.

The men seemed to share a quick glance.

"I don't think so," Charles said, walking to place a quick kiss on her forehead. "We would have felt a bump in the mine," he said, using the miners' term for an explosion.

Which meant that either Lydia and her protestors had been discovered, or there was some new emergency.

Charles squeezed her shoulders. "As soon as you get those biscuits out of the oven, I want you to go upstairs with Batchwell and the babies. Once we've figured out the cause of the emergency, I'll send someone to let you know. Otherwise, Batchwell will be insisting on getting down that hill."

"He'll want to be there anyway. If you could send a buggy as soon as you're able. I think that, between Shupe and I we can help him hobble as far as the drive."

Charles stroked her cheek with his thumb. "You're a wise woman, Willow Wanlass."

She leaned into the caress, ever so slightly. And then he was gone, he and his men rushing outside and slamming the door behind them.

"Ma'am, if you don't mind, I'll get that rifle."

She nodded. "Of course."

Untying her apron, she hurried up the back staircase, then along the hall to the huge double doors. She hadn't even finished flinging them open when Batchwell demanded, "What's going on down there? What's the problem?"

His booming voice startled the children, causing them to jolt from their sleep. Adam was the first to begin crying—a demanding, strong little bellow that indicated that any soothing should start with him. Eva quickly followed with a sad whimper that began to build as she sensed her brother's distress.

"Mr. Batchwell, shouting at the top of your lungs will not bring the answers any quicker. You'll only upset the children."

Judging by his shocked expression, Batchwell had never been chided in that manner—let alone by someone with Willow's stature and gender. Taking advantage of that moment of silence, she bent to scoop Eva into her arms and transferred the infant to Batchwell.

"Here. Since you woke them up, you can help to calm them."

Batchwell gaped like a fish thrown out of water, but his hands closed reflexively around the baby and he held her to his shoulder, one gnarled hand moving to automatically pat Eva's back.

Willow lifted Adam, then rocked side to side.

"What in the world is going on in town?" Batchwell tried again, his strident whisper only slightly softer than his shout.

"Charles has gone to find out."

"Charles! What was he doing here?"

Willow opened her mouth to explain, then closed it again. Since Batchwell had believed the fib she'd told him about the gunshot from next door, she saw no reason to explain anything more. If the ruckus from below had the women as its root cause, Batchwell would find out about it soon enough. If not, there was no reason to tell him any sooner than necessary.

"He came to see you," she prevaricated, knowing she'd never be able to carry off a lie with any manner of success. "When you were asleep, he sat down to a cup of tea in the kitchen."

Along with the rest of his blasting crew.

But Batchwell didn't need to know that.

"He said he'd send a runner back as soon as he had any information."

"I should be down there!" Batchwell thumped the arm of his chair, making Eva jump.

"Mr. Batchwell, you need to remain calm. I've told Charles to send a buggy as soon as he's able. When it arrives, we'll help you outside and down that hill." She pointed to the street below and the crowd that was beginning to gather from every corner of town. "They'll need you down there, Mr. Batchwell. You're the leader of this community and they'll need your strong hand. I promise. I'll get you to the heart of things as soon as safely possible."

The man blinked in surprise, and she reached down to squeeze his shoulder encouragingly. Despite her words, she expected him to continue raging until a buggy appeared. But to her surprise, he returned to absently patting Eva on the back while he studied the goings-on below.

"You remind me a bit of my wife, Mrs. Wanlass."

Wife?

Willow looked away from the crowd that now seemed to be dispersing to every corner of Bachelor Bottoms.

"I didn't know you were married, Mr. Batchwell."

Had he, like the other men, lived apart from his spouse all this time?

"It was a long time ago." Batchwell squinted up at her for a moment. "She had red hair, she did. Just like you." His voice trailed away. "A tiny slip of a thing, was my Fionella."

Briefly, Willow wondered if that was the reason why Batchwell had seemed particularly antagonistic toward her in the beginning.

"She was kind, like you. And shy."

He returned his gaze to the window, but she sensed he wasn't seeing the scene below.

"What happened, Mr. Batchwell?" Willow whispered, sensing a great sadness in his voice.

"We were so young. Too young. She died in childbirth. Neither she nor the little gel survived."

"Oh, Mr. Batchwell."

Willow touched his shoulder again.

Batchwell glanced down at the baby in his arms. Eva offered him a toothless smile and a gurgle of delight.

"I'd forgotten what it was like…" Batchwell murmured, so softly that Willow almost didn't hear him.

Not knowing how to respond, Willow bent to place a light kiss on the top of Batchwell's head.

"Children have a way of reminding us what's really important, don't they, Mr. Batchwell?" she murmured.

"Indeed they do, Mrs. Wanlass."

Chapter Sixteen

Gideon met Charles and his men at the bottom of the hill. As they brought their mounts to a stop, Gideon grabbed the reins to his friend's horse.

"We think the Tommy Gang is about to storm the valley in an attempt to steal the silver."

Charles's jaw worked and a steely expression settled over his features.

"How many?"

"Fifty or more. And they've got a cannon." Gideon allowed himself a slight smile. "But I'm hoping you and your men can help me with that little problem, Charles."

Charles's brow knit in confusion.

"Do you think you and your crew could set up some charges along the road? I wouldn't mind taking a few members of their gang out—maybe even a cannon—before they get to town."

The grin that Gideon had grown accustomed to seeing on his friend's face since his marriage to Willow returned full-force.

"You heard him, boys! Get into that storehouse and get a couple of cases of dynamite, blasting caps and a spool of fuse. Watkins and Ellis, you two round up the plungers from the mine."

"What about the buggy that your missus wanted?"

Charles shook his head. "They'll be safer on the hill. Find someone in town to head up there with a message. In the meantime, let's move as fast as we can!"

Gideon released the reins and stepped back. Immediately, Charles urged his horse into a gallop, heading down the lane that bordered the row houses where he could gain entrance to the storage house through a back door.

Dear Lord, please give them time enough to get things ready. And please, please, protect the good people of Aspen Valley.

Lydia and the other women burst through the door of the Dovecote.

Since it had proved easier to prepare the meals in the cook shack and complete some of the baking at the Dovecote, there were only a few women working in the kitchen. They must have heard the bell as well, because they began peppering Lydia with questions as soon as the brides entered.

Lydia held up her hands for silence. "The men think the Tommy Gang is going to raid the valley. I need everyone to gather baskets, pillowcases, crates—anything you can find. Collect every last bullet and shotgun shell and take it to the cook shack. Use the back path along the riverbanks. Gideon doesn't want us to be seen from the road."

"We'll never get the pumpkin cart through all that mud."

"Then we'll have to carry everything. Take as much as you can hold, then come back again. We'll do it as many times as necessary until the job is done."

The women immediately scattered.

"Miriam and Myra. How much clothesline do we have?"

The twins paused halfway up the stairs.

"Clothesline?" Miriam stared at Lydia aghast for considering the laundry during such a crisis.

"Yes. I know we don't have a lot of time, but do you think that we could tie the rope to the base of the aspen trees on either side of the road. The riders will probably head toward town with some speed. If we keep the line fairly low to the ground, and they aren't paying attention…"

Myra clapped her hands. "Brilliant! Leave it to us to set it up."

She and Miriam immediately changed course toward the rear entrance and the cords that had been strung from a set of poles.

"What else, what else, what else?" Lydia muttered to herself. "What else can we do?"

A pair of women were already clattering down the stairs. They labored beneath bulging pillowcases full of ammunition. "What about the weapons we were using, Lydia? Surely they'd be more useful in the hands of the men than with us."

"Those of you who can shoot, keep your weapons, but load them this time. Take the rest to the cook shack."

Lydia strode to the cupboard, removing a revolver that they'd stashed there. Then she reached for the flour bag sitting in plain sight on the shelf. Ripping at the thread they'd used to sew it shut, she grabbed a handful of bullets and began loading the revolver. After she'd finished, she filled her pockets with more. Once the revolver was loaded, she unfastened the top three buttons of her bodice and retrieved the tiny derringer that rested in a special holster sewn into her corset. Her aunts had always insisted that she be prepared for any eventuality. Should she need to protect herself, she had her hatpin, the derringer and oftentimes a small revolver tucked into her boot.

She quickly made sure the derringer was still loaded. Two tiny bullets rested in the double chamber. Then, she replaced the weapon in its hiding place, but left the buttons undone.

She'd help the others get the ammunition to the cook shack, but then she had her own bit of business. Having ridden with her father in the past, she knew how he liked to work—and she doubted he would have changed his tactics over the years. He wouldn't gallop into town. He'd find a vantage point above the action where he could analyze the attack and adjust his strategy as necessary.

She fought the taste of guilt on her tongue. It was her fault that the Tommy Gang had come to the valley. She had no doubts that her father's thirst for vengeance had spurred his desire to raid this particular town. He had come for her, and the stores of silver were merely the icing on the cake. Lydia had great faith that Bachelor Bottoms would rally against the force of the gang's attack.

But the man giving the orders?

She shoved the larger revolver into her waistband.

Lydia would take care of him herself.

As soon as Willow saw a horse and rider heading up the hill toward them, she handed Adam to Mr. Batchwell.

"I'll see what's going on, then I'll come right back and tell you."

Despite the warnings from Shupe for her to stay indoors, Willow stood at the gate waiting when the miner and his animal skidded to a halt.

"Charles wants you to know that the town may be under attack by the Tommy Gang," Craig O'Keefe rasped. "They've been spotted about two thirds of the way up the canyon. You and Mr. Batchwell are to stay here, where it's safer. He'll send a buggy as soon as he can."

The Tommy Gang.

Willow had read about the infamous band of outlaws long before coming to America. In the girls' school where she'd lived, some of the students had smuggled penny novels and periodicals into their dormitories. Sometimes, when they left for the holidays, Willow would borrow the forbidden texts. Although her reading skills were rudimentary, the thrilling stories of Indians and outlaws from the untamed territories halfway around the world had given her more than enough incentive to practice. She remembered the tales of the Tommy Gang quite well, most likely because there had been rumors that a young girl had ridden with the notorious band of men.

"What about Shupe?" she asked, pointing to the miner who'd followed her outside.

"He's to stay here and protect you and Mr. Batchwell."

"We can protect ourselves! Get on that horse, Mr. Shupe!"

Shupe reached for the other man's hand and swung onto the horse behind him.

"If you see anyone else," the miner added, "send them down to the cook shack for further orders. Miss Tomlinson and the women are gathering up ammunition and bringing it there to distribute. The way things sound, we're going to need every person we can get."

The words were barely out of the man's mouth before he pulled on the reins. Then, with a sharp "hiyahh!" he urged his mount back toward town.

Willow raced to Mr. Bottoms's cottage. Those women who had been guarding their "captive" met her halfway.

"Turn Mr. Bottoms loose. Those of you who know how to shoot with any degree of marksmanship, come with me. The rest of you are needed at the Dovecote to help retrieve the ammunition and take it to the cook shack. Hurry. Hurry!"

She ran back to Batchwell's mansion, three other women coming with her. She led them into Mr. Batchwell's study and pointed to the gleaming weapons that lined one whole wall of the room.

"I want you to take down every weapon and line them up on this desk." Without a second thought, she swept her hand across the surface, clearing it of ledgers and hand-printed stationery. "Load them up here. There's ammunition in that chest there. As soon as everything is prepared, bring rifles to Mr. Batchwell and me, along with a few boxes of bullets between us. Then, I want you to station yourselves on the upper balconies. Batchwell and I will take the ones facing the valley, you all take the rear of the house and the one over the side door. Whatever happens, no one gets inside, understand? They'll be looking for the owners to force a surrender, but they're not going to get them."

She was heading toward the staircase when Iona appeared.

"Where's Bottoms?"

"He's gone down the hill."

Willow had hoped to keep the two men together, but there was nothing she could do about that now.

"Go around the house and check the windows and doors. Make sure that everything is locked up tight and the shades drawn. Then head to Batchwell's bedroom. I might need your help."

Iona nodded and left in a flurry of skirts.

Willow stayed long enough to ready a pair of revolvers, then she ran up the stairs again.

To his credit, Batchwell didn't shout at her for having taken so long, but he clearly vibrated with impatience.

"I don't have much information," Willow said, rushing into the room and laying the revolvers on the bed. Without even asking for permission, she moved to Batchwell's large highboy and removed one of the drawers, upending the contents onto the floor. She quickly lined it with the babies' blankets, then set each of them inside.

The twins gazed up at her with wide eyes. They'd grown so much in the past few weeks that the two of them barely fit together in the makeshift cradle she'd made.

"I'll be right here, little ones." She kissed each of them on the forehead, then slid the drawer under the high tester bed, hoping that, if a gunfight ensued, they would be safe from any stray bullets. The babies whimpered at the unfamiliar setting, but Willow knew she didn't have the time to comfort them.

She scooped the revolvers from the bed and handed one to Mr. Batchwell. "The Tommy Gang was seen in the canyon."

Batchwell's face grew red, his brows pulling into the familiar scowl.

"From what I understand, the whole community is getting ready to defend Aspen Valley." She knelt so that she could meet him eye to eye. "Have you heard of the Tommy Gang?"

Batchwell smacked the arm of his chair with his free hand. "Of course!"

"Then you know what they'll do. They'll send the bulk of the gang storming straight through town. But a few of the men will be ordered to sneak around the back."

Batchwell's eyes glittered with a newfound respect. "How do you know all that, gel?"

"I—I confess to having read a sensational article or two in certain…women's periodicals."

A bark of surprised laughter burst from his throat. "Never knew that women had an interest in such things."

She regarded him wryly. "We do manage to keep abreast of the world around us, Mr. Batchwell."

"I don't doubt you do."

"Anyhow, I've sent Charles's man to help down below. That leaves you, me and four other women to guard you and your house, Mr. Batchwell."

"Me?" The word dripped with scorn. "I can take care of myself."

"I don't doubt that at all."

"I should be down there with the rest of them!"

"Normally, Mr. Batchwell, I'd agree with you. But we have to look at the facts. We don't have time to get a buggy, and there's no way, even with the help of the other women, that we could assist you in limping closer to the mine."

He seemed to sag a little when confronted with the truth.

"Mr. Batchwell, if the Tommy Gang runs true to form, they'll have researched this valley. They may have had someone watching us for days without our even knowing it. And one of the things they'll be looking for…is you."

Some of the redness eased from his cheeks.

"I've got the girls downstairs loading every weapon you own. In a minute, they'll bring us a couple of rifles and a few boxes of ammunition. I've told them to take the rear and side balconies. I'm going to head to the room next door and take up my position there. That leaves you to watch everything from this window here." She gripped the gnarled hand resting on the chair. "I'm trusting you to take care of my babies, Mr. Batchwell. If anything should happen, if someone manages to get into the house, I'm counting on you to stop them at the door, do you hear?"

Batchwell's gaze flicked from the guillotine windows,

to the drawer beneath the bed, to the revolver in his hands. When he looked up, his eyes were a steely blue.

"You have my word, Mrs. Wanlass."

She squeezed his wrist, then stood as Iona came into the room with a rifle in each hand. Her apron pockets bulged with boxes of ammunition.

"I was told to bring these up here. They're loaded."

"Thank you, Iona. Can you help me pull Mr. Batchwell's chair a little closer to the window? Then turn it slightly, so he has a proper view of the bedroom doors as well as the view below."

Iona gingerly set the rifles on the bed while Willow pulled Batchwell to his feet. He hissed when his broken leg touched the floor, but otherwise didn't complain. Bracing his weight with her shoulder, she waited while Iona moved the chair. Then the two of them supported the man on either arm well enough for him to hop the few feet necessary. When he collapsed back onto the tufted seat, Willow could see a thin sheen of sweat on his upper lip.

"How will that work, Mr. Batchwell?" He glanced in one direction to survey the street below, then back to the doors.

"Fine, fine. I just wish everything weren't so far away."

"I saw a pair of field glasses in the same chest as the boxes of ammunition," Iona said. "Would you like me to get them?"

Batchwell thumped the chair again, this time in agreement. "I like your way of thinking, Mrs. Skye."

While Iona ran back downstairs, Willow pulled the little table close and set the box of ammunition in the middle.

"Dump everything out loose. I can reload quicker that way."

She did what she was told, then grasped the rifle, leaning it against the window frame.

"Can you think of anything else you'll need?"

He shook his head. "You've thought of everything, it seems."

When she would have moved to retrieve her own weapons, Batchwell grasped her elbow. She looked down, wondering if he'd changed his mind about manning the room alone, but he merely stared up at her with quiet eyes.

"Forgive an old man?"

Willow shook her head in confusion. "For what?"

"I… I wasn't very kind to you. Especially that night when I found you and Charles and the twins…"

She shook her head.

"There's nothing to forgive, Mr. Batchwell. I think we've both moved beyond that first bad impression to become…friends."

His lips seemed to tremble ever so slightly. "Yes. I do believe you're right."

Iona rushed into the room panting. She set a pair of ornate brass field glasses on the table.

"Now what?"

Willow slipped from Batchwell's grip and reached for her own rifle. "You'll come with me. If we have to shoot, I'll empty the long gun first, hand it to you to reload, then use the revolver."

"Brilliant."

Only at the door to the hallway did Willow pause one last time.

Batchwell seemed to instinctively understand her hesitation.

"Don't you worry, Mrs. Wanlass. The babes will be safe with me."

"Thank you… Ezra."

Then, knowing there was no more time to waste, Willow forced herself to leave the room.

* * *

As soon as Lydia had ascertained that every last bullet had been taken from the Dovecote to the cook shack, she silently stepped away from the others and hurried across the street, then down the boardwalk to the stables.

Around her, Bachelor Bottoms looked like a ghost town. Granted, things had been quiet for the last few days as the men had been gathered up and locked away. But this…

A gusting wind had begun to blow, ruffling the surface of the puddles, bringing a chill from the upper slopes where the snow still coated the top half of the mountains. Even the sun had seemed to desert them, hiding behind thick black clouds that hinted a storm could be looming, bringing an artificial twilight.

If she hadn't known any better, Lydia would have thought the people of Aspen Valley had been whisked away. But the prickling between her shoulder blades warned her that her progress was being watched by dozens of pairs of eyes. She knew full well that there were men waiting behind the false fronts of the buildings and more behind every window. The narrow alleys that connected with the miners' row houses had at least one or two men peering out from the corners.

She knew the moment that the Tommy Gang appeared at the mouth of the canyon. One of the men posted on the edge of town offered the long mournful call of a barn owl. A staggered succession of bird calls passed the news over her head until the mine itself had been warned.

Dodging into the livery, Lydia hurried from stall to stall, looking for the mare that she'd ridden only days before, when she and Gideon had ridden to check the pass. She'd gone down one full side without finding it when she happened upon Gideon's strawberry roan gelding.

The animal would have to do.

She held out her closed fist, allowing the animal to become accustomed to her scent. He may have even recognized her, because his ears twitched and he obligingly shifted in his stall, tacitly giving permission for her to saddle him, should she care to do so.

"Good boy," she murmured, scratching his long nose, his ears, then his neck. "How about you and I take a ride?"

The horse nickered softly as if he'd understood.

As far as she could tell, the tack for each animal had been positioned on a series of pegs and rails at the front of each stall. She gathered up the heavy blanket and entered the stall, settling it over the horse's back. When he didn't object, she lugged the saddle in as well.

Within minutes, Lydia had the horse completely outfitted and led him into the center aisle. She drew him close to a pile of grain sacks near the back entrance. After pulling the sliding door open enough for a horse and rider to exit, she used the bags as a makeshift mounting block. Somehow, she managed to get her feet into the stirrup and swing herself onto the animal's back.

It took a moment to adjust the layers of her skirts and petticoats—and she rued the fact that she hadn't been able to change into her riding costume. But there simply hadn't been time.

Bending forward, she ran her hand down the horse's neck and closed her eyes.

Dear Lord, please help me. These people are so dear to me. They've become my family, and this valley has become my home. I know I'm not the only person to claim such a thing. You understand better than I that these are hardworking, God-fearing people. They've all banded together to protect one another. Please keep them safe. And if it be Thy will, please help me to find my father. It may be the only way to avert the violence that he has proba-

bly planned. In this and in all Thy blessings, I am so very grateful. Amen.

The moment her prayer was finished, she whispered, "All right, let's ride!" Then she and the strawberry roan burst from the livery and galloped toward the hills.

"Where's she going?"

Gideon looked up from his field glasses. Following the line of Dobbs's finger, he noted the rider galloping out of town.

Although he knew full well the identity of the familiar figure, he peered through the glasses again.

What was she doing?

He swept the glasses ahead of her, then onto the foothills above. Near as he could tell, she had no particular goal. For some reason, she was heading up the slope of the mountain, making a wide circle toward the mouth of the canyon. But other than a thick stand of pines and aspen, he couldn't see a logical objective.

Gideon felt his gut tightening in panic. Lydia had ridden out of town, away from the protection of the volunteer army that waited for the Tommy Gang to arrive.

It didn't make any sense.

For a moment, a traitorous thought flashed through his brain. She could be meeting the gang. She could be colluding with them. She could have feigned her panic when the so-called Pinkerton had arrived in town, simply to throw Gideon off the scent.

As soon as the idea took shape, Gideon thrust it away. No. He trusted Lydia. He didn't know how, he didn't know when, but despite her efforts to round up the men of the valley and attempt to overthrow its leadership, he knew she would never do anything to hurt the people of Aspen Valley.

She would never do anything to hurt him.

He panned the field glasses back toward the mouth of the canyon. Although the warning system they'd devised had already spread through town, he still felt a jolt of shock when the hills themselves seemed to darken, shift, then reform. What had been an ominous shadow on the ridge soon separated to reveal an army of men on horseback forming at the mouth of the canyon.

Gideon quickly whipped the glasses, searching for Lydia. She wouldn't have had time to hide herself.

But after scanning the entire area, he realized that she must have taken cover in the trees. And those trees…

Were nearly parallel to the men on the ridge.

Gideon checked again without the glasses, then peered through the lenses again. The warning prickle that he'd felt off and on for days exploded outward in waves of panic.

She wouldn't do it.

She couldn't.

He adjusted the focus on the field glasses. Although they weren't strong enough to pick out individual faces, he could tell by body language alone which one of the riders was in charge.

Clinton Tomlinson.

Lydia's father.

Gideon thrust the glasses in Dobbs's direction, then rose to a crouch position. "You're in charge of things here."

Dobbs nearly dropped the field glasses in his surprise. "Where are you going?"

Gideon pointed to the spot where Lydia had disappeared. "She's already three steps ahead of us, don't you see? When the Tommy Gang rides into town, Clinton Tomlinson hangs back like a general on a battlefield, usually choosing a spot above the fray. Soon enough, he'll be sending his army of men down that hill." Gideon pointed an emphatic finger at Dobbs. "When he does, *you* are going to take charge of the men under our direction." He waved his hand toward the upper slopes. "Meanwhile, she's going to do her best to sneak up behind Clinton Tomlinson and take him down. I aim to see to it that she doesn't have to do it alone."

Dobbs's eyes grew wide, but he offered a quick, "Yes, sir. God bless you both."

Charles and his men huddled in the copse of trees just off the main track. They'd had to rush to lay their charges and their cords—and he prayed that the advancing men wouldn't see their tracks in the weeds.

"You know what to do. Our main objective is that cannon. Keep your eyes on it at all times. If you see it coming into range, blow it up."

His men grinned in response. After years of carefully orchestrated blastings in the mine—where safety was paramount and hours of precise planning led up to each explosion—they were looking forward to a bit of mayhem. The eager expressions they wore reminded him of a congregation of arsonists being handed a box of matches.

Charles pointed to Al Meadows.

"Keep those coals hot. I don't want to have to rely on friction matches."

The man nodded. They'd made a small fire in a bed of gravel, and they'd been feeding it chunks of wood since they'd taken their position. A few feet away lay a crate of loose dynamite sticks, each one already prepared with blasting caps and a short fuse. Once the controlled charges had been set off farther up the hill, they'd start lighting the individual pieces of dynamite and lobbing them into the road.

"Stay alert and stay safe," Charles said. Then he moved to the first of the blasting boxes and placed his hands on the plunger.

Gideon had just managed to saddle a horse and exit the livery when the first explosion shuddered through the valley like thunder. Praying that the charges would provide a diversion, he pointed his mount up the hill.

As much as he wanted to ride full force to the stand of trees where he suspected that Lydia had hidden, he didn't want to give her position away, so he zigzagged from row house to row house, then kept to the trees as much as possible, waiting for the rhythm of the charges to move into the open.

Boom!

He managed to glance in the direction of the pass in time to see a cloud of dirt and broken tree limbs bloom in the air above the treetops. He burst forward several yards, then hugged the tree line.

Boom!

Another dash. He managed to close the gap between him and his objective to fifty yards. If Charles had managed to lay at least one more charge...

Boom!

He slapped the horse's rump with the reins, urging him forward, closing the last few feet until he went crashing through a stand of aspen. Pine boughs slapped and scratched him before he was able to rein to a stop. Ahead of him, he could see a dark shape in the shadows.

The unmistakable click of a hammer being locked into place caused him to freeze. Then he heard a gasp and "Gideon?"

He moved more carefully this time, weaving his way

through the brush until Lydia's shape coalesced in front of him.

"What are you doing here?"

He eased forward until they were side by side, their knees nearly touching. "I saw you ride out of town."

"Shouldn't you be with them? They'll need you."

He shook his head. "I'm right where I ought to be." Gideon reached out to touch her cheek, and a warmth gathered in his heart when he felt her lean into the caress. "You shouldn't have ridden out here on your own."

She opened her mouth, then closed it again, her jaw growing hard. "Go back to town, Gideon."

"Only if you come with me."

She shook her head. A glint of moisture pooled in her eyes. "You go ahead. I'll be along in a few minutes."

His hand slid to her nape, holding her there, forcing her to look at him.

"Why? So, you can confront your father?"

Her lashes lowered, shielding those expressive blue eyes, confirming what he had suspected.

"I need to do this alone."

His thumb strayed to the corner of her mouth. "Why?"

"Because this is all my fault."

Gideon shook his head, realizing that she truly believed that statement. "How can any of this be your doing?"

When she finally met his gaze, he was struck by the misery she'd tried so hard to hide.

"Don't you see? When I sent my father to prison, he vowed that he would get even. He means to ruin this valley and steal the silver as a…twisted sort of vengeance."

Gideon shook his head. "Maybe it started out that way. Maybe he wanted to find you, and all of the newspaper coverage about the avalanche and the missing mail-order brides gave him an inkling of where to go. But I doubt that's why he's here now. He'd have no way of knowing about the friendships you've made. As far as he's aware, this valley and the mine mean absolutely nothing to you." He leaned forward, willing her to believe him. "Frankly, I think all of his motives boil down to greed. He heard about the Batchwell Bottoms Mine and realized that, after the avalanche, we'd be vulnerable. We're cut off from communication with the outside world and low on supplies. None of those things can be laid at your door."

She blinked furiously, but even so, a tear plunged down her cheek.

"I still need to confront him, Gideon."

"All right. But we do it together. Charles is making enough noise down there to provide us with the element of surprise. The moment you find your father alone and wrapped up in what's going on in the valley, you can make your move. I'll follow your lead and hang back, keep the man in my sights."

He felt rather than saw the shuddering breath that escaped from her lungs.

"Thank you, Gideon."

Leaning forward, he placed a soft kiss on her lips.

"That's what friends are for," he said, then could have kicked himself. He'd long since passed the "friend" stage in regards to Lydia. Somehow, she'd managed to wriggle her way into his head and his heart. She'd converted a diehard, confirmed bachelor into a tongue-tied suitor who was suddenly thinking about finding a ring and planning for a future together.

Boom!

Their horses started, reminding Gideon that this was neither the time nor the place to wax poetic. They had a battle to win; a town to protect. And before it was through, Gideon intended to ensure that Lydia had the confrontation she so badly wanted. Maybe then, Gideon could find a way to banish the last of the shadows in her eyes.

"Come on. Let's get into position before Charles uses all of his dynamite."

Chapter Seventeen

Charles lowered the plunger on the last of the set charges and ran toward the crate of loose dynamite.

"We've knocked down at least a dozen riders, but we still need to take out that cannon!"

Some of Tomlinson's men thundered past them, but Charles knew that the cannon being pulled on its caisson had been toward the rear. Scanning the area, Charles realized that Tomlinson would place the heavy-duty weapon on the last ridge before the road swept down through town.

"Granville! Grab a handful of dynamite and follow me!"

Ruing the fact that he was about to lose a perfectly good hat, Charles nudged a few hot coals into the crown, then ran toward a spot in the road where they could get within feet of the wagon tracks, yet still be shielded by a large stand of boulders.

"On my mark, start lighting the fuses then hand the sticks to me!"

Hugh Granville knelt in the mud, a fuse hovering over the coals.

"Now!"

As soon as the fuse began to burn, Granville handed

the stick to Charles. Standing, he threw it in the direction of the pair of horses pulling the caisson.

Yards too short.

He grabbed the next one.

Almost within range.

He waited a second. Two.

Boom!

A glance at the dynamite at their feet reminded him that they only had three sticks left, and the horses were coming fast. Most of the riders had veered off the road to avoid the explosions or were fighting to control their startled mounts.

Boom!

The next stick detonated near the team's feet and the horses reared. For a moment, the caisson tipped, frightening the animals even more. Then the heavy cart flipped to its side, skidding through the mud and matted grass as the horses tore free of the traces and thundered toward the river.

Without thinking, Charles ran forward, tossing the dynamite directly beneath the cannon. Then, just as quickly, he dived for cover.

Boom!

He still had his hands wrapped protectively around his head when a strange pinging rattle filled the air. He looked up in time to see bits of metal and wood fly upwards before hurtling back down to earth amidst the acrid smell of scorched earth and gunpowder.

Granville slapped Charles on the back. "Beautiful! Absolutely beautiful."

Charles rose to his knees, allowing himself to take one last peek at the crater in the ground and the team running untethered along the riverbank. Then he pushed himself to his feet and whistled sharply to the rest of his men.

"Let's get back to town!"

* * *

The moment she heard the first charges, Willow closed her eyes for another quick prayer, asking the Lord to watch over Charles and his men.

Please, please don't let any of them get hurt.

Then, she was opening her eyes, trying to make sense of the army of men rushing into the valley.

At first, the figures were little more than a blur. Then, she saw a few riders fly into the air, their horses tumbling in grotesque somersaults.

Somehow, she felt no compunction at all for the men, but it pained her to see the horses' plight, and she was relieved when the huge animals righted themselves, many of them scattering, riderless, toward the hills.

Squeals of delight filled the air, and it wasn't until she heard Batchwell's distant, "Thatta boy, Charles!" before she realized that she'd been the one to make the noises.

She began counting the explosions.

Two.

Three.

Four.

Five.

There couldn't have been time for Charles and his men to have set more, could there?

Sure enough, the large reverberations were followed by smaller reports. Despite the smoke and grass and mud being thrown into the air, she could see that the explosions seemed to be tracking the arrival of the cannon.

Suddenly, the caisson seemed to waver, tip. Then, to her horror, she saw Charles racing into the open.

"No, Charles, no!"

Just as quickly as he'd left the shelter of the boulders, he turned and dived back toward them. Then the air was filled with dirt and chunks of what she supposed was the remains of the cannon.

"Do you see him, Mrs. Wanlass?" Batchwell called from his spot next door.

She squinted, trying to pierce the smoke and dirt and debris, then was finally rewarded with the sight of Charles and his men running toward the Dovecote.

"Yes! Yes, I see him. Charles and his men are running toward the riverbank!"

"No, Mrs. Wanlass. Do you see that rider? He's circling behind the row houses and heading straight up the hill toward you."

A burst of sheer terror shot through her system.

"Where?"

"Look slightly to your left, directly behind the steeple of the Meeting House."

She followed Batchwell's directions and zeroed in on a horse and rider picking his way up the steep slope. As he grew closer, her body tensed, a part of her recognizing his lanky frame before her brain could catch up.

The so-called Pinkerton who had come to the valley from the outside world no longer wore the distinctive blue jacket.

"We need help, Mr. Batchwell! I don't think I can get a clean shot from this angle."

Too late, she realized that Batchwell couldn't move, and short of bellowing at the top of his lungs…

Whirling, she ran from the room, taking the grand front staircase as quickly as she dared. Then she heard it, the strident jangling of the bell that had nearly driven Boris to distraction. It continued on and on until she heard other footsteps running toward her. Anna and Sophie ran into the hall from the rear. Iona from the side. Enid must have stayed at her post on one of the rear balconies.

"Iona, open the front door!" Willow whispered. "Just a few inches."

Willow eased backward into the bare space that would one day be Mr. Batchwell's music room. Except for an enormous piano, it had yet to be furnished. "Anna, Sophie! Get out of sight."

Iona unlatched the door, then dodged into the music room with Willow.

"What are we doing?"

Willow held a finger to her lips.

The gusting spring breeze caught the edge of the door, swinging it a little wider. As Willow had hoped, the hinges, rusty from a long, wet winter, issued a slow *squeeeak*.

From outside, she could hear the horse lunging up the last portion of the hill. The sound of the animal struggling to catch its breath after a nearly vertical climb helped Willow track the rider as he approached the front lane.

Willow doubted that anyone had ever entered Batchwell's home through the heavy front door. The only people who ever visited were mine employees and his business partner, Phineas Bottoms. As far as she knew, most of them preferred using the back gate and the smaller portal leading into the kitchen.

Willow heard the crunch of boots on the gravel. Then the hollow *thud* of a boot heel on the front steps.

Her heart pounded so loudly in her ears, she could barely hear the squeaky hinge as the door eased open, inch by agonizing inch. Then, the shape of a man's shadow slid across the marble entry.

She lifted the rifle, sighting down the barrel. As her finger wrapped around the trigger, she remembered how Charles had once protected their family with such a weapon. He'd been so careful not to take a human life.

Adjusting her aim ever so slowly, she waited, growing

nearly light-headed with nerves as the Pinkerton-who-was-not-a-Pinkerton stepped into view. She let him take one step. Two. Three.

Lord give me strength. Help me protect my babies, Ezra and my friends.

Her heart threatened to burst from her chest, but she waited until the man had reached the center of the entry hall.

"Don't move," she warned. Surprisingly, her voice emerged low and steady.

The man froze, his revolver still at the ready. Since Willow stood slightly behind him, he slowly turned to face her.

Keeping her eyes on his weapon and not his face, she made a sharp gesture with the tip of her rifle.

"Put the revolver down."

"Now, missy, I don't think I can do that. You see, I've been sent here to take care of some business, and I intend to do it."

"Put…it…*down.*"

Even through her peripheral vision, she could see the sly smile that spread across his lips. "I'm sorry, ma'am, but I've got orders to collect the owner of this here mine, and I intend to do it." He shrugged carelessly. "My own boss has a whopping temper, and there's nothing on earth I'd like less than to anger the man."

"Ladies!" Willow called out.

Anna and Sophie stepped from the doorways on either side of the entry.

Seeing that he was surrounded, Eddington offered a conciliatory, "Now, see here, there's no reason to get all feisty with me."

Lifting his hands, he seemed ready to surrender. Then suddenly, he dropped to his knee, firing in Willow's direction.

Before Willow could even react, a shot reverberated in the narrow space, the sound echoing off the marble tiles and arching ceiling. Then the man howled, the revolver dropping on the floor and skittering several feet away. He gripped his shoulder where a blossom of red appeared.

Instantly, Willow and the other women rushed to pin the stranger beneath three sets of weapons.

"Iona! Find something we can use to tie him up."

"I've already thought of that." Iona hurried to the figure on the floor, carrying the tasseled tie-back cords that had once held the drapes in the music room.

She and Sophie bound Eddington's arms and legs so tightly together that Willow doubted he would have any feeling left in his extremities. But she couldn't seem to feel sorry for him. Only when he lay immobilized did Willow relax, ever so slightly. But when she saw a bullet hole in the lintel nearby, she stiffened again.

"Who took the shot?"

She looked at Anna and Sophie, but the women shook their heads.

It was only when she heard a clattering from the grand staircase that she found Batchwell clinging to the railing.

He faltered, then half sat, half fell onto the upper step.

"Mr. Batchwell!" Willow cried out, hurrying up to help him straighten his broken leg to a more comfortable position. "I thought I told you to stay in the bedroom."

His features were pale, and she prayed he hadn't injured himself even more.

Willow set her rifle on the stair beside him so she could touch his brow. As she'd feared, he felt clammy and cold to the touch.

He grinned reassuringly. "I couldn't let a man with a gun come upstairs, Mrs. Wanlass. Not with those sweet babes up here. And I wasn't about to let any of you women feel the weight of a man's blood on your hands." He took a moment to catch his breath. "Now, if you wouldn't mind, I wonder if you and the other ladies could help me through the kitchen to the back gate. A few moments ago, I saw Boris and a group of men thundering up the hill with a team and a wagon." He pointed to the man wriggling on the ground. "We'll have them lock this miscreant in the cellar for now. Then, as soon as it seems safe enough, we'll head into town."

Gideon eased his horse a little closer to the edge of the trees, not sure where he should look. Much like Clinton Tomlinson, he and Lydia had a general's view of the battle down below. He saw the last of Charles's explosions, then the glorious sight of the cannon and caisson lifting into the air and disintegrating into pieces.

His gaze swept ahead to the riders who'd managed to make their way through the charges. They'd only gone a few yards when their horses began tumbling to the ground.

"What on earth?" he murmured.

He caught Lydia's secret smile. "Myra and Miriam strung a clothes line across the road."

"Landsakes! You women have displayed more strategy in the last few days than Ulysses S. Grant himself."

The group of men who followed split like a stream flowing around a sandbar. They avoided their fallen comrades, then coalesced again, heading straight for the center of town. By this time, they'd learned to slow their gait to a cautious walk. As they headed into the main thoroughfare, they looked puzzled by the fact that no one appeared to stop them. To them, the streets must have seemed deserted.

They rode to the spot where the lane leading to the Meeting House butted up against the Miners' Hall on one side and the cook shack on the other. For a moment, they gestured to one another, probably trying to decipher which of the many buildings and narrow alleys would lead them to the warehouse where the stockpiles of silver had been stored.

From his vantage point, Gideon could make out the dark shadows of the men crouching behind the false fronts or lying flat against the rooftops. If he hadn't known that they were there, he doubted he would have picked them out in the gathering gloom—and he hoped that Clinton Tomlinson hadn't noticed them, either.

"Why are they waiting?" Lydia whispered.

"They want as many of your father's men to congregate in town before they spring their trap."

The last of the stragglers finally caught up with their cohorts, and Gideon knew that Dobbs and Jonah Ramsey would soon make their moves.

"Are you sure you want to do this?" Gideon asked Lydia one last time, gesturing to her father.

"Oh, yeah."

A few yards below them, Clinton Tomlinson sat uneasily in his saddle.

Do it, Jonah. Do it!

As if Jonah had heard Gideon's thoughts, his men swarmed from the alleys and buildings near the mine. At the same moment, those on the rooftops stood, while Dobbs sent his contingent of men swarming in from the opposite side.

Gideon heard a few scattered shots, but then…

Nothing.

Realizing that they were surrounded by hundreds of men and women, the Tommy Gang reluctantly threw their weapons to the ground, held up their hands, then awkwardly dismounted.

At the same moment, Lydia clucked to her mount and left the shelter of the trees.

* * *

Lydia barely felt the movement of the horse beneath her. She moved as quietly as she could, stopping a few feet behind her father. Her pulse roared in her ears as she watched Clinton Tomlinson pull the hat from his head and slap it against his leg in frustration. He muttered to himself, then shouted, "Cowards. *Cowards!*"

Grasping the reins, he jerked them to the side, making the gelding beneath him stutter-step at the rough treatment, then balk altogether.

That moment of hesitation was enough for Clinton Tomlinson to realize that he wasn't alone.

"Hello, Father," Lydia said quietly. "Going so soon?"

She could see the muscles of his jaw clench and release, clench and release.

"I figured I'd find you here," he said coldly. "I take it that all this—" he waved toward the valley and the miners who had begun to round up his gang "—is your doing."

"No. This time, you picked the wrong target. The residents of Aspen Valley take care of their own."

Like the whip of an attacking rattler, he reached for his revolver. But Lydia, just as quickly, had him within her own sights. The years of riding with her father seemed to disappear, and the less than savory skills he'd taught her came as easily to her as they'd done as a young girl.

Her father offered her a grin, but there was no humor to it, merely a nasty streak of cruelty.

"I suppose that you mean to betray your own blood again. What kind of person turns on her own family?"

Lydia waited for the words to sting—just as similar statements had done when she'd taken the witness box and her father had cursed her for ever being born.

But as she stared at him, noting how the passage of

time had darkened his skin to leather, brought a hunch to his shoulders, and made him seem somehow…smaller…

She realized that she didn't feel guilty. She didn't feel… Anything.

If she'd learned anything during the years with her aunts Rosie and Florence, and her time here at Bachelor Bottoms, it was that families weren't always formed through birth. Sometimes, they were chosen.

The moment that thought whispered through her consciousness, Lydia felt as if her spirit grew, stretched, then wriggled free from years of guilt and turmoil. This man may have been responsible for bringing her into the world, but he wasn't a "father." Not in the truest sense of the word. Fathers were men like Charles, who openly loved and protected their children, or like Jonah, who would one day support his own offspring with as much enthusiasm as he supported his wife.

Or like Gideon had shown when he let her take the lead in this confrontation, but guarded her back, nonetheless.

"You've broken the law. For that, you'll go back to prison."

Her father laughed—a jarring, rasping guffaw. "And who's going to stop me?" His thumb hovered near the hammer of his revolver. "You?"

The grating sound of a revolver being cocked, didn't come from Clinton Tomlinson, but from Gideon, who had sidled up behind the older man.

"Don't move, don't flinch, don't breathe or I'll blow you away."

Clinton made the mistake of taking his eyes off Lydia and looking toward Gideon. In that moment, Lydia fired.

Suddenly, the gun flew from her father's hand. The bullet whistled as it ricocheted off the metal of his revolver. Tomlinson cried out, cradling his wrist against his chest. Lydia doubted the force of the weapon being shot away from him had broken any bones, but she might have sprained something.

"Well done!" Gideon said, obviously impressed. While Lydia continued to hold her father at gunpoint, he pulled a pair of irons from a pocket in his tunic. "Where'd you learn to shoot like that?"

"There wasn't much else to do while Pa and his gang got liquored up after their raids. I'd line up the empty bottles and take 'em down, one by one."

Tomlinson groaned as Gideon jerked the man's hands behind his back and secured them with the cuffs. Then, Gideon looked up at her, grinning, his dark eyes alight with an intoxicating mixture of relief, love and exhilaration.

"Good thing you didn't take up a life of crime," he said as he gathered the reins to Tomlinson's mount and tied them to the pommel of his saddle.

Lydia finally lowered her weapon.

"You can thank my aunts for that."

Gideon seemed to think a moment, then said, "Nah. You aren't the type. I think you would have found your calling even without their help: righting wrongs and fighting for the underdog."

That comment made her smile.

"How'd you like some company?" he continued.

"Company?" She wasn't sure what he meant by such a remark.

"Yeah. I've been thinking that it's probably not entirely safe for you to head to California for that speaking tour. Not on your own. I wondered if you might be interested in having an ex-Pinkerton, sorta-husband, private security team?"

"You can't mean that?" she whispered, so softly that she feared he wouldn't hear her.

But the smile that spread over his lips blazed in his eyes as well. "I've never been more serious in my life. So, what do you think?"

Lydia was sure that her heart would find a way to fly out of her chest. "I think I'd like that a lot."

She saw a wave of relief wash over Gideon. Had he really thought that she'd say no?

"But, if it's all the same to you, maybe we could wait until summer is over," she suggested. "There's still a lot of work for the two of us to do here in this valley. By that time, the railway lines should be repaired. We could head for California before avalanche season starts."

His gaze met hers, rich and warm and filled with the love that, in her stubbornness, she'd nearly refused to recognize.

"Sounds like a perfect plan."

By the time that Gideon and Lydia returned to town with their captive, Dobbs, the Pinkertons, Jonah Ramsey and a handful of miners had already decided how best to hold on to the Tommy Gang. Using a great deal of rope—and splitting the would-be thieves into as many separate buildings as possible, they began shepherding them to several secure locations in town. Clinton Tomlinson was given the jail cell from which Lydia had recently escaped.

As Gideon and Lydia emerged into the cool evening air after seeing her father safely locked up, a wagon rattled into town, and Lydia saw Iona on the bench next to Boris, with Willow, Mr. Batchwell and the twins in the box. At their feet, trussed up like a Christmas goose, was Eddington.

Boris called to the team, bringing the conveyance to a halt while Batchwell waved his walking stick in the air.

Lydia braced herself for the recriminations that were

sure to come. To her surprise, Batchwell yelled out, "Well done, everyone. Well done!"

Gideon reached for Lydia's hand as Charles and Phineas Bottoms converged on the wagon. Not at all shy about his feelings, Phineas pulled Iona into his arms, then rocked her from side to side.

"I was so worried when I saw that man heading toward you."

Iona laughed. "He didn't have a chance, Phineas."

Charles reached for Willow, gently setting her on the ground. Mindful of the baby she carried, he hugged her as tightly as he dared, then peered down at the face regarding him from a swath of blankets.

"What did you think of all the excitement, Eva?"

He seemed to suddenly realize that one of the twins was missing. When he saw Batchwell holding Adam in the crook of his arm, Charles's brows rose.

"You've got yourself a fighter on your hands, Mr. Wanlass," Batchwell said proudly.

"Adam tends to get what he wants, that's true."

"I was talking about the little missus."

Boris quickly enlisted the help of a few miners and they half lifted, half dragged Eddington from the wagon.

"Take him to the Miners' Hall," Gideon called out. "We've got room for one more there."

Batchwell pointed his walking stick at Gideon. "I guess we've got proof positive that the pass is cleared enough for travel, Gault."

Gideon stiffened, knowing what Batchwell meant to say next. For months, the cantankerous man had been issuing his order: *As soon as you can get a wagon down that canyon, I want the women gone."*

"First thing tomorrow, Gault—"

"Mr. Batchwell, I know you won't appreciate my interference, but I think you should know that there are quite a few people in this valley who would like to have it stated, for the record, that the women should be allowed to stay—"

"Women? Who said anything about the women? I'm talking about these infernal varmints who have destroyed the peace and well-being of our town. I want them hauled out of here starting at daybreak. Do you think you and your men could do that for us?"

Gideon hesitated only a moment, his brain struggling to change gears. "We'd be leaving the valley shorthanded. Maybe we should take them a few at a time so we can leave a contingent here to guard the silver."

"Nonsense! We've got enough able-bodied people in the valley to take care of security while you're gone."

Batchwell winked—he actually *winked*—in Lydia's direction. "If you let the ladies keep their weapons, they could take care of it themselves."

He brandished his cane to point in the direction of the cook shack.

"Fact is, I've got a few things to talk over with the leadership of this community. If I could get a helping hand, perhaps we can convene at the cook shack." His brows rose questioningly in Iona's direction. "I know that you ladies have had your hands full for the last little while, but do you suppose you could rustle up something to drink and a nibble or two?"

Iona disentangled herself from Phineas's arms. "Of course, Mr. Batchwell. It won't take but a minute."

She and several women separated from the group and hurried across the street.

Phineas folded his arms and pierced his partner with an unaccustomed steely gaze.

"Ezra, if you mean to hammer home your edict for the women to leave the valley—"

"Dash it all! Why do people keep putting words in my mouth before I can speak them myself!"

This was the Batchwell that Gideon was accustomed to seeing, blustery, loud and bristling with temper. He whacked the cane against the side of the wagon, causing Adam to jump, then offer a snuffling cry.

To Gideon's astonishment, the old man immediately softened his tone and bounced the baby in his arms. "There now, little man. I didn't mean to startle you."

As soon as Adam had settled into watching the commotion with wide eyes again, Batchwell looked up. "Well? Is anyone going to help an old man across the street? We've got plans that need making and I want you—" he pointed to Jonah "—you and you—" he indicated Charles and Gideon "—and you."

This time, he pointed to Lydia.

"Landsakes, this valley has been full of shenanigans and skullduggery for the past few days—and don't think I won't unearth the full extent of it!"

Gideon squeezed Lydia's hand when she shifted guiltily.

Batchwell looked down at the babe in his arms with an expression of tender melancholy.

"But it has come to my attention that our community could use some improvements. We've done a fine job, so far. The territories can be a harsh place, even for the strongest of men. But there comes a time and a place when the hard parts are conquered."

He looked up, scanning the crowd that had begun to gather around him.

"When you reach that point, you need to progress from a rough-and-tumble existence to a place we all can enjoy." His eyes lingered on Willow for a moment, and a secret message seemed to pass between them. "What we need around here is some genteel refinement, something that

can only come through the influence of our families. And
we have these fine ladies who were stranded in our midst
to thank for it."

A murmur spread through the crowd and Gideon felt
Lydia grow tense, barely breathing.

Was Batchwell saying that the women could stay?

Batchwell grunted, seeming to become aware of the
loaded statement he'd tossed their way.

"I think if we can sit down and talk, make some proper
plans—and get our housing issues in line…" He cleared his
throat. "Well, I think we could open the valley to anyone
who's willing to make a difference in this community."

When the crowd would have reacted, he stopped them
with a thump of his cane against the wagon—softer, this
time, lest he startle the baby.

"Just remember! We'll still be a God-fearing people,
and we'll hold strong to our principles! There will still be
no drinking, smoking or cussing in this town." He glanced
down at the infant he held and smiled. "But it's high time
we had some children running around to remind us why
we fight for those values…and what it's like to be young."

At that, there was no stopping the crowd. Some shouted,
some cheered. Charles Wanlass took Adam from Batchwell's arms and the older man was lifted up by a group of
miners, then carried on their shoulders to the cook shack,
looking every bit the conquering hero.

As the men and women of Aspen Valley crowded inside
to celebrate, Gideon and Lydia hung back.

"It seems your protest worked," Gideon murmured,
leaning down to rest his forehead against hers.

"I don't think so." A soft laugh bubbled from her throat.
"All that effort, all that sneaking around…and I'm pretty
sure it was the babies that changed his mind."

Gideon released her hand so that he could wrap his arm around her waist, pulling her close.

"Don't sell yourself short. It wasn't just the twins. It was everything and everybody. It was Sumner caring for wounded miners, the brides making and serving countless meals, Willow's kindness…"

He turned her to face him, holding her in the loop of his arms.

"And it was you, Lydia, stirring up the status quo, reminding us at every turn that things could be better. Reminding *me* that things could be better."

He stroked her cheek, her chin, then tucked a wayward strand of hair behind her ear.

"I thought I had my whole life mapped out. I thought that my experiences during the war had somehow…tainted me…for the rest of my days. I was so sure that the only way to keep the memories at bay would be to isolate myself—and anyone else—from those burdens."

His throat grew tight as he realized how solitary he'd become. Oh, he'd had friends, true. But even then, he'd held them at a distance, never letting them know about the experiences that still haunted him.

"But then I met you, Lydia, and you turned my whole world topsy-turvy. You challenged my authority, my capabilities—and yes, even my patience."

She opened her mouth to argue, but he placed his finger on her lips.

"In doing so," he continued, "you taught me that no burden should be shouldered alone. When you love someone, really love them, you share those problems and sorrows and triumphs. And in doing so, every step forward you take becomes even sweeter."

A tear plunged down her cheek, but she was smiling. Such a sweet, sweet smile. He knew in that instant that she understood everything he'd been trying to tell her, despite his clumsy way of explaining it.

She loved him.

She loved the good and the bad, what she knew about him and what she didn't. He knew without asking, that he could tell her every fear, every struggle, every mistake he'd ever made—and she'd be there to help him through it. Just as he would be there for her.

Lydia lifted on tiptoe, her hands resting on his chest, one palm flat against the place where his heart beat madly in his breast.

"And you taught me the true meaning of family, Gideon. Wherever you go, that's where I belong. With you… I'm home."

He bent to kiss her then, knowing that there was still so much to say, so many things to decide. But all of that could wait. Right now, he needed to reassure himself that this was real. That the woman he cared for more than life itself was really here, in his arms.

They had a lifetime together to sort out all the details.

Epilogue

October 4, 1874

Gideon shifted nervously, tugging at his vest, checking one last time to make sure his watch had been securely stowed in his pocket, and the chain looped smoothly to where he'd fastened it on one of the lower buttons.

"Hold still, or your tie will be crooked," Charles warned.

"You need to loosen it. It's too tight."

"It's not nearly as tight as you made mine the night I married Willow," Charles grumbled good-naturedly.

The door to the pastor's office burst open. "Isn't he ready yet?" Jonah groused.

"He's ready, he's ready." Charles scowled as he inspected Gideon, but he directed his comments to Jonah. "Have you got the rings?"

"Yep." Jonah patted his vest pocket. "Right here. Do you know what you're going to say?"

"Yes, Jonah. I swear, you're more nervous than Gideon, here."

Jonah laughed. "I doubt that's possible. He looks like he's going to keel over."

Gideon opened his mouth to refute that statement, then

closed it again. Truth be told, he'd been a little numb all morning, ever since his two friends had dragged him out of bed and hauled him to the Meeting House to prepare him for his upcoming wedding.

To Lydia.

The mere thought of his bride-to-be caused his heart to pound a little harder and the nerves to skitter into his stomach.

They'd waited so long for this day. At first, it had been important to get Clinton Tomlinson and his gang safely locked away in a territorial jail. After which, Gideon had needed to focus on hauling the ore out of the valley. At the same time, land had been secured for the new family dwellings to be built, and the railway lines had been repaired. Then Lydia's aunts had arrived along with the first of the wives and families who were being welcomed into the valley.

For a time, with all those concerns pressing in on them, it hadn't seemed right to focus on themselves—and in some ways, Gideon was glad. With a common goal in hand, Gideon and Lydia had spearheaded many of the changes that had occurred in Aspen Valley, and they'd grown closer with each accomplished task.

But finally, *finally*, things had settled down enough that they felt they could take some time off for themselves. This morning, they would be married in the new Meeting House—the first couple to ever say their vows in the gleaming white building. The old church had been converted into a schoolhouse, and Lydia's aunts had graciously volunteered to teach the first year, a fact that hadn't surprised Gideon. After months of wondering if Lydia had survived the avalanche that had sealed the pass, the older women had no desire to leave their niece yet. And since Lydia's speaking engagements had been rearranged for the following summer, she and Gideon had decided to remain in Aspen Valley for the intervening time.

The door to Charles's office burst open again and Sumner poked her head inside. "The bride is nearly here! He needs to go to the front of the church."

Gideon allowed himself to be pushed and prodded into the chapel until he stood at the end of the aisle and Jonah, as best man, stood beside him. Charles took his place in the center. In the months since the pass had opened, he'd done everything necessary to ease from his position as "lay pastor" to full-fledged minister, and this would be his first time officiating a wedding.

Gideon swallowed against the dryness gathering in his throat. This community had experienced so many "firsts" since routing the Tommy Gang. But as the last of the guests took their seats and the organ began to play, Gideon realized that these next few minutes would prove to be the most important to him.

His first look at his bride.
His first kiss as her husband.
Their first steps into the future.

Suddenly, the rear doors opened. There, illuminated in the light streaming into the foyer, stood Iona Bottoms—who was a new bride herself. Her butter-yellow gown set off her white hair and pink cheeks—making her appear girlish and vibrant. Immediately, her gaze swept the congregation, stopping only when she found Phineas on the front pew.

Phineas met his wife's look with a beaming smile. The older man had recently confessed that he'd been responsible for marooning the women in the valley. Knowing that the train holding their new company doctor would also be transporting a load of mail-order brides, he'd set a charge on a nearby slope, hoping to delay the women for a few days. Unfortunately, his plans had gone awry when the snow had completely filled the pass and stranded the ladies for months instead. Gideon thought it only fitting that the man who had hoped to influence his partner into changing the rules had been one of the first to be wed when the "no women" clause had been officially removed.

As soon as Iona took her place, Willow stepped into the doorway. Her red hair blazed in the sunlight, and her slight body had been accented to perfection in a pale green gown. Gideon saw the way that her gaze automatically skipped to Charles and a secret smile played over her lips. Then, she scanned the room, finding Adam, who was being bounced on Bottoms's knee, and Eva, who looked over Batchwell's shoulder and squealed in her mother's direction.

Willow had nearly reached the end of the aisle when Sumner appeared. She'd abandoned the sober, tailored clothing that she normally wore as her doctor garb for a pale pink gown. Despite the careful drape of an overskirt, the protrusion of her stomach was evident. Gideon saw the way Jonah straightened in pride at the sight of his wife, and Sumner, normally so cool and collected, blushed when her husband eyed her with open adoration.

Gideon lifted a finger to his tie, trying to loosen it, knowing that Lydia had chosen only three matrons of honor. He honestly didn't know why his knees trembled and his heart seemed to knock against his ribs. He wasn't nervous to begin his life with Lydia. He was more than ready for them to be together.

Then she stepped into view, a glorious vision in white. She wore a gown that could have stepped from the fashion pages. One with an enormous bustled skirt, a wasp waist, and willowy lines outlined with tiny pleated ruffles and sparkling beadwork. He knew that the women who'd remained in the valley had all shared the task of making the elaborate gown as a gift to their dear friend. Nevertheless, what caught and held his attention was the face beneath the gossamer veil.

Lydia.

His bride.

As soon as she met his gaze, she smiled—and in that instant, everyone else seemed to disappear. In her expression, he could see an echo of his own chaotic emotions—nervousness, eagerness, and an overwhelming certainty that nothing would ever feel as *right* as this moment together.

By the time she joined him at the end of the aisle, the last of his nerves had been chased away by the warmth of her gaze. His fingers were steady as he took her hand, and Charles began to speak.

As he recited his vows, Gideon tried to concentrate on each word, each gesture, each expression. He wanted to imprint this moment in his mind with such clarity that he would be able to relive memories any time he needed to remember what was truly important in life. He would focus on this day when wartime memories threatened to consume him, or when the pressures of work hung heavy on his shoulders. *This* would become his touchstone for the rest of his life—the delicate warmth of her fingers in his, the sweet tones of her voice, the joy radiating from her soul until she seemed to glow from within.

"You may now kiss your bride."

Gideon's heart thumped in his chest as he lifted Lydia's veil. With that final barrier removed, he could see her so clearly that his heart ached with happiness.

"I love you, Lydia," he murmured, for her ears alone.

"And I love you, Gideon."

Then he kissed her, softly, sweetly.

At long last, he took her hand, leading her out into the sunshine amid a shower of confetti, a crowd of well-wishers, and the sweet sound of children's laughter floating through the mountain air. They paused on the top step for a photograph taken by Mr. Batchwell himself and his new box camera.

As they waited for the bridal party to take their places, Gideon gazed down at his companion, and she, sensing his regard, looked up. For an instant, she took his breath away, and he could scarcely credit the joy and adoration that shone from her eyes.

Lydia Angelica Tomlinson, a woman he'd once thought would be trouble with a capital *T*.

Little had he known she would become so much more.

His sweetheart.

His bride.

His everything.

* * * * *

If you loved this sweet historical romance,
pick up the first two books
from author Lisa Bingham's miniseries
THE BACHELORS OF ASPEN VALLEY

ACCIDENTAL COURTSHIP
ACCIDENTAL FAMILY

Available now from Love Inspired Historical!

Find more great reads at www.LoveInspired.com

Dear Reader,

I hope that you enjoyed Lydia's and Gideon's story, *Accidental Sweetheart*. This is the third and final book in the BACHELORS OF ASPEN VALLEY series, and I wanted to make sure that I finished everything with a bang! To my delight, much like the characters themselves, as soon as I started writing, Lydia and Gideon hijacked the plot and decided to have a rollicking good time. In addition, characters from the first two books, *Accidental Courtship* and *Accidental Family*, decided to help out. I had so much fun bringing everyone together for one last happy ending.

I love to hear from my readers, so if you'd like to get in touch, you can reach me at my website, www.lisabinghamauthor.com, or through my social media sites, www.Facebook.com/lisabinghamauthor, and Twitter @lbinghamauthor.

All my best to you,
Lisa

We hope you enjoyed this story from
Love Inspired® Historical.

Love Inspired® Historical is coming to
an end but be sure to discover more
inspirational stories to warm your heart
from **Love Inspired®** and
Love Inspired® Suspense!

Love Inspired stories show that
faith, forgiveness and hope have the power
to lift spirits and change lives—always.

 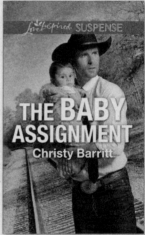

Look for six new romances every month
from **Love Inspired®** and
Love Inspired® Suspense!

Get 4 FREE REWARDS!

We'll send you 2 FREE Books
plus 2 FREE Mystery Gifts.

Love Inspired® books feature contemporary inspirational romances with Christian characters facing the challenges of life and love.

FREE Value Over **$20**